EVA EVERGREEN

SEMI-MAGICAL WITCH

EVA EVERGREEN
SEMI-MAGICAL WITCH

JULIE ABE
ILLUSTRATED BY **SHAN JIANG**

LITTLE, BROWN AND COMPANY
New York Boston

Copyright © 2020 by Julie Abe
Illustrations copyright © 2020 by Shan Jiang

Cover art copyright © 2020 by Shan Jiang. Cover design by Karina Granda. Cover copyright © 2020 by Hachette Book Group, Inc.

Little, Brown and Company
Hachette Book Group
1290 Avenue of the Americas, New York, NY 10104
Visit us at LBYR.com

First Edition: August 2020

Little, Brown and Company is a division of Hachette Book Group, Inc. The Little, Brown name and logo are trademarks of Hachette Book Group, Inc.

The publisher is not responsible for websites (or their content) that are not owned by the publisher.

Library of Congress Cataloging-in-Publication Data
Names: Abe, Julie, author.
Title: Eva Evergreen, semi-magical witch / Julie Abe.
Description: New York ; Boston : Little, Brown and Company, 2020. | Summary: Eva must travel to a seaside town to complete her training and earn the rank of Novice Witch before her thirteenth birthday, or be banned from using magic forever.
Identifiers: LCCN 2019021821| ISBN 9780316493888 (hardcover) | ISBN 9780316493864 (ebk.) | ISBN 9780316493871 (library edition ebk.)
Subjects: | CYAC: Witches—Fiction. | Apprentices—Fiction. | Magic—Fiction. | Adventure and adventurers—Fiction. | Fantasy.
Classification: LCC PZ7.1.A162 Ev 2020 | DDC [Fic]—dc23
LC record available at https://lccn.loc.gov/2019021821

ISBNs: 978-0-316-49388-8 (hardcover), 978-0-316-54045-2 (international edition), 978-0-316-49386-4 (ebook)

Printed in the United States of America

LSC-H

Printing 3, 2022

THIS STORY IS FOR YOU, READER,
BECAUSE YOU ARE MAGICAL.

DREAM WILDLY, AND KNOW THAT YOUR
PINCH OF MAGIC IS MORE THAN ENOUGH.

FOR EUGENE, MY LIGHT IN THE STORM.

CONTENTS

PART ONE

The Journey Begins

CHAPTER 1

THE ENCHANTED BOOKSTORE

The bell above the door chimed, and magic tingled at my fingertips. The scent of ink and freshly printed paper swirled invitingly in the air as I followed my parents into the bookshop.

Today was my last day as just an Apprentice Witch, the last few moments of being the unreliable Eva who summoned heads of cabbage instead of flowers or got a sunburn instead of calling down rain. Or, at least, I *hoped* it was the end of all that.

"Are you ready, Eva?" Mother nudged my shoulder.

I tightened my hands around the straps of my knapsack and summoned up a smile. "I'm ready."

A set of bright, spectacled brown eyes peeped out from a teetering stack of books at the counter in the center. "Welcome to Enchanted Ink, Rivelle Realm's one and only magical bookshop." Kaya Ikko, the bookseller, dipped into a bow, her black tunic fluttering around her. "Ah, Nelalithimus! And Isao! I did so enjoy the yuzu lemon trifles that Nela brought to tea the other day."

My stomach usually growled at the thought of Father's realm-famous pastries, but today, it churned queasily.

My father smiled. "My pleasure. I'll bring over my latest creations the next time we're in the city."

Kaya's warm eyes crinkled with delight when she spotted me behind Mother. "And Eva! So good to see you here."

"Hello, Elite Ikko!" My heartbeat fluttered as I paused in the wide aisle leading to her counter. Books lined the walls, all the way up to the dim window cut into the ceiling. One of these books would be mine, for my quest. So long as I could summon it.

"Go on, Eva. You can do this," Mother murmured, as if she had heard my thoughts. She adjusted my pointy hat, smiling down at me.

At first glance, Mother and I almost looked like mirror reflections. We had the same inky black hair resting slightly below our shoulders, rounded brown eyes, and slight tans from summer afternoons in the garden. We even had the same black witch's dresses.

But that was where the similarities ended.

The delicate jewel brooch at her neck and her black dress were laced with a diamond-like shimmer, marking her Grand Master status. My dress was plain black, as I was only an Apprentice, a level so low I wasn't even considered an official witch.

And most days, it seemed, all other witches and wizards were more like Mother than me. Magic rushed through their veins, with just a drop of blood.

I definitely had more blood than magic.

Father wandered over to the non-enchanted cookbooks, and Mother picked up a book at random and pretended to be absorbed in it, to give me a chance to slow down the pounding in my chest. The book's pages flipped without Mother turning a corner, and my heart thundered faster.

"Oh, Kaya, would you like to walk over to the Council Hall together?" Mother called.

Kaya popped back out, clutching a stack of books. "Of course, of course. But I'm waiting for the soon-to-be Novice's book summoning, as you know."

She'd kept her shop open for my sake. A smile tugged at my lips.

It was now or never.

And I was ready for my quest.

I stood straight in front of Kaya and stretched up as tall as I could, though I didn't surpass even the smallest piles of magical tomes. "I'm ready to summon my book." A shiver ran down my spine with excitement. "Can you please open the enchanted bookshelf?"

The books clattered out of Kaya's hands. She pushed her glasses up her nose and squinted, her eyebrows knitting with confusion. "Eva? Oh, no, Eva. I—I thought you were going on your quest next year...."

I sucked in a breath. "Next year?"

She rummaged under a stack of books, one smoking at the edges, and pulled out a square of parchment stamped with the Council's official crescent-moon seal. Her eyes searched the page. "Eva...you're not on the list. There's only one wizard this year and...it isn't you...."

My heart pounded. "But I've got magic"—it had *finally* manifested—"and I turned twelve years old three moons ago."

"Kaya—truly?" Mother asked, her hands clenching the book, now rattling in her grasp.

Kaya flipped the parchment over, as if expecting to see my name on the back. "In all my twenty years, this has never happened before...."

I stammered, "How can that—I *have* to be on the list."

My lungs tightened, and I could barely breathe. What could she mean? The summons I'd received from the Council had stated: *Evalithimus Evergreen is hereby summoned to the Council of Witches and Wizards meeting on the first day of the fifth moon, for discussion of her witch rank.* Mother, Father, and I had prepared my knapsack, Mother had gifted me a shiny new broomstick, and we'd had everything ready except my ensorcelled book from Enchanted Ink and my ticket from the Council.

Kaya shook her head with confusion. "The only person the Council listed this year—" From behind me, the door chimed, but I couldn't pull my gaze away from Kaya. Her eyes widened at the sight of the person opening the door. "Is him."

My heart pounded in my throat. Who—

"Elite Ikko, I'm here for my book," said a familiar, haughty voice.

I spun around and bit down a groan.

Conroy Nytta and I eyed each other with barely concealed dislike. Even though he was only two moons older, he always acted above me. He brushed off an invisible speck of dust from his pristine black long-sleeved shirt and trousers that fit him so perfectly it looked as if they had come straight from the queen's own tailor.

He nodded at my father, then strode to Mother and bowed over her hand, a lock of straight, dark hair falling over his eyes. "Wonderful to see you, Grand Master Evergreen."

As if an afterthought, he added, "And Eva."

I promised myself he'd have to call *me* Grand Master someday. Still, his greeting stung.

"Hello, fellow *Apprentice* Conroy," I said, addressing him properly.

"Did your magic truly show up?" Conroy flicked his eyes to the knapsack slung over my shoulders.

"Conroy!" Father and Mother scolded in unison. He'd apprenticed under Mother, and living with him when we were both ten had been the worst year of my life. Conroy used to whisper—only when my parents weren't around—how mind-boggling it was that the daughter of the most powerful witch in Rivelle Realm was magicless. My magic hadn't manifested until I turned eleven, after he'd left for his next apprenticeship.

Conroy leaned close, out of earshot of my parents. "I'd heard rumors, but…Oh, wait, was it you who fell asleep in the stream instead of stopping the rain? Classic." He snorted.

As if answering my thoughts, magic tickled faintly at my fingertips, longing to show off a spell or two. But unlike Conroy, I couldn't waste a drop of it.

"I manifested last year," I said quickly. "Mother's been training me as her Apprentice since then."

"*Last* year? And a single apprenticeship?" He raised an eyebrow. "You've got only one chance to pass your quest, you know. Can you even *fly*?" Conroy had started an enchanted snowstorm on the day he was born. Ever since, he'd been training all around the realm. Mother's friends in the Council whispered that he'd most likely earn his Grand Master status by the time he reached sixteen. Most witches and wizards only reached the Elite rank, the third and middle tier.

"I—I can fly. Well enough," I said through gritted teeth. "And I'm aware I only have one chance."

One chance, one chance. Those very words had echoed in my mind every time I'd thought of my Novice quest. But I *needed* my powers. I'd do anything to keep my magic.

For any other witch or wizard, not passing the Novice quest, the easiest of the Council's ranking quests, was unthinkable. I wasn't so lucky.

Mother cast enchantments as she walked, talked, and even slept. Most times, she didn't even need her wand to channel her magic. Just yesterday, within a handful of minutes, she had charmed the house to dust itself up, the sponge to scrub the dishes, and her piles of books to alphabetize themselves. Half an hour later, I had finally thought of a spell—*A mean clean is in need*—and summoned up enough magic for a rag to wipe crumbs off the stovetop and then fling itself into the waste bin. And then I'd slipped into a nap on the kitchen floor.

Casting charms pulled magic out of my blood far too quickly. And I, unlike most, paid a consequence for every spell. Whenever I overused my meager stores of magic, I fell asleep.

"We've got the Council meeting in a few minutes,"

Mother said placatingly. "They'll clear it up, as I'm sure it was just a mistake."

"What was a mistake?" Conroy asked.

"N-nothing," I said quickly, and he narrowed his eyes. My fingers curled around my wand, my nails biting into my palms. I wasn't going to give up on becoming a Novice Witch that easily.

"I know what's a mistake—any spell Eva casts." Conroy snickered under his breath.

Kaya looked nervously between us. "I'll summon the bookshelf now, especially since we've got two of you." I beamed with relief. At least Kaya would let me get my book. Conroy glowered, likely not wanting anything to do with me. She raised her wand and chanted, "*The right book for a quest, at the journeyer's behest.*"

The circular counter turned and turned around her, sinking into the wood floor with a rumble. The air sucked out of my lungs. My quest was finally beginning.

Kaya stepped to the side as a gilded structure rose in its place, gleaming under the faint light shining in through the overhead window. Magical tomes glimmered on the ten shelves. Pristine gold-stamped covers were mixed with well-loved books, big and small, old and new.

I breathed out a quiet, reverent "*Oh.*" It was beautiful.

"I'll go first. I haven't got time to wait." Conroy's sharp eyebrows rose in condescending slashes, as if he'd issued a challenge I couldn't possibly meet. I leveled a glare back. He flicked his wand and chanted, *"My journey is to begin, endow the knowledge within."*

The magical tomes shifted and fluttered like a thousand paper wings, but hushed as a book with a rich bronze cover floated up into the air. It fell neatly into Conroy's outstretched hands, and he tucked the slim book into the pocket of his black tunic before I could see the title, probably just to irritate me.

"Good luck summoning your book, Eva." Conroy's eyes flicked to my broomstick resting against a shelf. "I mean, assuming you have magic."

"Enough magic to give you a wart," I retorted, but he'd already turned away.

"A pleasure to see you, Grand Master Evergreen and Mister Evergreen. And of course, thank you, Elite Ikko," Conroy said, bowing again. He didn't bother saying the same to me. "Well, I shall see you at the Council Hall."

He brushed past, and I clenched my fists in the folds of my skirt, wishing I could magic away the smug look on his face.

Conroy twirled his wand with one hand and aimed it toward the doorway. His wand shimmered. *"A light so bright, for the one that's right."*

The door flew open, and a beam of sunlight shone down on him, illuminating the bits of gold in his dirt-colored hair as he strolled out.

"What a waste of magic," I grumbled.

The shop darkened as soon as he disappeared. I wanted to turn into a tornado, to tear down the walls and race after him, and challenge him to a magical duel. I slumped my shoulders. Compared to his powers, I was nothing but a faint spring breeze.

Mother sighed. "He can't help being Hayato's nephew."

"He can stop being *awful*, though," I protested. Mother hid her laugh, but Father let out a chuckle.

"I'm ready for my spell." I stepped up to the bookshelf and tapped it with my wand. *"Book for me, please be seen."*

My head spun slightly as magic pulled out of my blood. The tip of my wand lit dully. Instead of flying into my hands, books leaped on top of the shelf and began swirling around, like dancers at one of the queen's balls.

"Curses! I didn't mean 'be seen' like *that*," I groaned. Kaya's lips twitched. She'd probably never seen a witch like me before.

A loud *ring!* chimed through the city, and I stiffened.

"It's the first bell," Mother said. "Remember, choose only the words that will help you concentrate on what you want to have happen. Rhymes are always good as they're easier to remember and will help you focus. Create a spell that homes in on your desires. Hope for it. Believe in it."

I nodded, but my mind had been wrung clean of ideas. I'd heard those exact instructions time and time again from the moment my magic had manifested, but creating spells still never came easily, particularly because of how hard it was to find my magic inside me. It was there, somewhere in my blood, but whenever I tried to cast a spell, my magic seemed to shrink away and hide.

All my carefully crafted spells in preparation for this very moment seemed to have flown out the door along with Conroy. The only thing I could think of was how they'd misfire.

"We've got a few minutes..." Mother added slowly.

But not much more.

I clutched my wand tightly, feeling my head spin. My limit was about five simple spells, which had seemed a lot until I followed Mother around one morning. In a few minutes, she'd cast twenty charms as easily as snapping her fingers.

With today's one spell, somehow, my magic had seeped from me. And my ideas for spells with it.

My mind was blank.

All I could see were the books taunting me, spinning in circles and kicking up the dust. If Conroy had stayed, he would've been crying with laughter by now.

Maybe *"Come on a journey, book on a tourney"*? No. The books would probably start dueling. My words had shriveled into useless scraps.

But Father and Mother moved to my side.

"You can do this, Eva," Father whispered in his deep,

calming voice. And Mother squeezed my shoulder, her cool hand reassuring me.

My parents had never given up believing I'd pass my quest. As long as I hoped to be a witch, they hoped, too. I couldn't let them down. Blood pounded in my ears as magic poured out.

"Bestow what I need, for this journey to succeed."

The books rumbled, just like they had for Conroy, and I perked up. Had my spell worked?

I held my hands out, expecting a tiny book like Conroy's.

The books shifted, spines popping in and out as if they couldn't figure out which tome to dispense. Then, one after another, book after book shot out, throwing themselves into my hands with a resounding *smack, smack, smack.*

By the time the books were finished, thirteen magical tomes towered over my head. I teetered to a side table, and Mother helped stuff them inside my knapsack. I snatched up my worn copy of *The Guide for Questing Witches and Wizards*, which I'd brought from home, and placed it carefully on top. "Did you have this many tomes during your quest, Mother?"

"If it sits, it fits!" As usual for Mother, she quickly thought of a spell to expand my knapsack further and waved her wand with ease. The canvas bag obediently swallowed up the books, though it was already crammed

with food and other supplies. "I had a thinner book. But these are simply recommendations. You aren't required to read all of them."

"Books have a way of making themselves known," Kaya added. "When they're meant to be read, they'll appear. When you need them, you'll always be able to find the right book for you."

With a swish of her wand, Kaya magicked the enchanted bookshelf away.

The second bell rang, chiming throughout all of Okayama. The sound echoed in my ears, as if it had rooted itself in my heartbeat. Mother met my eyes with a quick nod.

We needed to hurry to the Council Hall. I had to find out why I hadn't been included in the Council's letter to Kaya.

The list *had* to be a mistake.

CHAPTER 2

RIVELLE REALM'S COUNCIL OF WITCHES AND WIZARDS

My future depended on the Council Hall in front of me, a magnificent stone and glass building at the edge of the capital city. West of Okayama City, the Torido River split into two, as if the waters had been forced to flow around the magic-infused glass and head out to the sea in two separate paths.

Mother, Father, Kaya, and I hurried across the courtyard leading up to the shimmering building. Mother and Kaya stopped, bending in a deep bow toward the Council's enchanted trees. I followed their lead, and the light flickering on the metal and glass leaves tugged at me, as if charming me to walk closer.

"We have to go in," Kaya said, nodding toward the hall. I stopped, trying to resist the urge to inch closer to the trees. "There's only one bell's worth of time before the meeting starts."

"We'll head inside shortly," Mother said, waving her along. My parents smiled at me. "Go on, take a look."

I reached out to the Novice tree with a hesitant, quivering hand and whispered, "I'll be up there soon." When I ran my finger along the rough bark of the tree, it was cool under my touch. Eleven bronze leaves, engraved with the names of the realm's current Novices, clanked in the breeze, ringing with a lonely sound. Knowing Grottel's favoritism, he'd give Conroy his license before me. I would become the thirteenth.

Or, at least, I hoped so.

Spray misted the courtyard, coating everything with slick dew. In the shade of the hall and raised by the breath of the twin rivers, the five magical trees swayed in a line, their metal and glass leaves twinkling like chimes.

I whispered the names like a spell. *"Novice, Adept, Elite, Master, Grand Master."*

Five levels. If—no, *after*—I passed my Novice quest, I had to fulfill the quests assigned by the Council to progress from Novice to Adept, Adept to Elite. Most witches and wizards stayed as Elites, unable to beat the three incredibly difficult quests required to become a Master.

Or pass the mysterious tests to become a Grand Master.

The magic in my blood tingled at the thought.

"I can't believe it. My daughter's going off on her

Novice Witch quest," Father said, nervously shoving his hands into the pockets of his sand-colored tunic. "You're going to have your own guardian watching over you, and you'll forget all about us."

My throat tightened at his words. "It'll only be a moon's time. And I'd *never* forget your croissants or cakes, Father," I reassured him, solemnly.

He let out a small laugh, and it felt like the faintest rays of sunlight had peeked out of the clouds. Mother patted his shoulder, probably itching to cast a spell to ease his worries, but it was against the Council's laws to spell the magicless without their consent.

"I'd best get going, so I can be here when you get out." Without magic, Father couldn't go into the Council Hall; the current leader of the Council had decreed this years ago in his hungry need to control as much as possible in the realm. Now, the magicless were only allowed in if they accompanied the queen. The Council, after all, had been formed to serve all requests from the ruler of our realm. Father shot us one last smile as he headed out the iron gates, toward Okayama City, to meet one of his baker friends.

My eyes stayed glued to him as he hurried down the hill. Father disappeared into the crowds on the smooth, wide cobblestone road winding through spindly wood buildings, topped with vermilion roof tiles curved like nightdragon scales. Shopkeepers hawked their wares as the occasional truck puttered through. All roads led to the queen's castle. The swooping pure crystal arches and glass spires of the castle shone like a heart in the center of the city. Someday, perhaps, I'd serve the queen. But if the queen's castle was the realm's heart, the Council Hall was the realm's blood.

The branches of the Grand Master tree swayed in the wind and mist, catching my eye. It was at the far end of the line of trees, closest to the door of the Council Hall. The mere two leaves were on opposite sides of the tree. Hayato Grottel, head of the Council, had his marker on a branch that pointed out toward the sea. Mother's was directly across, in the direction of our cottage in Miyada. A ray of sunlight streamed onto the tree, and I could make out Mother's name, *Nelalithimus Evergreen*, cut into the diamond leaf and lined with gold.

Someday, I dared to dream, my name, *Evalithimus Evergreen*, would be on that tree with hers, sharing that very branch. And like Mother, I would serve the queen in one of her crystal spires. I took a deep breath, as if I could absorb the thick air that felt full of hopes and dreams, even though magic wasn't in the land anymore, not in the way I had read about in history books: plants bursting with enchanted blossoms and rivers flowing with charmed strength. Magic had trickled out, year by year, and the number of witches and wizards had similarly dwindled.

"They were once full of leaves, you know," Mother said, gazing at the Elite tree in the middle. "Ages ago, when magic floated in the air and was infused into the very soil of the realm, families were unsurprised when their newborns could charm their toys to life. Those children attended schools to help them hone their magic. Almost anyone could create a spell to mend a wound—or curse an enemy. Until magic seemed to shrivel away throughout the land, and the Council was created to organize the remaining witches and wizards."

I couldn't imagine a time when these tall, angular trees were heavy with enchanted leaves. The leaves, inscribed with the names of the current members of the Council, barely chimed in the wind. Even the Elite tree, the middle tier, held less than a hundred. According to the trees, just about two hundred witches and wizards covered the thousands of cities and villages in Rivelle Realm.

"We do not need the powerless vying for our roles," a voice sneered over Mother's shoulder.

Hayato Grottel.

The head of the Council towered over me, casting a dark shadow. He flicked his narrowed, hooded eyes past me, at the trees, like I didn't exist. The twin rivers roared in my ears like a warning.

Norya Dowel, his assistant and an Elite Witch, hurried over, nearly tripping over the hem of her black witch's skirt, and hastily bowed, throwing a nervous smile toward

Mother and me. She seemed more interested in staring down at the stone pathway leading up to the hall than meeting our eyes. "G-Grand Master, sir, the meeting's about to start—we mustn't waste any time. The whole realm's worrying over our preparations for the Culling."

A chilling breeze whipped my dress, and I shivered. Mother stiffened. "Respectfully, Hayato, that is all the more reason for me to be assigned to the Culling."

"I thought you preferred being at the queen's beck and call," Grottel sniffed. I didn't know what *he* was smelling, but I caught a whiff of sour jealousy reeking from his scowling face. Queen Alliana and Mother had become close friends, back when the queen was only a village girl. She and Mother had banded together to rescue the villages in the farmlands from a particularly furious four-headed nightdragon that had risen out of the abyss at the Constancia border and broken through the protections. Together, Mother and Queen Alliana had saved the realm's precious crops from burning down.

Grottel, on the other hand, had been on the team responsible for the break in the border that had suffered heavy losses. It seemed he'd never forget that. Especially since Mother had been the one to swoop in to rescue him.

"I can respond to the queen's requests *and* investigate the Culling," Mother replied. "Have me and Eva work on it. We'll solve it."

I gulped. We would?

"The *queen* put me in charge of the investigation on the Culling. And you're not planning on going against Queen Alliana, are you, Nela?" At Mother's pained silence, Grottel smirked. He spun on his heel, his black tunic snapping in the wind. "Well. *I* have duties to attend to. Such as meetings that don't require the *magicless*."

As he blew past, his disdainful eyes flicked toward me, finally, but they were as icy-cold as the Torido Rivers. A deep shudder ran down my spine. Had he—I glanced over at Norya, who was shifting her weight from foot to foot by the entrance—had he somehow changed the Novice list and removed me from it?

"And do your duties include researching the rumors that rogue magic is at work?" Mother called after him. "Possibly even blood magic?"

"Rogue magic like that does *not* exist anymore." Grottel slammed the door shut, rattling the glass panes.

"It was worth a shot," Mother said, shooting me a wry smile. Then her eyes widened, and she turned to Grottel's assistant. "Curses, I meant to ask—Norya, might you know why Eva wasn't listed—"

A loud, solemn bell clanged over the rush of the twin rivers. I jolted, prickles running along my skin.

"The final bell! I'm terribly sorry, but I must go." Norya smiled nervously as she yanked at the iron knob. "Oh, drat, he's sealed it!" Grottel's assistant jabbed her wand at the door. "*Let me in, so this meeting can begin.*"

The tip of her wand flashed a faint yellow, and the hinges creaked wearily as she scurried inside.

I stared at the wide-open doorway. In the stone hallway leading to the meeting room, witches and wizards chatted with one another, all outfitted in sleek black with hints of colors showing their ranks. They turned to me with curiosity, studying my knapsack and broomstick slung over my shoulder. Some of Mother's friends waved, beckoning us in, and my heart thumped strangely in my chest. I would have my place within the Council, *finally*.

"I'm sure that oversight with Kaya's list won't be an issue, but we can check with Grottel after the meeting so it won't happen to anyone else in the future." A smile lit up Mother's warm eyes. "Ready?"

Once I went inside, I'd get my ticket and my Novice Witch quest would start.

My heartbeat pounded in my ears, but I grinned back. "I've been waiting for this all my life."

From the moment I entered those doors, I'd have to fight all I could to keep my powers. Because not completing my quest meant something so bone-chillingly awful that I had spent all twelve years of my life trying desperately to avoid it.

CHAPTER 3
THE TICKET

This endless meeting was going to be the start of the best adventure of my life. I was sure of it. If only Grottel would finish droning on about his so-called attempts to investigate the Culling and read out the Novice announcement.

Beyond the ceiling-to-floor windows that framed Grottel's greasy head, the twin rivers roared past, toward the rest of Okayama City. By the magic of a trio of Elites, the glass stayed pristine and untouched by the drizzle, and I watched the water foam and froth as it sped on its own journey. I bounced my toes, jostling my knapsack, and *The Guide for Questing Witches and Wizards* slid out. I dove to catch the book before it hit the stone floor and smoothed out the corners, dog-eared from being read cover-to-cover countless times.

"He should be announcing it any moment now," Mother whispered from the seat next to mine.

"Next," he sniffed, as if he'd heard Mother, but was reluctant to agree with her. "Promotions."

I perked up. This was it. This was my chance to fulfill the Council's mission: Do good. I stared at the wobble in Grottel's chin, waiting for him to speak the magic words.

"Conroy Nytta is now eligible for his Novice Wizard quest."

The crowd roused up a big cheer, echoing against the tall glass windows. I slumped down. Of course darned Conroy, the only other twelve-year-old wizard in the realm, would be announced first.

Norya charmed a piece of paper in a flash of golden light, and Grottel rearranged the greasy clump of hair barely covering his bald spot as Conroy sauntered up. As Grottel handed over the ticket, he leaned down to Conroy's ear, sharing something, and they both smirked. Conroy passed by, raising an eyebrow at me before throwing my mother a bright, cheery smile and waving his golden ticket. "Thank you for your help, Grand Master Evergreen!"

I raised my chin. I didn't know why Conroy had to show off; I'd be getting mine next. I scooted to the edge of my seat, clutching the tome to my chest, ready to hurry to the podium to accept my ticket as soon as Grottel called my name.

Grand Master Grottel's beady eyes scanned his scroll. After the longest second in all of eternity, he cleared his throat.

I leaned forward in anticipation.

"I will send out invitations to celebrate Conroy's Novice ceremony, in one moon." He rolled his scroll back up. "That is all. Meeting adjourned."

I froze, my body turning still as a statue.

Mother sucked in a hiss. "Hayato, *no*—"

My heart pounded as the room spun around me. This was worse than falling asleep from casting one too many spells. It was like I'd plunged straight into my darkest nightmare. He couldn't possibly mean...

Chairs scraped the floor as witches and wizards started gathering their things, picking up their broomsticks, and heading out the door.

I gasped for air. "But..." I turned to Mother. Even her normally rosy cheeks were ashen.

My mother shook her head in disbelief. "It's just an oversight, it *has* to be." She raised her voice. "Hayato!"

He ignored her, sticking his scroll into his pocket and striding toward one of the side doors.

Fear zipped through my heart, like an arrow straight into my chest. I scrambled up the aisle, squeezing past Kaya and Mother's other Council friends, whose heads all turned when they noticed me. "Wait! Please! The meeting can't be done yet!"

"Eva!" Mother called after me, her voice rising in surprise.

The crowd stared as I shouted, "Please, Grand Master Grottel!"

He turned, the force of his glare as mighty as a storm. "What?"

I skidded to a stop. "The last item!"

"I have missed nothing," he spat coldly. Flecks of saliva splattered at my feet. "Are you trying to insinuate that I am not doing my duties as the leader of the Council?"

"No, no, you just forgot—I mean, um, I mean…" I blushed madly and swept into a bow. "Sir, my apologies, but I was summoned to this meeting."

Grottel stared down from the raised stage. "Who are you?"

His words stunned me more than any spell. I'd been to Council meetings before. He'd just seen me outside with Mother. I couldn't be so below his notice. With so few witches and wizards in the realm, he should've at least had an inkling of who I was.…

"E-Eva Evergreen, Apprentice to Nelalithimus Evergreen." I fought to keep my voice from trembling. "I received a summons. I'm due to receive my ticket for my Novice Witch quest."

"That's right, I remember you now. Norya set up that request, didn't she?" he said. "Go to the infirmary."

With a wave of his hand, two burly, oafish-looking guards stepped forward. I shrunk back.

"What? Why do I need to go to the infirmary?" That didn't make any sense. I'd only need to do that if—

"You've hardly done anything particularly, well, magical, as an Apprentice, have you, hmm?" He stared down his sharp nose. Some of the other witches and wizards nodded. By the door, Conroy crossed his arms, eyes unreadable. My blood froze in my veins.

I shook my head, slowly backing up.

No.

No, no, no.

My very worst fear was coming true.

"It won't hurt *that* much. The extraction spell is quite simple, really." He snorted. "Wish it was so simple to give magic to others."

"They're—you're—going to take away my magic?" I whispered.

If the Council deemed an Apprentice magically unfit— a potential rogue witch or wizard—their powers got taken away. Pulled out of their blood, erased from their future…

The pain of that extraction spell would be nothing compared to the pain of losing my magic *forever*. "There must be some sort of mistake. I've created tons of spells, I swear. I've done plenty of good."

"Some magic is not *enough* magic," he snapped.

"There was that time I helped my father with an oven

that combusted—I enchanted a box to hold in the heat so he could keep baking. I'm handy with repairing things."

"Once," he sniffed. "Is this what we should let our magic be reduced to? The realm needs us to do real spells, not cook up party snacks."

I squeezed my arms around my book, as if it could shield me from Grottel. "But I—"

"Aren't you the witch who summoned a field of cabbage instead of flowers when you attempted creation enchantments?"

"The farmer didn't need to worry about harvesting anymore! Plus, it's because I have an affinity for repairs rather than creation magic—I mean, at least I think I do."

He shook his head in disgust. "I have received reports from some of the citizens you have 'helped.' The only reason you have a so-called affinity for repair magic is because you keep breaking things, is it not?"

"Well, I—"

He spoke over me, magnifying his voice throughout the hall. "And when you tried weather magic, you brought down a thunderstorm instead of sending off rain clouds?"

In one of the rows behind me, Conroy snickered. My blood boiled.

"But I fixed it!" I protested.

"And for all of these cases, you took a nap before you 'repaired' the problems you created?"

"I didn't want to, I just…"

I had run out of magic before I could fix the thunderstorm, and Mother, who usually helped sweep up my mistakes, was off on the queen's business. So when I'd fallen asleep, drained of magic, a crack of thunder had woken me up. It'd been the talk of the town, but I hadn't realized word had gotten to Grottel, too.

I glared at Conroy, who sneered as he twirled his ticket in his hand.

But then I looked around the hall. Nearly a quarter of the witches and wizards were shaking their heads more and more vigorously, rumbling with disapproval.

I felt like a piece of dust, about to get charmed into oblivion. I'd dreamed of being a witch like my mother all my life. I needed to be Eva Evergreen, Novice-Witch-in-Training.

If the Council took my powers, I'd be just Eva, a magicless girl.

I tried to speak. "Sir, Grand Master..."

The rest of the Council overpowered my words, muttering as loud as the Torido Rivers rumbling on by.

But Mother's voice soared above the rest. "I believe Eva deserves a chance to become a Novice Witch."

She stepped to my side, the worry on her face mirroring mine. "There's a shortage of us, Hayato. We need all the magic we can get, especially with the Culling coming."

Grand Master Grottel shook his head. "She's a liability. As if a girl with a pinch of magic could shield the realm against the Culling. Go to the infirmary, girl."

His henchmen reached for my arms, one of them stepping between Mother and me.

"Wait, wait!" My throat tightened as tears pricked the corners of my eyes.

One of Grottel's cronies reached out to pluck away my witch's hat, and I scrambled backward, my chest pounding as I bumped into a chair.

My precious book, *The Guide for Questing Witches and Wizards*, tumbled from my arms and fell open to chapter five, with the familiar drawing of a girl heading off on her Novice quest, a broom resting on her shoulder and her hat set at a jaunty slant.

This was my favorite chapter. I had always imagined myself to be just like her. I swallowed the lump in my throat and held back my tears.

"Chapter five..." I murmured, kneeling to gather the magical tome in my hands. "Chapter five."

"Move," growled one of Grottel's henchmen, towering above me.

"Chapter five. The rules for our quests."

"Huh?"

"Grand Master Grottel," I said slowly. Wild hope bloomed in my chest, as if I'd cast a spell on myself. I reached out and picked up my dear, favorite book and brushed it off. "I may have peculiar magic. I may only have a little bit compared to Mother or you or any of the witches or wizards here, but I still *have* magic."

"Not enough."

Slowly, I stood up. "Even a pinch of magic is enough."

I turned the book around and pointed at the top of the page. My blood felt like it was dancing from a spell, zipping from my heart straight down to my fingertips. "Chapter five, section twenty-three."

I read it out:

REQUIREMENTS TO PASS THE NOVICE QUEST

All those with magic must go on a quest.

To show themselves worthy of passing this test.

☙

ONE: Help your town, do good all around.

TWO: Live there for one moon, don't leave too soon.

THREE: Fly by broomstick, the easiest trick.

☙

The rules are simple for the valiant, clever, and strong.

But if you cannot continue, you do not belong.

I shivered as I read the last line. But the law was absolute. The Council lived by these rules. Without them, our realm would be weakened by those using rogue magic, meaning some sort of magic that wasn't overseen by the Council. A spell gone wrong by an unchecked witch or wizard. A mistake that turned deadly.

There'd been incidents years back, as magic waned

and some witches and wizards cast magic unchecked. A
rogue witch had, with one wayward spell, decimated an
entire town. Now, apprenticeships and the quests ensured
that witches and wizards were trained and licensed and
swore by the mission of the Council: Do good.

"It says that any Apprentice gets to go on their journey.
As long as they have magic." I stared down Grand Master
Grottel. "Let the judge be the leader of the town that I end
up in. I swear I'll uphold the Council's rules and do good."

Those who hadn't sided with Grottel nodded in support.

Grottel scanned the hall, a vein throbbing in his forehead. Then his eyes narrowed at me. I fought my nervous
urge to try to charm myself into the ground. He couldn't
possibly disregard the rules of the quest—it would be like
disregarding the rules of the Council.

Kaya and a handful of Mother's closest friends shifted
closer toward us. The air brewed thick with a heaviness,
like clouds forming before a thunderstorm.

"The rules are much too lenient," Grottel snapped.
He flicked his hand at Norya, who scribbled something
onto a paper and tapped her wand, casting a quick spell.
She bowed low, the paper held high as she raised her
hands above her head.

He jabbed his wand at the paper. It glowed gold and
lifted up into the air. The crowd hushed in surprise.

Grottel growled, "Evalithimus Evergreen, although you have yet to show any noteworthy enchantments, we hope to see that your pinch of magic is not a fluke."

He flicked his wrist and incanted a spell. *"Fly to the girl."* Grottel, like my mother, was powerful enough to be able to use the barest of commands for simple spells. The golden ticket shot into the air and fluttered down to my fingertips.

I clutched the ticket, my hands shaking with excitement, and read it out:

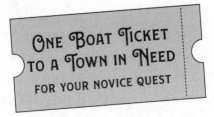

My heart soared. "Thank you, Grand Master Grottel. I promise I'll do good by the Council."

"Good luck with your attempt. Your boat leaves in an hour," he sniped. He turned on his heel and stalked away.

Norya hurried up to me, a kind smile warming her eyes, and handed over a black tube. "Your Novice quest rules and application—keep it safe, and make sure to get the application properly signed. Best of luck to you, Apprentice Evergreen. I hope to call you Novice Evergreen when we meet next."

As Norya hurried off to follow Grottel, Mother wrapped her arm around my shoulder with a cheeky grin. "You've made Hayato listen for once. You'll be a witch like me in no time."

I smiled as if I was as certain as she was.

But sweat trickled down my back as I stumbled out of the Council Hall, in Mother's footsteps and to Father's awaiting arms. How in the realm was I going to pull this off?

ᗞo Good

The wind fluttered the brim of my witch's hat and it lifted up, as if it was planning to fly off on its own adventure, but I tugged it firmly down. I clutched my knapsack and broom, staring in awe at the tall boat bobbing in the water. We had rushed from the Council Hall to the docks, so I could catch the midday boat from Okayama, and made it just as they'd started boarding.

"All packed? Got the croissants?" Father patted my knapsack and then blinked quickly, staring at the foaming peaks of the river as if it was to blame. "Darn that water, spraying in my eyes."

"All packed," I echoed.

"I saw you got a copy of *Potions of Possibilities*." Mother frowned, prodding her cherrywood wand at the buckles of my knapsack, checking that they were latched and secured for the thirtieth time. "I know potions are out of fashion, but you may find that tome useful."

"Along with the smoked mackerel, the huge bag of rice, the *Do Good* needlepoint, and the thirteen jars of odds and ends you've already snuck in?" I said. "My knapsack will probably sink the boat." Father hid his laugh.

"I just want to send you off right." She raised an eyebrow and pointed her wand at me. "Don't make me charm you into staying."

I knew she'd never do that. With every wish I'd made hoping to become a witch, she'd also believed that I'd become a witch like her, too. I whispered, quieter than the rush of the river, "I'm going to miss you both so much."

Mother pulled me in for a hug, resting her head on top of mine. The smooth silk of her dress brushed my skin, and I breathed in her spicy cinnamon scent, slowing down my racing heartbeat.

"One last thing that I made for you," she said, and pulled something from around her neck. A tiny hourglass smaller than my thumbnail, made of two glass stars meeting together, dangled on a bronze chain. Bronze, like the color of the Novice rank. My heart swelled; Mother must have picked the color wholeheartedly believing in me. "It's charmed to your quest window, so sand trickles down as time passes, and the top star will empty out when your time is up."

I slipped the chain over my neck. "Thank you, Mother." Now I had a bit of her to take with me, wherever I got sent.

"One moon will pass in no time." She brushed at the droplets of mist forming on my hat, smiling gently. "Don't forget to meet with your town leader as soon as you get off. And have the best time with your guardian, too. But more than anything, never forget the mission of all witches and wizards, Eva."

The first day of the Novice quest would be simple enough: meet with my new town leader, secure a guardian as the liaison between me and the town...and, always, do good. "I won't forget." I didn't need a needlepoint to remember that. Even with just my pinch of magic, even if I was a fluke, I wanted to do good just like my mother.

"The Culling will hit the realm before the end of the year, though." Father rubbed the stubble on his chin thoughtfully. "Come back before then."

"It's still early summer, Father. I'll be home in one moon, well before it starts." I waved the star-shaped hourglass at him, yet prickles ran down my neck.

Seven years ago, the Culling, a strange, cursed force of nature, struck the realm. Every year since, it pelted the land each autumn with anything from a sudden blizzard on a once-sunny day to an earthquake that deepened the abyss between Rivelle Realm and Constancia, the realm to the south.

In previous years, witches and wizards had tried to

spell the Culling to weaken its hold on the land. Those enchantments had only enraged the Culling, which sucked up the powers of the charms to ravage the realm with an unstoppable fury.

The scrying witches and wizards could only see the rising force of nature hours before it slammed against the realm. Each time they scried for a source, something—or someone—had blocked them.

Mother believed that rogue magic was at work. Or even something far more sinister...

At previous meetings, she'd pled for Grottel to look into the possibility that the Culling had been formed through blood magic. The Hall had been in an uproar, but her words had rung true to me. It could very likely be a rogue witch or wizard sacrificing their own *blood* in exchange for terrifying amounts of power. But Grottel refused to listen. He'd said that the Culling was because of the current imbalance of magic within the land. That the Culling showed there were too many weak witches and wizards who couldn't help the realm in times of need. He pointed to the other six realms as an example. Most of the other realms had less magic than us. Since Rivelle had been the first to form a Council to organize its magic users, he claimed that our Council had helped Rivelle keep the most magic.

And Grottel pointedly argued that all blood magic had been stamped out hundreds of years ago. He insisted that the source of the Culling came from one of our neighboring realms. To placate the concerns, he had sent out convoy after convoy of scrying witches and wizards, to traverse past the borders of Rivelle Realm.

Years later, they'd found nothing.

But the Culling—whether as a tornado, earthquake, or other disastrous form—continued to plague the realm every year, wrecking everything that dared stand in its path.

Although I had an affinity for repair magic, my unreliable fixes wouldn't stand a chance against the Culling.

"Even if the Council frowns upon you returning home early, come back anytime," Father added. "Don't listen to those stuffy witches and wizards."

Mother laughed. "That's exactly what you told me years ago, isn't it?"

I couldn't laugh. Returning home without passing my Novice quest would mean I'd failed. The Council would strip away every last drop of magic from my blood.

I couldn't imagine my future without magic.

As we waited for my turn to board, a little girl stumbled into me and I barely caught myself from tumbling into my father. Mother scooped her up before she could fall. "Careful now, dearie."

The girl's cheeks dimpled. "Thank you!" She scurried away.

My skin prickled.

"Where are her parents?" I craned my neck.

The little girl had slipped through the hordes until she stood at the end of the long pier. "Mama?" The girl waved her hands up at the grimy ship windows. She looked only two or three years old. "Mama!"

A worker walked past, heaving a tower of boxes. I tried to call out but I was too far away. He bumped into the girl, clipping her on the forehead.

Her smile melted into tears. I gasped as the girl's arms flailed as she blindly wobbled toward the rushing river. "No!" I cried, grabbing my wand. *"No harm...on ground..."*

Orange light spluttered out. My magic wasn't strong enough.

"What are you charming?" Mother spun around.

Trapped air burned in my lungs. I had to do something....

The girl teetered over the edge and her shrill cry shot through the pier. Time seemed to slow as she fell, her eyes frozen in fear while waves licked at her, about to pull her under.

Mother whipped out her wand. *"Stay safe and sound, fences all around!"*

Golden light flashed. Vines sprouted from the wood, weaving into a net. It caught the girl and pushed her back to safety. The branches wove along the length of the pier until the warm glow faded, leaving behind a fence.

A pale-faced man pushed through the gathered crowd

and folded the girl into his arms. "Izu! Don't ever run off again!"

The little girl pointed over his shoulder. "Witch!"

"Izu, it's rude to point—" He turned around and his mouth dropped open. "Are you—are you *the* Nelalithimus Evergreen?"

Mother tugged the brim of her witch's hat. "At your service."

"Thank you so much, Grand Master." The man bowed deeply. "It's an honor." His eyes flickered to me, at her side, and the wand in my hand. I stepped back into the crowd, letting curious onlookers push past. This was Mother's work, not mine.

"Thank you, thank you." The little girl stared up at my mother in awe.

My chest tightened. If only my spell had worked right, they would've been thanking me.

After one last bow of thanks, the man settled his daughter on his shoulders and headed back to the boat, still shaking his head in wonder. "*The* Nelalithimus Evergreen..."

The crowd slowly broke up, shooting final glances at my mother. They were probably trying to memorize every last detail of her to tell their families back home.

Mother slipped her wand back into her pocket as a smile danced on her lips. "I've been telling the dock captain to put up a barrier for years. Stick-in-the-mud wouldn't pay the carpenters' guild, yet didn't want to ask for an enchantment because he was afraid the carpenters would be insulted." Then her eyes sparkled. "I think this counts as a valid reason, right?"

Father's grin matched hers. "They'll have to accept it now."

My fingers tingled, as if my magic longed to help, too. But my charm had spluttered out.

A horn blew. "Last call!" shouted the attendant at the loading ramp. I jumped. I couldn't miss the boat. Mother's hand curled around mine in a tight squeeze as Father helped me hoist on my knapsack and sling my broomstick over my shoulder. Mother's eyes misted as she and Father wrapped me in one last hug. She didn't pretend it was from the river's spray. "We'll miss you, Eva."

As I hurried to the line, the shadow of the boat loomed over me. My stomach roiled like I was about to get swept out into the waves like that little girl. After I boarded, I wouldn't have Mother's spells to save the day.

When I got to the foot of the ramp, the attendant paused. "A witch?" She had jet-black hair clipped at her shoulders in a sharp bob, and a bottle-green, fitted uniform with sharp trimmings that matched the honey-brown of her eyes. She looked maybe ten or so years older than me, but the way she spoke made her seem much older.

"Yes, Apprentice Evalithimus Evergreen, going to my new town for my Novice quest." I tried to match her mature, assured air, but it didn't quite seem to fit.

The attendant examined my golden ticket, glinting under the bright sun, and then neatly punched a hole into the corner. "It's a pleasure to meet you, Apprentice Evergreen."

"Oh, everyone calls me Eva."

She smiled as she handed back my ticket. "I'm Rin. Let me know if you need anything, okay?"

I tipped the edge of my hat. "Thank you."

Inside, the boat was cool and dark, like diving into deep water. Dust motes danced in the faint light streaming through the dirty windows. The lower deck was packed with people settling into oak benches long enough to sit two or three people. I skirted around a businessman and his rustling newspapers, past a family arranging their rolling trunks under the benches, and to the first empty bench.

Sliding into the window seat, I put my knapsack on my lap for warmth as I shivered from a breeze. One of the side effects of magic was that my blood always ran cold. I had tried to fix it with everything from spells to heated bricks on winter nights. Despite all my attempts, I still felt the chill, even with the warm summer air.

"May I?" From the aisle, a portly man gestured his wrinkled hand at the bench.

I nodded. "You're welcome to sit here, sir."

He sighed in relief as he eased a rickety-looking crate to the ground. I jumped when something scratched at the slats.

"Hush now," the old man said, patting the crate.

The horn blew twice. Peering through the dirty window, I spotted my father, placing his arm around my mother as she leaned into him. "Do good, Eva," my parents called, even though they couldn't see me through the grubby panes. "Safe travels!"

A strange pang tightened in my chest.

I traced the outline of their faces on the glass. Their upturned faces disappeared into the crowd as the boat rumbled down the river, pushed by the fast-moving currents and the steam engine puffing thick clouds into the wind. The boat was scheduled to stop at a handful of towns before the river poured into the Constancia Sea, and then the route led south along the coast, pausing at a dozen more towns along the way.

Outside, the familiar plains and hills shrank into the distance. The grime made the scenery sepia-toned, like an old photograph.

I checked my pocket. My golden boat ticket peeked out, the letters shimmering even in the faint light:

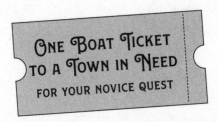

ONE BOAT TICKET
TO A TOWN IN NEED
FOR YOUR NOVICE QUEST

Council tickets were different from magicless tickets. Because Rivelle Realm had so few witches and wizards, a clever witch had the idea of using a charm to disperse us equally around the realm. There were all sorts of magical tickets—boat tickets and train tickets and automobile tickets, and I'd even heard that one wizard had gotten a horse ticket.

When the ticket sensed a town where a wizard or witch like me might be needed, it would tell me to get off. The paper would flash from gold to red and crumble into dust when the boat got to my new town.

A few minutes later, the boat attendant's voice rang through the deck. "Next stop, Tsudanuma!"

I let out a yelp of surprise, and the creatures in the crate happily yapped in response.

What if—what if it was already time for me to get off?

If Tsudanuma was my new home...I would be close to my parents, but it was one of the moderately big cities, almost as big as my hometown. I'd be overwhelmed with requests from the instant I stepped onto the docks. Grottel would probably pop by just to laugh at the piles of requests I'd left unfulfilled.

I screwed my eyes shut before I could see my ticket.

CHAPTER 5
A Magical Mend

Taking a deep breath, I peeked down. The ticket shone bright gold, and I slumped back into the seat with relief. This wasn't my new town.

After the ship made a few more quick stops—without a flicker from my ticket—my stomach started growling.

I unbuckled my knapsack and the smell of buttery croissants wafted out. For a second, I felt like I was back at home, waiting for Father to pull the baking sheet out of the oven. The thought of my parents heading home without me made my throat tighten. I looked over to offer some to my neighbor, but he was snoring with his chin tucked on his chest.

Balancing my small jar of redbud jam in my left hand, I scooped out a ruby-red dollop onto a croissant. It melted in my mouth with a burst of vanilla and citrus, as if I'd captured falling redbud blossoms on my tongue.

Mid-bite, a scratching sound came from my neighbor's crate. Then a wood panel on the box cracked loudly. A wet snout poked out, sniffing the air.

I tugged my neighbor's sleeve. "Sir, um, I think your dogs are escaping."

The man shot up, rubbing his eyes. "These trouble-makers," he growled, as a puppy popped its head out of the hole.

"Ohh, I've never seen a dog like that," I said in awe. The pup had reddish-gold fur and pointed ears that were bigger than its foxlike face, with a white starlike mark on its forehead. Small white patches of fur were dotted above each eye, like little eyebrows, and its lips curved up in a clever smile, as if it was saying, *Are you proud of me? I figured out how to escape this box!*

A larger puppy with black fur craned its head out to look at the old man, whining. "That's 'cause they're not your average puppies," the man replied, shifting the small glasses perched on the edge of his nose. "These are flamefoxes. They're part fox, part dog, part flamethrowing nightdragon, and most days, they're the worst parts of each."

He lifted the bigger pup out of the crate, and it licked his nose. I yelped as he patted its tail—flames flickered around his hand. I'd only read about flamefoxes in books;

they were the four-legged, very distant, and far more mischievous cousins of phoenixes and nightdragons.

"Here!" I cried, grabbing my canteen. "I've got water!"

He laughed. "That's the trademark of a flamefox, missy. Their tails give off light, and sticking your hand in their flames just feels warm. It's when they start *breathing* fire that it's an issue."

"Wow," I whispered.

The smaller pup whimpered for attention, and when I looked at it, it seemed to crinkle its eyes in a smile.

"He's probably hungry again." The old man shook his head. "That one's a bottomless pit."

"I have pastries," I offered. "My father overpacked my bag."

"He'll never leave you alone now," the man warned. "This red runt isn't interested in anything other than eating, sleeping, and causing trouble. His tail isn't even producing flames. I've never seen a flamefox without a fiery tail, to be honest."

I knew how the red flamefox felt. I was a witch who wasn't very magical.

"Where did they come from?" I asked.

"I picked them up in Okayama. Their old owners thought they'd be cute, but this pup gnawed on everything in their house—including the house itself—like it was all his own chew toy, until their owners threw 'em out."

The wood panel cracked in half as the red-gold pup

stuck his head out again, eyes sparkling as he pushed his star-marked forehead under the man's hand for another rub. The old man grumbled. "Dragonsharks! The darn crate's no use if they're not *inside*."

"Want me to fix it?" I asked. My magic itched to be let out, like little bubbles in me that wanted to pop. I could repair this—hopefully. Mother guessed that I had a slight affinity for repair magic, so when I fixed things, my powers flourished. Well, as much as my pinch of magic could flourish. Mother's affinity was creation magic, so she would have created a new, unbreakable carrier out of thin air with a flick of her wand.

I couldn't make things out of nothing. But even if my magic was messy, I did my best to make it work.

"Are you really a witch?" he asked, pursing his lips. "I've only met a handful of you folks. And, well, you look so young."

"I'm on my Novice quest." I drew myself up as tall as I could.

Suddenly, the red-gold pup wriggled out and jumped onto my knapsack, snuffling loudly.

"My croissants!" I yelped and dove for my pack. The man grabbed for the pup, raking his hand against the edges of the broken wood, crying out in pain.

The red-gold flamefox lifted one paw to jump into the aisle. I dove, snatched the flamefox—it felt like I was grabbing onto a fire-warmed brick—and shoved him and his friend back inside. I could've sworn the red flamefox rolled his eyes. Then I plopped my knapsack on top of the hole.

I turned to my neighbor and sucked in my breath. A wicked gash extended from his palm up to his elbow.

"May I cast a healing charm on you?" I offered hesitantly, pulling out my wand.

"Ooh, the witch is performing magic!" a boy called out. Heads popped up from all around the boat to watch, and my cheeks burned.

Ideas for enchantments flickered through my mind. *Slow as you go* might backfire and make the whole boat stop.... There had to be another spell I could use.

The old man winced looking down at his arm, but he shook his head. "Please, could you help with the crate first? They'll escape again."

My chest tightened as I quickly examined the crate. There was never a one-size-fits-all spell. Mother created clever charms, sometimes in rhymes, that made her magic more focused—though she didn't really need it. She and Grottel were the only ones in the realm who could utter one- or two-word spells. I couldn't use her incantations, though. When I tried her enchantment for making dust fly out of the house, the dust swirled around in the corners and clumped up. By crafting my own incantations, I created a spell that was all mine, and that connected to the magic in my blood far better than borrowing charms.

This was why it was so important for me to venture out on my own to become a Novice Witch.

At my side, the old man was pale, wincing again as he pressed a handkerchief to his gash. I had to fix the crate, fast. Pulling my own handkerchief out of my knapsack, I laid it over the gap.

"Knit, whipstitch, mend." I tapped my wand on the cloth. This charm patched up minor tears I'd gotten in my dresses after falling asleep a few too many times from overextending my magic—but I wasn't sure it would work in this pinch.

Pale blue light flowed out of my wand, and the handkerchief stretched and knitted to the wood, and when I knocked on it, it was stiff. I sighed in relief.

"Ah, thank you, missy," the man croaked. His forehead gleamed, and sweat beaded on his bulbous nose.

"Er, are you sure you're okay?"

"Strange, eh?" he said faintly. "I run a wild-beast shelter, yet I get woozy from a speck of blood...." He held his arm out and turned his face away.

The cut looked surprisingly deep, and splinters were embedded in his skin. He grimaced and tried to make light of it. "When you get old like me, a simple cut isn't so simple anymore."

I tried to smile, yet I couldn't. The next stop was still half an hour away—what if I couldn't heal him?

I'd fail my quest before I even got off the boat.

"You can do it!" the boy called, his eyes shining. Around the boat, passengers bobbed their heads in agreement.

All I had in mind was a spell I had used on paper cuts, not wounds the full length of my arm. Still, I couldn't think of anything else. I chanted, *"Heal a slice that isn't so nice."*

I chanted the charm again and again, and a surprising amount of magic poured from me until the splinters had eased out and only a faint pink scar remained.

"You did it!" The riders on the boat cheered for me and I blushed. Thankfully, most of them, deciding the show was over, sat down or went back to their newspapers.

"Ah, thank you." The old man clutched his arm, splotches of color returning to his cheeks. "You don't mind if I rest a bit, do you?" Without waiting for my answer, he closed his eyes with a wheeze of relief.

Moments later, as he let out a gentle snore, the flamefoxes started whining. Fearing they would wake up the old man, I fed them bits of flaky crust through the cracks, saving one last croissant for later. Their soft tongues tickled as they lapped up every speck.

The attendant stopped by. "Nice work, Eva," Rin said.

"Oh." I smiled at her. "I just did what any witch or wizard would've done."

Rin tugged at her cap as she headed down the aisle.

I released a deep breath. Before boarding, I had been

wound up and excited, but using magic had sapped my energy. I curled up against the window and yawned.

A ticklish feeling in the back of my mind reminded me of the ticket in my pocket. But the drain on my magic tugged at me, and the boat rocked me gently into a peaceful rest.

CHAPTER 6
THE TOWN OF LIGHTS

I was having a lovely dream. I had set up my own magical repair shop, and customers kept pounding at the door, flooding me with requests. *Please help me fix this, Elite Witch!* cried my guardian. Even my mother knocked, calling out, *Eva, we need a repair that'll save us from the Culling!* I flung open the door and—

"Eva? Eva?" A salty breeze tickled my nose, and I rubbed my eyes. Rin, the boat attendant, leaned over the seat, her luminous honey-brown eyes twinkling. The old man with the flamefoxes was already gone. "Time to wake up, little witch."

The knots in my neck protested as I sat up. The boat bobbed up and down instead of jetting through the waves. "W-why've we stopped? Did we make it to the sea?"

Rin glanced around. "What do you mean—oh!" She tilted her head back and laughed. "We're at Auteri!"

"Auteri?" I echoed. "The home of the Festival of Lights?" The curtains were drawn on the windows, so I couldn't see outside.

She beckoned me toward the door. "Come outside, you'll see."

It was too quiet. A creeping sense of dread crawled down my spine. "Doesn't this boat keep going?"

"You mean you're not supposed to be here? Auteri is the last stop of the route. The next boat won't head back toward Okayama until morning."

Her words rang in my ears. *Last. Stop.* I shot to my feet. The cabin was empty except for me and Rin and a handful of crumpled sandwich wrappers in the aisle, tumbling in the gentle wind.

My heart plummeted as sweat beaded on my forehead. Where was I supposed to have gotten off? Was I at the wrong stop?

"Maybe my ticket will show—" I dug into my pockets.

They were empty, except for a fistful of dust. A breeze blew and the remains of my ticket fluttered away in the cool air.

"Well, then." Rin stared at my trembling hands and then cleared her throat. "I guess that means you're meant to stay here, right?"

I curled my fists in the folds of my skirt. It felt as if I

was drowning in the black depths of the sea. I gasped for air, but I couldn't breathe, as if water flooded my lungs.

How was I supposed to figure out where I had to get off? My ticket had blown away in pieces, and I couldn't scry like a fortune-telling witch.

"Come along, everyone in Auteri will be excited to meet you!" Rin waved at me to follow her. My knapsack tugged down on my shoulders, feeling heavier than it had in the morning, though I'd finished off nearly all the croissants and a jar of jam.

I gripped my hands around the straps of my knapsack. All I had to do was find a town that didn't have a witch or wizard. The ticket was just a guide to help me find a town. As long as I fulfilled the requirements of the quest, I could stay as the town witch.

There was only one moon's time left, and I needed each and every day to win over the town leader.

I *had* to stay here.

A few people walked through the cabin—a group of cleaners pushing their rattling carts along the aisles and stray passengers yawning and heading out to the deck to disembark. Most of them were tourists with wide floppy hats and big rolling trunks. Unlike me, all of them looked like they expected to be here.

"Eva?" Rin called, from outside the door.

I stood as straight and as tall as I could, the way Mother would. It felt like I was barely treading water, but at least I wasn't sinking into the sea. Breathing deep, I whispered, "I'm a witch, just like Mother. And I'm going to keep my magic, too."

With that, I followed after Rin.

The moment I stepped outside, a blast of salty air hit my face. Above, pricks of stars glinted in the vast red-purple evening sky. But bigger than the sky was the rippling water.

Back at home, we had a stream that trickled next to the garden, and we always traveled down to Okayama by riverboat. The other shore had been a stone's throw away. I'd never seen anything like this.

I gasped. "Is this—"

"The one and only Constancia Sea." Rin grinned at my astonishment. I ran to the railing and leaned over.

Taking a deep breath, I gazed out at the splendors. Water stretched out and out, until it mixed with the sky at the faraway horizon. I turned around and gaped at the strange new world in front of me. On the other side of the ship, rocky cliffs reached toward the sky, looming over us. Beyond some of the moored boats, there was a gap in the cliffs, about the length of five sailing ships, as if the rocks were two hands reaching for each other yet forever apart.

Through the opening, a town was nestled in a bay. Skiffs zipped to and fro, ferrying cargo and passengers to land. Inside the bay, it looked like a witch had cleared out a circle within the cliffs and filled it half with water and half with land.

"Why don't we dock by the town?" I asked.

Rin shook her head. "The ships can't make it into the rocky shallows, so we have to switch to a smaller boat." She handed me a pair of binoculars from her pocket. "Go on, take a look at Auteri."

Through the lenses, the half-moon shape of the town glimmered, huddled between the circle of cliffs and dark blue bay. Stone roads crossed between the white homes and stores with dark blue and gold tiled roofs, and lights sparkled from windows, making the town look like a cluster of sapphires and diamonds peeking out of stone. On the farthest edge of town on the top of a small hill, a huge building towered over Auteri, capped with a gold dome. Behind the town, a narrow road led up and over a steep peak.

"Welcome to Auteri," Rin said. "Home of the Festival of Lights."

She motioned me toward a skiff. We settled onto the plank seats, surrounded by crates, as the sailors shouted to one another, grunting as they pulled on ropes to lower the skiff.

We bobbed in the slight waves, and the skiff workers began rowing us in. I ran my fingers through the cold water, and goose bumps prickled all over my arm. "It's beautiful here."

"Isn't it?" Rin smiled. "Still, the sea is a fickle one. Won't listen to what any sailor, nightdragon, or witch says. It's gorgeous now, but it grows vicious in autumn. Even more so with the last Culling."

I shivered. Last year, Mother and nine Elite witches and wizards hadn't been able to get to Kelpern, one of the cities on the coast between Okayama and Auteri, until hours after a blizzard had started. By then, the damage had already been done. Hail had shattered the windows, and the buildings had caved in under the weight of the ice. They barely managed to combine their magic to create a bubble-like shield over the broken city as the blizzard raged on.

A few days later, the storm dissolved into thin air.

But the ruins remained.

Shivers tingled down my spine.

"Staying for a while, are you?" one of the rowers asked, squinting at my plump knapsack, and shaking me out of my thoughts.

"I—I don't know," I said honestly. "I'm on my Novice quest, and so I'm looking for a town that needs my help."

"Well, I definitely hope you'll stay," Rin said.

The rower wiped the sweat off his neck with a handkerchief. "We sure could use your help getting our dear town into fighting shape before the Festival of Lights."

Rin nodded, smiling at the man. Then she lowered her voice. "He's right, Eva. We do need help. The realm may be scared of the Culling, but for us, a town on the waterfront, it's the shadow to every beautiful day out on the sea. I wish there were more of you. Last year, though the blizzard hit Kelpern, some of our buildings near the docks flooded. These white buildings were stained with mud, up to the windows. Even worse, some of the stores got knocked down. An old cobbler's shop near Seafoam Sweets Shoppe got completely wiped out, and the orphanage took some damage."

I shuddered. This town was too beautiful. I couldn't imagine the sparkling buildings flooded with saltwater.

The skiff passed through the gap between the towering black cliffs. "Don't these rocks protect the town?"

"We've made a thick wood-and-iron gate to stop waves and wind from rushing through this gap, but it got blasted off in the past storm like a piece of paper. Nothing's going to be able to bridge a gap this big, not unless there's magic involved."

I didn't want to say that my Novice Witch quest would end long before the Culling. Or, even worse, that my magic might not be enough.

"Oh, look!" Rin pointed to the right of the boat, where three fins stuck out of the waves.

"Dragonsharks?" I gasped, jerking my hand out of the water and peering down for a glimpse of their razor-sharp fangs.

She shook her head with a light laugh. "Watch."

A dolphin soared out of the water, droplets sparkling on its gray skin. It arced, spun a circle in the air, and dove back into the sea. Its friends joined it, and the dolphins frolicked alongside us, flying in and out of the waves. When we got close to the pier, they turned after one final jump, as if they sensed the rocky shallows.

"It's a good sign." Rin sighed with a quiet joy as the dolphins swam out to open sea. The rest of the rowers nodded, too.

The workers docked the skiff, and Rin motioned me out. I stood, but the overpowering smell of sweaty sailors and piles of fish made me sit back down.

Rin grinned. "When I've been away from the docks too long, the smell is a punch in the face."

"Hey, Rin." One of the sailors scowled. "You don't smell so sweet after a day on the ship, either."

"I'm sure you smell like roses." She raised an eyebrow. "I'm too scared to smell my own clothes."

I subtly sniffed the air. The skiff worker blended in with the rest of the sailors—smelling like briny fish. The faint scent of sun-dried laundry drifted from Rin.

Rin turned toward me, and I wrenched away.

Her eyes crinkled at the corners. "Ready to go?"

My cheeks warmed. "Definitely." I hefted up my sagging knapsack.

"So, where should I take you?"

I sorted through my list of priorities. "First, I need

to meet the town leader." All witches and wizards were supposed to meet with the leader to understand how they could best help the town, and that's where I would receive my guardian assignment—if I was allowed to stay.

"That's not going to happen." Rin shook her head. "When the sun starts to set and the dinner bell rings, Mayor Taira closes up the town hall to encourage workers to go home for dinner with their families."

My chest pinched. "I can't fulfill my duty to see the mayor?"

The Council would be appalled. Conroy would say I was charming myself onto the path to failure.

Rin chuckled. "Believe me, it's better to meet Mayor Taira after a good night's sleep." Then she studied my broomstick and lumpy knapsack. "But we should get you a place to stay.... You're young enough.... Maybe there's a spare bed at the orphanage?" She glanced at a two-story white stone building at the edge of the docks. "Ah, wait! It's been so long that I almost forgot.... You don't mind living alone?"

"Not at all." Or at least I didn't think so. I gulped. It finally sank in that my parents were terribly far away; Father would've befriended everyone on the ship with his croissants by the time we had landed, and Mother would've found a way to charm Mayor Taira to an audience. My cheeks burned. I doubted that they would have fallen asleep on the boat, either.

"How do you feel about a fixer-upper?"

"I'm handy, I'm good with fixing things," I said, drawing myself up.

Rin's lips curved into a smile. "Then I know of the place for you."

∽

I followed Rin away from the town and on a narrow path up a cliff, stumbling over the moss and rocks. In the crevices, pale purple dusklight flowers had unfurled in the evening glow, swaying in the sea breeze. To my right, the wall of black rocks towered over me; on the left, the path dropped straight down to the sea.

I had never been scared of heights, but there was something ferociously wild and *other* about the sea. I stuck close to the cliff and the stiff brush that grew in the crevices. I was used to grassy plains and lush forests, not this turbulent blue-black water. I breathed in deep, and the salty sea spray settled into my dress and onto my skin.

Rin disappeared around a corner marked by a lonely patch of stiff brush. I hurried to catch up. I turned around the cliff, and the path opened up to a small house built into the rocks, with vines of dusklight flowers covering its front.

"Ah, it's been years since I've been here." Rin stretched out her arms. "I used to sneak out here with my friends."

I stared at the tiny cottage. Under the vines, it was

painted some sort of brownish color. Or it was simply very dirty.

"Who lived here?" I wondered aloud.

"This is Auteri's cottage for witches and wizards like you. We haven't had one in more than a dozen years, so this place has been a bit neglected."

The cottage definitely was a fixer-upper. It would require a lot of magic to clean it up, but something about the place felt so right.

"I'm sorry....It doesn't look like much." Rin tugged her cap down to cover her eyes.

I blinked and shook my head fervently. "No, no. That's not it."

My magic bubbled up inside me, itching to mend the storm shutters dangling off the hinges, to scrub the windows caked with dirt. With a good cleaning and some repairs, the glass would shimmer with the reflection of the sea. I could stay in Auteri and help the town, starting with this cottage.

I turned to her and grinned. "It's perfect."

CHAPTER 7
A Ghostly Visitor

Hours later, past midnight, I sprawled on the floor. My bones ached from cleaning the cottage with a simple spell and a whole lot of elbow grease.

I had charmed a handkerchief to scrub the house from floor to ceiling with *"A mean clean is in need."* It had run out of magic halfway through, and I had finished scouring the floorboards with the limp cloth and a bucket of soapy water.

There were only two rooms: a square washroom and a main area with windows that looked out onto the sea. The central room had a tiny kitchen area, a rickety bed frame with a lumpy mattress, and a small closet that I had tossed my knapsack into. I had fixed up the broken sink and started a fire in the stove to cook a late dinner.

While I waited for water to boil, I scribbled out a quick letter.

> Dear Mother and Father,
>
>   I'm in Auteri. I was wondering... Is there any way to check whether I'm in the right town? I don't think I got off the boat too late or anything, just to confirm.
>
>   And Mother, don't worry—I'll do good by my town, I promise.
>
>   With love,
>   Eva

My fingers carefully folded the paper in and under to create a paper bird. I wasn't very good at folding—one wing was bigger than the other—but it was all I needed for letters. I wrote *To Nelalithimus and Isao Evergreen* in my best cursive on the right wing.

"*Resist the water, resist the wind, resist until your path desists*," I chanted, and tapped my wand against the letter. I scooped the paper bird into my palm and brought it to the window.

"Give my love to my parents, little bird." I blew lightly on the paper and the bird-letter jumped up onto the sill, arching its neck. Fluttering its thin paper wings, it leaped into the night.

For a second, I imagined I could fly like the bird, back home. I glanced at my broomstick propped in the corner. I'd told Conroy that I could fly, but that was a bit of a stretch. Like my magic, I'd practiced and practiced but never quite gotten the hang of it. "I have to learn how to properly fly first. I should name you—how about Fiery Phoenix?"

I had always been fascinated by phoenixes. When I read Mother's magic tomes, I had traced my fingers over the painted yellow-red eyes and the majestic gold-leafed plumage, like a glowing flame. If a witch or wizard was lucky enough to receive a phoenix feather, their magic blossomed, but no one had found a feather in more than a hundred years. I'd always wanted just one feather. Just last year, rumors spread of a sighting in the east of the realm, by the Walking Cliffs. Almost all of the realm's witches and wizards had swarmed the cliffs, Mother included. Not a feather was to be found. After weeks of crawling over the rocks that were almost as tall as the Sakuya Mountains, the Council chalked it up to a fireside fable.

The stiff broomstick didn't look anything like a phoenix. "A different name, maybe." I put it away in the closet.

I rummaged in my knapsack for the smoked fish, the canvas wheezing with relief as I took out my kitchen supplies and poured a handful of rice into the boiling pot. Before long, the familiar smell of the bubbling rice wafted through the cottage. I scrubbed a chipped plate from the dusty shelves and brought my simple dinner to the front step of the cottage.

My tired body nearly melted when I sat on the stone slab. The night sky sparkled with more stars than I'd ever seen. I peered to my left, and the golden lights from town flickered comfortingly.

"I'll do my best to take care of you, Auteri," I whispered. As long as Mayor Taira would let me stay, of course. But nearly every town in the Realm appealed to the Council for help, so Auteri was likely in need, too. As long as they didn't mind an inexperienced witch.

I went to pick up the plate. It wasn't where I had left it.

It had moved behind me.

And, somehow, the plate was polished clean.

There was no one in sight. Was there a ghost?

A few grains of rice led into the cottage. I followed the trail, one by one. My heart beat unsteadily. Mother kept me awake with ghost stories on too many a dark night. When she told me tales of the haunted forests of the north, where she'd grown up, I almost sensed the presence of the villagers' wailings carried on the wind. But she'd never told me stories about ghosts that stole rice.

The trail led straight into the closet, where I had left my knapsack on the floor. The three shelves on the walls were all empty. I leaped back when my knapsack wriggled.

"W-what?" I croaked.

I snatched the Fiery Phoenix and used the stick to prod my knapsack, and it *squeaked*. I lifted the top flap.

Nestled among the crumbs of my last croissant, the red-gold flamefox from the boat stared up and let out a loud burp. He cocked his head with his huge ears perked up. A grain of rice stuck to the tip of his muzzle, and his tongue flicked out and polished it clean. I wasn't sure if he was smiling or laughing. Probably both.

My eyes focused on something underneath him. "My scroll!" I dove for my knapsack and grabbed the leather tube containing my Novice Witch application.

The flamefox jumped out and landed gracefully. He padded over and sat docilely at my feet. The black tube had some nibble marks on the corners, so I popped off the top.

REQUIREMENTS TO PASS THE NOVICE QUEST

All those with magic must go on a quest.

To show themselves worthy of passing this test.

ONE: Help your town, do good all around.

TWO: Live there for one moon, don't leave too soon.

THREE: Fly by broomstick, the easiest trick.

The rules are simple for the valiant, clever, and strong.

But if you cannot continue, you do not belong.

The rules parchment was unscathed. I held my breath when I turned to the application page, and I wanted to let out a sigh of relief because it was all in one piece—but my stomach knotted back up. At the top, a huge blank line waited expectantly—in order to pass, I needed Mayor Taira of Auteri's signature. I put the tube on the highest shelf, far out of the flamefox's reach, feeling like I was pulling a rug over a mess I was trying to hide.

Then I sat on the ground, staring back at the fiery little mischief-maker now sitting in the middle of the cottage. His eyes glimmered, and he started trotting toward me.

"What trouble are you up to now?" I asked, but it was too late. He leaped.

Even though he was tiny, his jump knocked me off balance. I waved my arms like a windmill as I toppled backward, falling flat on the ground. His wet, warm muzzle bopped my nose, as if to check whether I was okay. Satisfied, he then let out a loud burp that smelled suspiciously mackerel-like, crawled onto my stomach, and curled up, as if to say, *This is* my *place now.*

I'd never had a pet before. My parents traveled too much for them to get a dog, and Mother was allergic to cats, most witches' and wizards' favorite companions. The flamefox raised his head and nudged my hand over the star-shaped mark on his forehead, and I started petting him, running my hands down his sleek coat. He was a bundle of heat, and for the first time since my magic had manifested, I was warm, too.

He stretched his jaw open in a yawn and his sharp, tiny teeth glinted in the lantern light.

I lifted him up and put him on the foot of the bed. He plopped down, tucking himself into a cozy, tight curl with his bushy tail wrapped around him, snuggling into the mattress with satisfaction.

I groaned. "What have I gotten myself into?"

PART TWO

The Semi-Magical Repair Witch

Business Reason.

To save the town...

CHAPTER 8

THE MAYOR OF AUTERI

The next day, I woke before the sun peeked over the horizon and stretched my arms. Magic usually tickled at my fingertips in the morning, but today I felt only the faintest of sparks. I had used too much magic helping the man on the boat and repairing the cottage.

Mother believed that the more I used new spells, the more magic I would have to draw upon in the future. Right now, I could barely cast a simple charm. I wanted to rest, but I needed to meet the town leader first.

When I checked on my food stores, my smoked mackerel stash looked suspiciously lower than it had yesterday. I chewed on a piece, wandering back over to check on the flamefox, now sleeping on his back. His plump, pink belly and paws stuck up as he snored lightly.

I wafted my mackerel over his nose and he woke with

a squeak, rolling onto his legs. I grinned and tore my mackerel in half. He shook his bushy tail so furiously that he toppled over and contentedly lay on the bed to chew on the smoked fish.

I scratched behind his ears. "You probably don't understand commands, do you?"

The flamefox's dark eyes twinkled with mischief. *If you feed me more, I'll listen.*

"Okay, maybe you do." I raised another piece of smoked mackerel. "See this, flamefox?"

His ears perked up as he stared hungrily.

"If you promise to stay here and wait for me, you'll get this now and another snack after I return." I dangled it in front of him and he nearly turned cross-eyed. "When I see Mayor Taira, I'll ask if anyone knows where your owner lives. Don't wander off, though."

The flamefox wagged his tail, leaped up, and grabbed the fish. He put it on the bed as if to say, *This is mine now.* This time, though, he didn't eat it right away.

He followed me into the washroom and watched as I smoothed the loose hairs around my face. My brown eyes were firm and set, even if I felt like melting from nervousness inside. I was as ready as I'd ever be to meet Mayor Taira. I slipped my wand into the pocket of my dress and adjusted the angle of my hat.

I left the front door propped open. The flamefox ran around the cliff, chasing the shrieking seagulls and sniffing at the closed buds of the dusklight flowers. "Stay here, okay?"

He skittered to a stop. Before I turned the corner, I looked back. The flamefox sat in the middle of the clearing, whining softly when I waved. His head turned questioningly, as if saying, *Do I really have to stay here all alone? That's no fun.*

"Remember our deal—no trouble," I called. "I'll see you later."

Rin had given me directions to Mayor Taira's offices. "You'll see the town hall before you get there," she had told me, but she'd scribbled down the instructions on the back of an old magicless ticket and pressed the scrap of paper into my hands.

I followed the map into the winding, bustling streets of Auteri, dodging trucks and swarms of workers in billowy trousers and blue or gold tunics, scurrying back and forth between the docks and shops. I walked up a slight hill, until the path opened up to a square lined with merchants, hawking everything from the latest fashions from Okayama to piles of golden corn and sacks of almonds to delicate dusklight flowers.

When I stepped into the middle of the town square, a shadow loomed over me. I looked up and gasped.

I'd found Mayor Taira's offices. The building looked like a palace, with five stories of smooth white stone and a gold cap that glimmered against the black cliffs.

I trailed behind a man carrying a pail of fish in each hand and followed him through the enormous gold doors. The main room was big enough to fit a whole sailing ship. Countless doors and hallways sprouted off the cavernous room, and four stairways branched up to different levels. The floor was paved in polished, dark gray stones hewn from the cliffs. The snow-white walls were unadorned except for wide windows rimmed with gold that looked out onto the sea. The view of boats floating in the waters looked more beautiful than any painting I had ever seen.

Streams of people hurried in and out of doorways. Clearly, they all knew where they needed to go. I inched back toward one of the windows.

A girl leaned on a stairwell, studying everyone walking by. She looked like she was around my age, and she had wavy hair, rich as sun-soaked barley, braided at the crown of her head and tied back with a blue ribbon. She wore a navy tunic cinched at the waist with a belt heavy with pouches, and tan pants with ample pockets. Her cat-like gray eyes narrowed when she saw me. She sauntered over and looked down her snub nose.

"Are you the witch?" The girl turned her head to the side. "I thought you'd be...older."

I stood as straight as I could. Still, I wasn't very tall. "I'm twelve years old, just like any other witch going on their Novice quest."

The girl shrugged. "Well, I promised Rin I'd show you in since she's working. I'm Charlotte. Follow me."

She led me up one of the stairways, down a few hallways, pulled open another set of huge, gold doors, and disappeared into the room. I had to hurry through the gap before the doors slammed shut.

In the room, a line of people waited to talk to a man sitting at a small desk. The man was dignified, with gray hair and a sky-blue uniform with gold buttons and trimming. He talked briefly to each person and sent them to the doors to the right, left, or behind him.

Charlotte waved. She was already in line. I hurried over. "Is he Mayor Taira?"

She raised an eyebrow. "Of course not. The mayor doesn't have time to meet with just anyone. You'll have to plead your case with Kyo, her guard and her secretary, first."

The man holding the fish pails was arguing at the desk, but he frowned when Kyo motioned him to the right. "Next." Kyo gestured at the woman waiting at the front of the line.

"The fish quality keeps degrading!" the man with the pails shouted, waving his arms. Seawater splashed over the rims and onto the stone. "We won't be able to sell to the rest of the realm if this keeps happening! I need the money to restore my boat!"

I stared as two attendants firmly escorted the man out.

"That's one of the owners of the fishing boats. He's like that all the time." Charlotte shook her head at the man's retreating back. "Complaining about the fish quality even as he commissions a new fishing boat every year. He's whining to get Mayor Taira to lower the taxes."

I hoped Kyo wouldn't march me out, too.

"Have your plea ready," Charlotte warned. "Kyo doesn't listen to babble, and Mayor Taira hates it even more. Get to the point quick."

"Oh, thank you." I hadn't expected her to give me advice. She seemed like she had other things she wanted to do rather than chaperone me.

"Don't thank me, thank Rin. I had to skip my last day of school for this," she muttered, toying with a strand of hair that had escaped its braid. "It's your turn."

She placed her hand on the small of my back and shoved me. I stumbled forward; I was face-to-face with Mayor Taira's secretary.

He smoothed his mustache. "And you are?"

My words spilled over one another. "Ah, yes, um, I'm Apprentice Evalithimus Evergreen, here to meet Mayor Taira." I bobbed into a bow.

The man scrawled my name on his sheaf of parchment and tapped his fountain pen expectantly. "And your reason for meeting with the mayor?"

I stammered, a flush of heat burning my neck. "I'm— I'm trying to pass my Novice Witch quest...."

The man kept tapping his pen. By my name, there was a huge, gaping blank for *Business Reason*.

Charlotte leaned over. "Kyo, Eva's the witch that Rin found. She's staying at the cliffside cottage, and she needs Mayor Taira to sign off on her paperwork."

I stared at her, stunned. "Um, yeah, that." *Thank you, thank you, Charlotte!*

"Eva will *save* Auteri from the Culling." *Wait, wait—what? How am I going to do that?*

Kyo glanced at his paperwork, and the corner of his mustache twitched. "All right, all right, Miss Charlotte. No need for dramatics. Your witch friend can meet Mayor Taira." Kyo scribbled *To save the town* for *Business Reason*.

Charlotte grinned, looking like a cat that got the cream. "Okay, Eva, you're in. I've done my duty." She turned and headed out.

"Didn't Miss Rin ask you to stay with your witch friend?" Kyo called to Charlotte, his salt-and-pepper eyebrows rising knowingly.

She slumped her shoulders and sighed, looking completely different from when she had pled my case only seconds ago. "Rin only asked that Eva got an appointment. I figured Davy would be a better match."

I winced. I was an errand she wanted to check off her list. "I'm fine on my own."

"Did someone say my name?" cried a boy's voice.

"Speak his name and he appears," Charlotte grumbled, but the corner of her lips pushed up slightly. "Almost as if *I* was the witch."

A lanky arm slung around Charlotte's shoulder and a pair of light brown eyes peered at me underneath messy black hair. Davy was around my height and age, utterly disheveled in a pair of worn canvas overalls over a yellow shirt, and he smelled like the briny sea.

"Gross, get off me." Charlotte peeled his freckled arms off her.

"Hi-yo, Uncle Kyo," the boy said cheerily.

"How are you and your father doing, Davy?" Kyo asked, his steely face softening slightly.

"The usual." Davy shrugged. "Pa talked this morning, though. A bit."

Kyo looked as if he meant to say something consoling, but the look on Davy's face made it clear that he didn't want to talk anymore about his father. The secretary pointed to yet another line waiting at the door behind him. "You'll get called in when Mayor Taira is ready for you."

"Thank you, sir." I bowed again.

Davy trailed me and Charlotte over to the next line. He glanced at me, his excitement picking up again. "Char, is this your new sidekick?"

"This is the girl that Rin asked me to take care of." Charlotte stood straighter when she mentioned Rin.

"I guess she figured you needed a buddy other than me." He clasped his chest. "Ah, and as Charlotte's best and only chum, I would've sworn I'd never see the day that our 'Princess' of Auteri makes another friend!"

"Oh, stuff it." The tips of Charlotte's ears turned pink. "I'm not a princess."

"I'm not a princess, either," he confided to me. From behind him, Charlotte shook her head. "I'm Davy." He stuck his hand out and shook my hand like his life depended on it. My arm flopped numbly at my side when he let go.

"I'm Evalithimus—I mean, Eva."

"Evalithimus—are you related to *the* Nelalithimus Evergreen? *The* Nelalithimus that even the queen calls on?"

Queen Alliana was one of the most popular rulers of Rivelle Realm in recent history, renowned for keeping peace at our borders and fairness across all regions of the realm. The former queen had selected Alliana and two others from the Queen's Advisors, the group of twenty-one princesses and princes that each watched over a specific region of the realm. The final decision was made by a committee of ordinary citizens. And to everyone's surprise, it was Alliana, the girl who'd once thought she'd never leave her village, who ascended the throne. Mother had explained the crowning process to me a long time ago, though I'd never really paid attention because I couldn't imagine being anything other than a witch, but the whole realm adored the queen in the way that I looked to my mother as my idol.

I nodded. "Grand Master Evergreen's my mother."

Davy's eyes widened. "Whoa. If you're *her* daughter, what're you doing at a place like Auteri?"

"I'm on my quest to become a Novice Witch."

"A quest!" Davy's face gleamed. "You hear that, Char? A quest, a—"

"Heard the first time. And the second and third, for that matter." Charlotte raised a sharp eyebrow at me. "You better figure out how to make your case, or else this will all be for nothing."

"My sailor friend placed a bet that he'd spotted a witch-girl walking through town." Davy studied my black dress, as if he expected a tail or a third arm to pop out. "I guess I lost my copper."

I desperately wanted to charm a fake third eye onto my forehead to see if he'd scream, but I figured that if I did, the attendants definitely would escort me out. And, unfortunately, mischievous spells were forbidden, as they could be mistaken for rogue magic. "I'm only an Apprentice trying to become a Novice Witch. My strongest affinity is for repair magic. But...I can only perform a pinch of magic compared to a Grand Master like my mother. *She's* the one who's barely got limits."

"Some days, I wish I had magic, 'specially that time

I got caught trying to stow away and tried to escape by climbing up the topmast. When the captain caught me— he's my friend, now—he was going to unfurl the sails so I'd go flying into the waves. If I manifested, I'd sail the seas and discover new lands."

I blinked, my head buzzing. "You stowed away?"

"I wanted an adventure. There's so much to see beyond Auteri."

"Just work on the boats like Rin." Charlotte crossed her arms. "Isn't that your plan?"

Davy nodded. He blew out a breath, ruffling the hair curling over his forehead. "Rin's the coolest ever. Except for your mother, maybe. From the stories I've heard, she's pretty amazing." He peered at the wand sticking out of my skirt pocket. "How's your magic work?"

"I have to create an incantation, usually in the form of a rhyme, to focus the magic," I said. "I chant the charm and use my wand to channel it."

"Did Grand Master Nelalithimus teach you any spells?" Davy asked.

"My mother taught me the basics, but reusing others' incantations doesn't work well. I have to create the charm on my own for it to work."

Davy checked a big gold-rimmed watch strung on a strip of leather and wound around his wrist. The watch was sticky with grease. He saw me looking at it and explained,

"I'm working on testing different waxes for making it waterproof." He rubbed at the glass. "Yikes! Got any charms for turning back time?"

An attendant stuck her head out the door. "Next?" She did a double take when she saw my witch's hat. "Come in, miss."

Davy nudged Charlotte to follow me through the door and then waved his waxy watch at us. "I gotta go. The *Hyodo* should be docked, and I promised my sailor friends I'd help ferry in the crates."

He shook my hand again—it felt like I was getting rattled on a rough train ride—and then dashed out of the room.

I stared after him. "Is he always—"

"A walking terror of words and thoughts?" The corners of Charlotte's lips tugged up. "Always. Come on, I'll go in with you to meet Mayor Taira, but you have to talk for yourself."

I chewed on my lower lip nervously.

She glanced at me and wrinkled her nose. "She doesn't treat us as anything less than adults, which is a blessing and a curse. You'll see."

Taking a slow, deep breath, I stepped past the tall gold doors, with Charlotte following close behind.

"Be quiet, please." The attendant motioned for us to stand at her left.

On the far end of the long, rectangular study, the

late morning sun shone in through an opened window. Under the streaming light, an older woman sat behind a desk that had carvings of waves etched into the wood. She wrote down notes as she listened to a young mother speaking in a trembling, soft voice, clutching her son to her shoulder. To the side, two scribes wrote on scrolls as they listened to the conversation.

Even from afar, the woman at the desk commanded the attention of everyone in the room.

Just about a year ago, after my magic had manifested, my mother had brought me to a Council meeting. The witches and wizards were bickering over whether to cast charms on both sides of the abyss to also protect Constancia, the realm south of us. Mother tapped her wand against the back of an oak chair and her voice had rung like a clear, sharp bell. "As witches and wizards, we must do good. We must take care of our neighbors and help them understand we can protect them with our magic."

She had raised her head high, staring evenly around the room and daring anyone to challenge her. Not one of them did.

I had thought she had cast a spell. Now, though, I realized the way my mother and the mayor drew the attention of everyone in the room with a single look was a magic of its own.

Mayor Taira rose out of her chair with her skirts

shifting as she moved, like a rose unfolding. She had jet-black hair streaked with white, twirled into a bun. Deep wrinkles carved frown lines around her mouth.

Mayor Taira put her hand on the woman's shoulder and said in a voice as rich as honey, "I am sorry for your loss. Remember that the people of Auteri will stand by you in this time of need."

The woman clutched her son tightly to her chest, even as he squirmed. She ducked her head and said huskily, "Thank you for your benevolence, Mayor Taira." As she passed by me, her face glistened with tears.

Her pain was raw. I wished to enchant her grief away, but Mother had warned me that even the best of charms never properly healed sorrow. When I'd asked her once, when Father was crying after his brother passed away, her voice had cracked as she'd said, "We remember shooting stars for their shine, not the darkness of the night. Trying to wish away grief extinguishes those memories that glow so bright." And she had warned me there was a chance sorrow might come back twofold. There were limits to magic, as I knew all too well.

Charlotte swallowed. "Looks like the sea took another sailor. The Constancia Sea is unforgiving. If I ruled the realm, I'd stop sea trade when storms are scried." A slight shadow darkened her eyes. "But who am I to say as an orphan girl living on the benevolence of Auteri?"

She stared coolly, as if daring me to respond. I said softly, "I'm sorry."

Charlotte jerked her head away, craning over her shoulder to watch the woman leave.

Mayor Taira pulled out a new scroll from a pile on her desk. "Next."

I walked up to the desk and bowed. "Mayor Taira, it's a pleasure to meet you."

The woman examined me through the glasses perched on her nose. It felt like her dark eyes were picking me apart and judging me, seeing that I was nothing more than a witch with a scrap of power.

I gripped the folds of my skirt. "I am Apprentice Eva-lithimus Evergreen, daughter of Grand Master Nelalithi-mus Evergreen. And I have traveled from Miyada to earn the rank of Novice Witch in Auteri."

Charlotte's stare burned between my shoulder blades. I shifted uncomfortably, imagining her growling, *Get to the point.*

I swung my knapsack off my shoulders and set it against the wall. I popped open the black tube and dug out my application paperwork. Mayor Taira plucked the parchment from my trembling hands, scanned the front, then flipped to the second page, her eyes narrowing at the empty signature line.

"Town leader's endorsement!" She stared at me over

the papers. "And what exactly will we receive from your services, Apprentice?"

"I'll support the town in any way I can," I said earnestly. "I'm here to help Auteri."

"You're on your very first quest, aren't you? I requested an Elite or Master from the Council." She leaned over the desk and stared down. "Are you an Elite Witch?"

"No…"

"Or a Master Witch?"

I hung my head.

"Each town can have only one witch or wizard. It's the queen's law. I'm not here to solve your problems. I'm here to find solutions for my town, before the Culling strikes this autumn, and we need a skilled witch."

This would've been the perfect moment for me to cast some sort of spell. Maybe make the whorls on her desk turn into water and then back to wood. Something, *anything*, to show my powers.

But I couldn't think of the right spell. She was right. I was inexperienced. Weak.

"We cannot support an *Apprentice* who cannot properly serve our people."

Each word she spoke slammed me down, making me feel small.

"But—"

I bit back a gasp as she tossed my application to the corner of her desk.

My heart burned with pain. I had expected the gracious woman who had taken care of the mother and son before me, not this disapproving leader.

One of her attendants went to take the papers off her desk—to throw it away, to burn it, I wasn't sure—but I darted forward and snatched my application from under her hand, almost knocking over a small silver bell on a thin chain. Mayor Taira lunged for the bell, holding it by the clapper so it wouldn't ring.

"This is our town's charmed bell," she hissed, stringing the chain around her neck. "It is imbued with powerful magic. And there's probably more strength in this bell than all of you."

I swallowed, my hands shaking. "But I can help the town.…Please, may I have a chance? I'm a fully trained witch."

I glanced back at Charlotte and my heart dropped more. Even she looked at her feet, as if the force of Mayor Taira's words was absolute.

But…if that was the truth…I'd have to leave this town empty-handed.

I would become magicless.

My voice cracked as I swallowed back my tears. I tried one last time. "I can fix things. I'm really handy. I can set up a magical repair shop that'll help the town—" I clutched my skirt in my fists. She scribbled on her parchment, probably finishing up notes from her last case.

She was done with me.

"*Mother!*" A shout came from the reception room, and I spun around. The door shot open and Rin collapsed against the doorframe, panting. She wore her green uniform, but the buttons were undone at her neck and sweat plastered her hair to her face.

"Rin?" I said, confused, looking from her to Mayor Taira.

The mayor pursed her lips, eyes narrowed. "Well, look who decided to show up—"

"Mother, no matter how angry you are at me—please, listen. A ship's crashed into the cliffs. Passengers and workers are trapped under the main deck and the boat's sinking." Rin gasped as she caught her breath. Then she saw me. "Oh, Eva, thank the fates that you're here."

Mother? At first, I couldn't see the slightest resemblance. Looking closely, I realized they both had the same honey-brown eyes, but where Rin's were gentle, Mayor Taira's eyes were sharp.

"What happened?" The mayor stood quickly.

"The *Hyodo* was trying to avoid a skiff that shot out in front of the ship. The captain overcorrected and crashed into the cliffs."

"My daughter is supposed to be heading in on that boat," one man cried out. He started shoving his way through the crowd.

A woman clutched her chest. "My husband's working on the skiffs right now, dear fates."

The horde of panicked townspeople pushed toward the door, crying and shouting.

Mayor Taira strode into the reception room and slammed her fist down on Kyo's desk, sending his pot of ink flying to the ground. Her face was white as she roared, "*Silence!*"

As good as a spell, they stopped and stared at her.

"We'll mobilize the rescue team." Mayor Taira turned to her secretary.

Rin's hands curled into fists. "They're already at the cliffs, yet there's only so much they can do. . . . The ship's sinking, fast. We need to open up the stairway for the trapped passengers, but there are rocks blocking the top deck."

I slid my application back into my knapsack. My stomach fluttered nervously, like it was growing wings.

"I'll go," I said loudly, standing in the doorway. The crowd's stares drilled into me.

Mayor Taira shook her head. "You're just a child."

My heart beat wildly as I stepped in front of Mayor Taira. "Please, let me go. I may be young, but I'm still a witch. Let me help, for the sake of the people of Auteri."

Mayor Taira pressed her lips and stared at me for a long second. She turned to Rin with a trace of reluctance. "Can you take her?"

Rin nodded. "Let's go, Eva."

She grabbed my hand and pulled me out of the room. Passersby jumped out of our way and stared as we ran through hallways, out the grand gold doors, and down the stone stairs.

"I want to go with you, too," Charlotte called, rushing behind us.

Rin paused. "My motorcycle only takes two, Char. Stay safe here, okay?"

"Can't the witch take her broom or—" Charlotte muttered. The roar of Rin's motorcycle cut out her words, but the girl's gaze pierced me.

Rin wheeled her motorcycle in front of me, engine howling, buckled a helmet onto my head, and slipped onto the bike. "Hold on tight," she yelled, and then we jetted off. I clung to Rin for dear life.

I couldn't even secure a spot for myself in this town. How in the fates was I supposed to save a whole boat?

CHAPTER 9

A Cry for Help

Rin revved her motorcycle as we raced to the cliffs. I laced my fingers tighter as we swerved through the boulders and zoomed along a path to the top.

"We're going to go a little faster now," Rin shouted over the wind.

Gray-black jagged rocks stuck out of a thin path that was meant for adventures on foot, not motorcycles. Less than fifteen paces to either side, the cliff dropped down to the water. I gulped. "We're already going pretty fast—"

"No time. I used to ride this path when I was younger. It's not the easiest, but I can do it."

We curved up to the summit, twisting and turning, jolting over stones. My insides felt like they had scrambled with my brain.

"Can you tell me what the damage is like?" I shouted, my teeth rattling as I tried to speak.

"The stairway's blocked by huge boulders. About forty passengers and sailors are stuck below the deck. Some are injured, too."

I gripped my fingers around my wand. Mother would shrink the rocks with a flick of her wand. Conroy would summon a gust to blow off the boulders. But—I couldn't do *that*.

Finally, Rin screeched to a stop.

She helped me unbuckle my helmet and tossed it onto the bike. "C'mon."

We sprinted to the edge. I gasped when I saw the boats below us.

Skiffs clustered around the crashed ship, like moths fluttering to a dying light. The front of the boat, the bow, had crumpled into the rocks, far below us. Part of the cliff had collapsed onto the deck, covering the front with a mountain of rocks.

"How're we supposed to get there?" I fought to hide the quaver in my voice.

"There's a trail." Rin pointed to a narrow ledge that led downward. "Follow me."

Pebbles skittered under our feet, falling over the edge and into the water as we rushed down. Paths crisscrossed the walls of the cliffs, widening where they met. We ran along the closest route that took us to the water.

Rin and I skidded to a stop on a ledge ten or fifteen feet above the ship. A cry wedged itself in my throat. There was so much damage. The deck was buried under an avalanche of boulders taller than a grown man. And water gushed into the gaping opening in the hull. The boat was sinking, inch by inch. Voices shouted from inside, pleading for help.

I stepped closer, to crawl down to the ship. Rin held out her hand. "Stay here, Eva, where it's safe. I don't want you to get hurt, too."

A handful of ragged sailors, plump storekeepers, and skiff workers were trying their best to clear out the wreckage. Others dove into the sea in failing attempts to patch up the leak. "C'mon, crew," one of the men shouted, "we gotta get them out!"

Davy was on a skiff, helping a few unharmed passengers climb down rope ladders and onto the skiffs ferrying them away to the docks. He saw me pacing the ledge and shouted, "Hey, witch-girl!"

The rescue team paused from pushing at rocks to look up, expectantly, and I inched away. Boulders pressed down on the deck and water poured in through the cracks. The cries of trapped sailors and passengers made my chest wrench with fear.

What if I couldn't save them? What if they *died*? My failure would cost people their lives. My mind was drawing a blank when I tried to think of something...anything....

I didn't have enough power.

"Aren't witches supposed to do *magic*?" snarled a sailor, no more than a handful of years older than me. "Why are you just standing there?" The boy's thin lips curled disapprovingly, and a thick, raised scar on his jaw twitched as his fingers dug under a rock and strained at it. Another two sailors joined him, and they tossed it down into the waters.

My eyes stung.

"Got any ideas?" Rin said, her face pale.

A passenger's muffled shout rang from below. "Please! The water's rising! Help!"

"Hold on!" a woman on the rescue team called back. "We're going as fast as we can."

I chewed on the inside of my cheek, until I tasted the metallic tang of my blood.

Mother would have barged in and cast a spell on the spot. The rocks would disappear into thin air, she'd magically knit up the leak and heal the wounded, and the whole town would be drinking her special redbud lemonade by now. But I didn't have enough magic to repair the whole boat.

Davy dove from a skiff and swam up to the cliffs, pulling himself onto the closest ledge. He hurried up the trail toward us, his boots squelching.

"Don't they need you at the skiffs?" Rin asked Davy.

He shook his head, eyes downcast. "Soma said I'm not

a fast enough rower." Plucking a strand of green-yellow seaweed off his shoulder, he chucked it at the ground. He kicked at the slimy blob with his soggy boot, but he put too much weight on his leg and slipped instead, his arms windmilling as he caught himself. "Yech! Stupid seaweed. Stupid Soma. I can row fast, but he said I'm too small...."

Rin grabbed him by the shoulder, steadying him. "Don't listen to that hired crew. They used to be pirates, and being polite wasn't part of the job. They only listen to money."

Davy squeezed seawater from his shirt. "That's a nice way to phrase it."

Pirates? I hadn't seen any bandannas or eye patches, but then again, I was a witch without the proper marks of the Council. I glanced down, and the sailor boy's beady eyes met mine in a glare. I dropped my eyes to the path.

"Stay with Eva, would you? I'll go down and help." Rin turned to me and whispered, "You can do this." For a second, I didn't see her; I saw Mother's warm eyes gazing into mine.

Davy barely had time to nod before Rin unbuttoned her jacket and kicked off her boots. She scaled down the rocks and dove into the water thick with seaweed, bubbling up to talk with the divers and examine the broken hull.

I picked up a small rock from the ledge. It was light

in my hands, but the boulders on the ship were definitely not pebbles. The rescue team struggled to untangle the tightly clustered boulders and push them overboard.

What would Mother do? What kind of spell would the others cast?

"How about some sort of charm that makes the rocks disappear?" Davy asked. I jumped. I guess I'd been speaking out loud.

"It's tricky—I don't want to make this whole cliff disappear."

Davy whistled. "Yeah, I prefer standing on two feet." He untangled another strand of seaweed out of his hair, chucking it at the cliff. Instead of sticking, it slid down.

"I have an affinity for repair magic, so I can fix things...." My eyes narrowed.

I'd been asking the wrong questions all along.

What can I do?

"What?" he asked, patting his face. "Do I have a crab on my nose or something?"

I tugged out a piece of seaweed dangling from the front pocket of his overalls. "Something better than a crab."

Cupping the rock and seaweed in my left hand, I pulled my wand out of my skirt pocket. *"Become one with seaweed, make rocks slip with speed."*

The small rock trembled in my palm, glowing yellow-green as the seaweed dissolved onto the rock. I fumbled around, trying to get a grip on the thick, slimy coating. As I closed my hands, it slipped and shot straight out, with a *splosh!* as it hit the water.

"You can do that for the deck!" Davy cried, and I nodded, a tiny spark of hope kindling inside me. "I'll pile seaweed onto the boulders!"

Without another word, he scaled down the cliff and jumped into the water. I took a deep breath. I hoped this would work.

Taking a knife out of his pocket, he flipped it open and hacked at the long fibers swirling in the waters. "Rin!" he shouted. "Haul this to the deck! Eva needs these on the rocks!"

Rin, her forehead wrinkled with confusion, ran to the railing and lowered a bucket on a rope. Davy piled seaweed into the bucket and knocked on it with the handle of his knife. "All up!"

Some of the rescue team glanced at Rin spreading seaweed around, and then up at me. They started nudging one another. "Is the girl gonna do something, eh?"

I rolled my sleeves up. Cupping my hands around my mouth, I called, "Rin, can you please clear everyone off the ship?"

She nodded and put her fingers between her lips, blowing out an ear-piercing whistle. "All hands—off the deck!"

The majority of the rescue team scrambled past the

broken railings, diving into the water. But the crew in gray, along with the boy-sailor, stayed. "I don't believe it." The boy's teeth showed jagged and yellow as he growled. "You expect a pile of seaweed to help this?"

Rin stared straight at the boy. "Well, Soma," she said evenly, "you can keep pushing the boulders around and get nowhere, or we can see what this witch can do."

He sneered, his raspy voice like nails scratching down metal. "Witches don't put *seaweed* on rocks. If I had magic, I'd actually do something."

Soma and his friends glared at me one last time before jumping off and clambering onto the gathered skiffs, rowing back to give the ship ample berth.

Up on the cliffs, high above us, an automobile screeched to a stop. I paled as Kyo, the salt-and-pepper-haired attendant, jumped out of the driver's seat and pulled open the back door. Mayor Taira stepped out, and Charlotte slid out of the car after her.

Rin jumped up onto the rungs of the mast, above the boulders. "All clear, Eva!"

I tried to grip my wand, but it felt like my palm was coated with seaweed-slick sweat. My heart pounded in my chest as Mayor Taira's heels clicked down the rocky trail, with Kyo and Charlotte close behind her. The mayor's gaze bored into my back. If I looked at her, I'd probably freeze from fright.

"Do good." Repeating the Council's mission felt like

lighting a fire within me. Taking a deep breath, I raised my wand straight at the rocks at the top and chanted, *"Become one with seaweed, make rocks slip with speed."*

Yellow-green light shot from my wand to the top, encasing the rocks in glowing light. Nothing changed.

My face bleached of all color.

Then the rocks wiggled and the seaweed disappeared with a satisfying *pop!*

"Try pushing it!" Davy hollered, from the safety of a skiff.

Rin leaned out and nudged the stone mountain with her foot. A boulder and a handful of rocks slipped down the pile and off the side of the ship.

The rescue team cheered, but sweat trickled down my neck. I had only transformed a handful of stones. A mountain of rocks towered before me.

I cast the enchantment again. *"Become one with seaweed, make rocks slip with speed."*

More rocks shivered, popped, and slithered down. Magic dribbled out of me. My throat felt like something was stuck in it.

The ship and the sky spun around me, and I stumbled backward, pressing my hand against the cliff. My skin was icy cold and growing even colder.

Turning toward the ship, I pinched my arm. I needed to stay awake.

The pile was getting smaller. I kept going, one at a

time...another spell... *"Become one with seaweed, make rocks slip with speed."*

Rin pushed at the rocks again, and more slipped over the sides and cascaded into the water. Finally, a gap revealed a corner of the stairway.

"You're almost in!" A sudden shout came from within the boat. "A few stones more!"

"Please, before the water level rises!" another voice cried, ragged.

The rescue team climbed back aboard, swarming toward the opening, straining and straining to drag away the last rocks. They shoved at the largest boulder, pushing with all their might, until the wood under the boulder creaked.

I tried raising my arm, but I could barely stand straight. Breathing heavily, I whispered, "I'll help...."

"Whoa, whoa!" one of the sailors shouted. The boulder rolled into the sea, creating a wave that rocked the ship. The rescue team shouted, gripping onto the broken railings, and water gushed onto the deck.

"Wait, wait, I'm not done—" I protested, my voice coming out as a wheeze. The sparkling sea wavered in front of me. I needed a new charm to patch up the leak, so the boat would hold up for everyone inside. Taking one shaky step forward, I pointed my wand at the boat. *"Stand up, stand tall, this boat will stay strong and protect all."*

Suddenly, there was a flash of blue sky and yellow sun, and then everything went pitch black.

I heard a voice—Rin's?—calling my name.

My vision kept blurring and blacking out, but someone held me up, cradling me from hitting the rocks. With a flush of disappointment, I realized what had happened.

I had collapsed from using too much magic.

Rin spoke gently. "We've got you, Eva-girl. You've done enough. The rescue team is in the ship, and they've gotten almost everyone out."

"The ship isn't safe," I insisted, struggling to stand up. "I didn't put enough magic into the enchantment, so it may be temporary. The ship won't be able to hold up if water keeps pouring in. I need to reapply the charm...."

My sight flickered black again, sleep pulling at my consciousness.

Mayor Taira's voice rose with alarm. "Temporary? We can't have temporary—"

"Don't worry," Rin said. "Don't worry, Eva. Rest now."

CHAPTER 10
A MAGICAL REQUEST

My muscles screamed with pain as I stirred awake. I leaned against the rocky cliffs and faced the open sea, with Rin's green jacket tossed over my shoulders. Ragged tears ruined my black dress, and falling had left my palms scraped raw. My teeth rattled from shivers; I was drained of all magic. Pulling Rin's jacket around my shoulders, I trembled from the cold coming from within me, even though the afternoon air was still warm.

Ships drifted gently outside Auteri's cliffs. Down on the *Hyodo*, in the midst of the sailors, Rin carted away broken wood from the deck.

I crawled down the cliffs. The ship's hull was cracked, but it floated, and the stairway had been opened up. I jumped the small gap from the rocks to the deck of the

Hyodo. Some of the rescue workers stared as I stumbled aboard.

I made my way over to Rin and asked, "Rin, where are the passengers? Are they safe?"

Rin's honey-brown eyes widened when she realized I stood next to her. "Eva, thank goodness you're okay," she cried, grabbing me by the shoulders and pulling me into a hug. "They've been taken to the infirmary. We were going to take you there, but we've never taken care of a witch, so we weren't sure if we should move you."

"I'm okay," I said, summoning up a small smile. "I just get, um, tired after using spells."

"Is that usual for witches and wizards?" Rin asked, frowning. "I've never heard of that before."

I blushed, tongue-tied. "Not with most."

A throat cleared from behind me and I turned around. Mayor Taira nodded her head stiffly. "Thank you for helping us, Evalithimus."

I wanted to tell her that everyone called me Eva, but even in my foggy head, correcting her didn't seem like a bright idea.

"I'll grant you a boon on behalf of the town of Auteri," Mayor Taira continued. "We can outfit you with new clothes for you to continue your journey, perhaps?"

From behind her, the rescue team elbowed one another and hushed, leaning closer to hear our conversation.

"A boon?" I echoed.

From behind Mayor Taira, Charlotte stopped, a pile of broken wood in her arms. She lifted her head, staring down her snub nose.

My mind wasn't thinking fast enough. I needed to ask for something, something meaningful. "Ah, yes, I do have a request, Mayor Taira."

Her voice was polite. "Yes?"

"Mayor Taira, may I...may I stay?"

"Here?" Mayor Taira asked, her thin eyebrows rising.

I squared my shoulders. "This is where I want to earn my rank as a Novice Witch."

"That's a lot to ask, for a witch who is too weak to cast proper spells."

"Mother!" Rin said sharply.

"Rin," Mayor Taira snapped back. "This is *my town*. Not yours, not after you chose to work on the boats."

"No matter how much you don't want to see me, don't direct that anger toward Eva!"

Mayor Taira reared her head back, and I swore I caught the briefest flash of sadness—and, seemingly, regret.

I clamped my hands into fists. I couldn't let Rin fight my battles, especially not at the cost of ruining her already rocky relationship with her mother.

The magical ticket might've told me where to get off,

but Auteri needed me just as much as any town in the realm. The cottage had been buried in grime and dust, and I knew no witch or wizard had taken care of Auteri in a long time. The Council had forgotten about them. This would be the perfect place for me to become a Novice Witch—if Mayor Taira would let me.

Rin hissed at her mother, "We've been waiting for someone to help the town for more than a decade—"

I cleared my throat, and Rin's eyes shot to mine; she clamped her lips down.

"I'll only stay here for one moon, and if I do help the town of Auteri sufficiently, then I would ask for you to sign off on my Novice Witch application."

Rin cleared her throat. "What do you need in order to pass your quest?"

Mayor Taira lifted her chin. "We cannot—"

"We cannot go another year without help, Mother. Look at how Eva's saved us here. Remember what happened last year with Kelpern and the Culling. You've heard the news. It's not like the Council has enough witches and wizards to grant one to every town in the realm." Rin smiled encouragingly. "What do you need, Eva?"

My eyes darted between Rin and Mayor Taira.

"Fine, I'll listen," Mayor Taira snapped. "But that doesn't mean I'll agree to it."

Rin's shoulders sagged, and she spoke so softly that I could barely hear her. "Thank you, Mother."

Mayor Taira's gaze flickered, softening. Her hands, stiff at her sides, seemed to reach out toward Rin for the briefest instant, but they curled up into fists again. Instead, Mayor Taira's eyes narrowed at me. "What do you want, Apprentice Witch?"

"I would like to request three things," I said.

The mayor crossed her arms.

"First, I'd like a storefront to start a repair shop in Auteri. And I'd like to stay in the cottage on the cliffs."

"I counted two items. And?"

"And I need a guardian." I gulped. "The guardian's a contact between the townspeople and the Novice-in-Training. Most times…most times…it's the leader of the town."

"Well." She turned away. "That's an easy answer—no."

"No?" My stomach slid down to my feet.

"I will not be your guardian. I do not have time to take care of a child."

I stared, at a loss for words. The sailors and townspeople ducked their heads so they wouldn't meet my eyes.

Rin stepped forward. "I'll be Eva's guardian. The other requests are simple boons, Mother."

Mayor Taira tapped her chin with her thin fingers,

stretching out the painfully long silence. "You said you wanted to travel the coast and see the realm, and *now* you choose to stick around?"

"I don't love Auteri any less for wanting to be on the boats," Rin replied. Then, almost quieter than the sea breeze, she added, "Or you any less, Mother."

Mayor Taira jerked her head away, toward the crowd that had quieted and was waiting for her answer. Finally, not meeting Rin's eyes, she slowly inclined her chin. "Very well, then. Evalithimus, I grant you a space for this repair shop of yours and permission to live in the cliffside cottage. And, since she offered, Rin will be your guardian. I will grant you these boons on one condition—you must prepare Auteri for the Culling."

Her words slammed into my chest, knocking the breath from my lungs. *The Culling?* Even Mother had to band together with nine other witches and wizards to barely save Kelpern from the Culling.

What was I supposed to do as a lone, weak witch?

"The Culling doesn't come until late autumn, though. We've got five or six moons, at the earliest." Rin frowned. "Her quest is only for one moon."

Mayor Taira sighed, as if tired of having to explain it. "She'll have to figure out clever ways to fix up our town to withstand the brunt of the Culling before she leaves. I'll only sign her application if she shows me proof of these safeguards *and* her overall contributions to my townspeople."

Ideas sparked in my mind. Perhaps I could strengthen the buildings and cliffs to withstand a rockslide or heavy rains. Or maybe I could use my repair magic to craft tools to help the townspeople.

Mayor Taira turned to me and her gaze darkened. "If you cannot help Auteri in its times of need, I will not sign your papers."

If she didn't approve my application, I would *never* become a Novice Witch.

Grand Master Grottel would act on his threat. The Council would strip my magic away from me.

But...even those thoughts and her deep frown couldn't keep delicate tendrils of joy from blossoming inside my heart. I had a chance. The *smallest* of possibilities, but it was still a chance.

The Culling was far enough away that I wouldn't be here when it hit. And after I left, I could appeal to the Council to arrange for my mother or Conroy or any other wizard or witch to watch over Auteri.

If I stayed here, I could pass my Novice Witch quest. I'd get to keep my magic.

"Understood." I clasped my hands together and fought to keep from spinning and dancing around on the spot.

"Welcome to Auteri," she said, her voice still cool. "I expect only the best for my town, Evalithimus."

I swept into a deep bow, ducking my head down. I needed to keep my magic. I loved magic more than breathing, even more than Father's croissants or redbud jam. I would have to do everything possible to help Auteri prepare for the Culling.

CHAPTER 11
THE MAGICAL REPAIR SHOP

Rin drove me back to town by motorcycle. She parked at the town hall so I could pick up my knapsack. After that, she had planned to take me back to my cottage to rest, but I couldn't wait. I wanted to see my new shop straightaway.

We threaded through the main square outside the town hall, bursting at the seams with tourists visiting the stalls even in the dusky late afternoon. She waved at a few shopkeepers and glanced at me apologetically. "Your store is by the docks, on the other side of town. That was the most Kyo could manage last minute."

"That's fine." My heart thrummed with excitement. Just like in my dream, I would layer thick carpets on the floor and make my store inviting, a haven where the townsfolk could relax with a mug of steaming barley tea, like back at home, and leave with their things fixed and feeling rested. "Thank you for volunteering to be my guardian, Rin."

"You remind me of when I set off on my journey to work on the boats. I was just about your age, and all the other captains didn't want a scrawny thing like me. Only one captain took a chance, and to me, that one chance was the world." She squinted at the setting sun as we walked down the long main street. "Ah, we're this way."

Rin guided me to the right as we walked onto the docks. The afternoon glow danced on the water as the sun slowly dipped below the horizon.

"At home, it's all dainty houses and rolling hills." I stared out at the water. "This is dizzying, with all sea and no land as far as I can see." I shook my head, trying to break the sea's enchantment on me. "So, where's Ten Corsair?"

"It should be over here. Here's Eleven Corsair—oh, it's Seafoam Sweets, their sugar sculptures always draw folks to our town. Seafoam's sugar dusklight flowers are the best souvenirs, along with our sweet corn and cloudberries. That's why there's always a line."

So many people were shopping inside that more than a dozen people waited at the door. The shop's huge window displayed a honey-gold trading ship, no bigger than my handspan, with white sails unfurled. The ship sailed on a foaming sea, breaking through a blue-white wave and tilting up, as if it was flying.

"Is that made of sugar?" I peered closer in awe. "Or glasswork?"

Rin breathed out. "All sugar: the sails, the water, the boat itself. It's beautiful, isn't it?" We walked a few steps past a gap between the buildings. "Ah, and here's the orphanage—it's Nine Corsair. You're neighbors."

A few kids, maybe six or seven years old, sat on the porch steps, laughing with one another as they played a game of light-paper-water. "Rin, Rin," they cried. "Come play!"

"Maybe later," she called back.

"We want to play now," one of the boys grumbled.

"Ask Char for a new paper animal. And if you all behave, I'll be by later with cloudberry cookie drops."

The kids cheered and clambered off the steps, pushing one another as they raced inside. The girl shouted, "Last one to find Char gets turned into a frog!"

One of the boys hollered after her, "That was the witch! Char said the evil witch is gonna turn *you* into a frog!"

Rin grinned. "Better not tell them whether or not you *will* do that. They'll listen better if you keep it a mystery."

I stifled a laugh, looking around again. "Wait, where's my shop?"

We backtracked between Seafoam Sweets and the orphanage, stopping in front of the empty lot.

In the middle, a small sign on a stake pierced the dirt.

I walked closer and read the painted, peeling words. "Ten Corsair…?"

It was a rectangle of dirt and patches of weeds, enclosed by three white walls from the neighboring buildings. Rin swallowed. "It looks like this…is it."

I wanted to sink into the ground. I balled my hands into fists and dug my nails into my palms, the sharp pain reminding me not to cry.

This empty lot wasn't anything close to my dream shop.

Over our heads, seagulls screeched as a boat pulled in. The fishermen tossed buckets full of fish onto the dock. My stomach turned as traces of the sun-warmed fish guts they had used for bait wafted out, sour and rotten.

"I'm sorry." Rin bit her lip. "Mother refuses to forgive me for running off to work on the boats, instead of working in the town hall for her. And now she's taking it out on you. Maybe Kyo will have somewhere else that'll open up? I mean, you helped us so much today."

I had already tested Mayor Taira's patience. I could only imagine her telling me to go home if I asked for an actual storefront.

I shook my head. "It should never have taken so long to think of a spell. The Council would be appalled if they knew." My face flamed. "And I fainted."

"We couldn't have gotten them out as fast without you—if at all. So thank you, Eva. You changed our fates for the better when you decided to come to Auteri."

I lowered my eyes. The rest of the town didn't know what a real witch was like, but Mayor Taira knew what a poor bargain she'd gotten with me and my pinch of magic.

I couldn't keep asking for more. Turning to Rin, I forced the biggest smile I could summon. "I like this spot. You can't beat the view."

"I bet you'll enchant this lot into a palace before I know it."

Even if I had to magic a smile onto my face, I'd manage it for Rin. "Will you come visit when my repair shop opens?"

"As your guardian, of course. I would break things just to create a reason to visit you," she said, and then my smile didn't feel so fake anymore.

@

When I got home, the flamefox was curled up on the windowsill. His ears perked up as soon as I turned around the corner of the cliff. He streaked out of the cottage, like a sunset-red bolt.

He barked, and I groaned. I had forgotten to ask about his owner. It had completely slipped from my mind the instant I'd heard of the sinking ship.

"Hello, little flamefox." He pranced around me, weaving in and out of my legs as I dragged myself slowly up the steps.

I stopped at the doorway and leaned down. I brushed

my fingers against suspicious gnaw marks on the white wood door.

You told me to wait, he seemed to say plaintively. *I got bored.*

"Don't tell me..." I was too drained to fix it. I slumped on the cottage floor. The wind blowing in through the door was icy cold, but I didn't have energy for another step.

"You're not supposed to chew on the door. This place isn't yours to wreck—it's not mine, even." A familiar purple book lay on the ground with its cover gnawed. "Don't tell me that's *Potions of Possibilities*."

The flamefox licked my hand, as if sort-of-not-really apologizing. His tail wagged fast, like glowing embers in a fire.

"It's been a long day, Ember. I'll fix the door tomorrow." Then I stopped. "Did I just—"

And now I had named this fiery spark of trouble.

Pressing my cheek against the wood floor, I mumbled, "I promise to ask around tomorrow, when I'm setting up my new shop, okay?"

And then I fell asleep on the floor.

◌◌

I woke a few hours later. A gust of salty wind blew over me and I shivered.

The cold night air coursed through the gaping open

door. I should've been frozen to my bones, but my body was strangely warm.

While I slept, Ember had curled around my body, between me and the door. He was as hot as a furnace, with his head leaning on my shoulder.

He whined when I blinked.

"Thanks, Ember." I cracked a small smile. "I guess I forgive you for breaking the door."

The flamefox stood and stretched, then leaped up on the mattress. I pushed the door closed and pulled out a bag of slightly squashed contomelon rolls and a tiny round of herb-coated soft cheese from my pocket. I was about to set it on one of the kitchen shelves—surprisingly, Ember hadn't already helped himself to it—but my stomach protested immediately.

I crawled into bed and Ember curled up next to me. I was too tired to cut up the mouthful of cheese, so I nibbled on it, chewy herbed rind and all, alternating with mouthfuls of decadent bread. The sweet, buttery rolls were formed in the shape of round contomelons, with a hint of juicy melon flavor woven through their fluffy insides. I fed wisps of bread without the crackly sugar crust to Ember, who lapped them up hungrily, but he also seemed to be listening carefully, ears turned toward me, as I told him about the boat wreck and everything I had planned for my shop. "I'll need so much to get the shop started. There's got to be something I can use for counters...."

He pushed his warm muzzle against my cheek insistently, so I dusted the bread crumbs off my fingers and started petting him. The flamefox stretched out under my hand.

"I need to help the town, too. But you know what the issue is?" My voice cracked. "I'm not sure...how."

Ember growled under his breath, as if telling me not to wallow in my worries.

"Right, right. Father always says to think of a fix. And Mother says to make a list. Okay. Maybe I can strengthen the buildings?" I sat up. "Maybe a twist on that spell I made today—*Stand up, stand tall, this boat will stay strong and protect all.*"

Then I sighed. "No, I'd probably turn the buildings into solid rock or something."

The flamefox swatted at me with his paw, as if telling me to think of something else. I snuggled back under the sheets. "In the meantime, I can repair things to help the townspeople...."

I fell asleep mumbling about ways to fix up my store, with Ember close to my side, keeping me warm.

CHAPTER 12
𝒯ICKING 𝒯IME

K *nock, knock.*

"Who's there?" I mumbled sleepily. The sun hadn't risen through the foggy darkness. A paper bird was perched on my windowsill, pecking at the glass, carrying a package on its delicate back.

I jumped out of bed, pushed open the window, and cupped it in my hands. The bird jabbed at my skin insistently. Ember barked at it, growling and jumping on the mattress.

"Ow!" I cried. "C'mon. *Let the seal be broken, let this letter open.*" I blew on the paper and the bird froze. The paper wings unfolded in my palm, the small cloth-wrapped bundle tumbling into my other hand.

To our dearest Eva,

Perhaps writing to the Council would confirm, but Hayato might just kick up dust and cause trouble. If there aren't any witches or wizards in town, then it's a perfect sign to stay.

Stuffy Hayato would never—or, at least, should never—turn down a witch who's truly done good. You'll just have to prove you're doing so well that he can't say no.

Time flies when you're having adventures, so keep an eye on your hourglass so time won't fly away from you.

A thought—Auteri is terribly south, isn't it? Come home fast, before the Culling can possibly start, dear. We want you safe.

All of our love,

Mother and Father

PS. Don't forget to practice flying! Also, Father made some of your favorite yuzu cookies—we hope they survive the flight!

The familiar, citrusy scent of home floated up as Ember snuffled at the package, and my heart clenched. I missed Mother and Father terribly.

I lifted the star-shaped hourglass at my neck. It dangled in my hands, time dribbling away. With Mother's powerful enchantments, sand from the top star trickled into the emptier glass star even when I turned it upside down. My heart beat faster and faster each time another dot of sand fell. A small tingle of magic tickled my fingers, but I was still weak after yesterday. My black witch's dress was full of tears, but rather than wasting magic on a repair for myself, I'd have to conserve every drop of my magic for setting up my shop.

I dug through my knapsack. Under thirteen tomes, a few sparking at the touch, and several black witch's dresses with Ember-shaped teeth marks, I found my wrinkled dark gray blouse and black skirt from two years ago, before I'd manifested. I slipped them on. The shoulders were tight and the waist slightly pinched, but it was the only outfit I had, without mending the holes in my dresses. After hitching my knapsack over my shoulders, I peered at my reflection in the window. Even with my pointed hat, I didn't quite look like a witch.

I left Ember at the cottage with a stern warning. "Don't you mess up anything, okay? Stay here."

Ember whined loudly as he plopped down on the front step, following me with his mournful, dark eyes.

The thick fog swallowed me up. It felt like I was walking through clouds, and I inched down the stone path, clinging to the cliff around the corners where the path narrowed and my steps sent small rocks tumbling off. The ledge rose so far above the sea that I couldn't hear them hit the water.

Once in town, I walked past the beach and along the docks, dodging sailors with arms full of crates and nets. I squinted through the fog. Was that the orphanage—

Lost in my thoughts, I bumped into a man staring out at the sea and knocked something out of his hands. It fell to the ground in a flash of gold. The man startled as if I had woken him out of a trance, and he scanned the ground, his eyes widening in panic.

"I'm so sorry!" I cried and scrambled to pick up his delicate gold wristwatch, pressing it back in his hands.

"Ah...thank you." His voice creaked, as if it had been unused for too long. He blinked, eyes returning to his trance.

"The fog was so dense that I didn't see you," I said. The man didn't seem to hear me. He was transfixed by the sea. It was almost as if he had been cursed, but that couldn't be right. Rogue magic had been stamped out years ago. "Are you lost, sir?"

"A'coming, a'coming." His words were gentle as a drop of water on the sea, yet echoed hauntingly in the mist.

Shivers ran down my spine, worse than during any ghost story Mother had ever told me. I skittered to my lot and stopped with surprise.

Instead of an empty patch of dirt, crates were stacked neatly into the shape of a long counter. Wide, stumpy boxes sat in front and behind the taller crates, like benches, covered in plump canvas cushions. A note was pinned on top:

Eva,

    Some of the sailors volunteered a few crates, and I found a few cushions. You may need to sand down the wood, though. I'll drop by again as soon as I can.

    Good luck setting up shop!

                Rin, your favorite guardian

I breathed out a sigh of delight, drinking in the beautiful sight of my own repair shop. It wasn't a proper store like Seafoam Sweets next door, but it was far more than the bare patch of land it'd been yesterday.

As the sun burned through the morning fog, I used a bit of parchment, a handful of sand from the beach, and a spell—"*Sift in the sand, mend what I can*"—to create sandpaper to smooth down the splintered wood. My vision swam as magic leached from my blood, and I sighed.

Around me, fishermen tossed buckets of reeking bait onto their boats and pushed off. Out on the water, skiffs zipped between the massive ships anchored outside the bay of Auteri. On the cobblestone street leading to the main square, townspeople scurried about, heading to their shops, up to the town hall, or down to the docks. The white buildings sparkled in the morning light.

I gulped. I couldn't imagine the town wrecked by

a force of nature like the Culling. Mayor Taira's words echoed in my mind: *If you cannot help Auteri in its times of need...*

I didn't want to think about the possibility of having my magic taken away. I had to set up my shop and figure out how to help the town, fast.

I arranged jars of odds and ends from my knapsack on a small crate directly under the counter, with everything from globs of wax to parchment to sticks of charcoal. Since I wasn't powerful enough to magic things out of thin air, I always liked to keep a few supplies on hand.

By the time they were in place, the sun had risen, burning my skin. The smell of caramelizing sugar wafted from Seafoam Sweets. My stomach growled. I'd forgotten lunch. To keep my mind off the mouthwatering scents, I worked on a sign:

FOUND:
FLAMEFOX. RED-GOLD, CURLY TAIL.

I was tempted to draw Ember like he really was, trying not to look guilty with specks of croissants all over his fur. But I drew his face the way he had looked this morning when he sweetly cuddled close to my side, listening as I talked to him about my plans for the day.

As a finishing touch, I scrawled EVA, WITCH on a piece of stiff parchment. I propped the sign so that it stood up on the wood.

There. Ready for business.

A line reached out the shop door, and I could see people looking at me. I cupped my mouth and called, "Magical repair services!" When I tried to meet their glances, their eyes seemed to slide away. "Need help with any fixes?"

Silence. Even the sailors stopped, stared, and quickly walked away.

My stomach twisted. I knew Auteri hadn't had any magical help in a while, but these folks examined me like they had never seen a witch. And, to be honest, what if they came up to my counter and asked for a fix I couldn't perform?

A seagull screeched and swooped at my head and I ducked. The people in line hid their laughs.

"Magical repair s-s-ser-bises," I stammered. "Um, ser-services! Magical repair services!"

Again, silence.

I sat down, feeling like a fish flopping on the docks and preparing to be slaughtered.

What would it feel like for the Council to strip the magic from my blood? Maybe someone would have to learn to wield the spell—I'd never heard of it being used on anyone before. Did it hurt? Would I feel empty after

they took it away? At that thought, my stomach didn't
growl anymore.

The hourglass dangling at my neck warmed, as if it
could hear my very thoughts. When I pulled it out, the
sand continued to trickle down—time would not wait
for me.

CHAPTER 13

THE FEEBLE FIX

After the lunchtime rush, the crowd thinned out in front of the sweets shop. But no matter whether the store was packed or empty, everyone seemed to pass me by.

To my right, the door of the orphanage swung open. Charlotte darted out, stuffing rolls of parchment into a sack slung over her shoulder. A trail of younger kids followed her.

"Stay here," she told the eight or so kids right on her heels. As if it was a familiar warning, they groaned collectively and slumped on the steps of the orphanage.

"Do you *have* to go?" one of the boys grumbled.

Her eyes flickered over to me as she lowered her voice. "Later, if I hear that you all behaved, I *might* give you a new paper animal."

They all perked up and babbled over one another.

"Really? I want it now!"

"What'd you make?"

"Is it a rockcrow?"

"We *never* get enough toys!"

Charlotte spoke over them. "Only *if* you all behave. And that means not being rowdy! The customers lining up at Seafoam Sweets are looking over, and we can't have that."

The kids sighed and nodded mutely, slinking back into the orphanage where, seconds later, a boy's voice screeched. "Get it out!"

"Soggy rice does *not* belong in tunics!" an old woman's voice snapped. The other kids burst into snickers.

"Well. Guess I won't show them my new paper turtle after all." Charlotte shut the heavy white wood door, shaking her head. She adjusted the strap of the bag on her shoulder and clattered down the steps.

I waved at her. It felt good to know someone's name. "Hello, Charlotte."

Charlotte skittered to a stop and walked up to my store, her eyes scanning the crates. "Well?"

"Hmm?" I said, confused. "Oh! Do you have a repair job for me?"

She raised her eyebrow. "For you? No—when people wave me down, that usually means they have a job for *me*."

"What do you do?" I glanced at the pouch slung over her shoulder and the leather belt tied around her waist, with different shaped pockets all knotted closed. My fingers itched to craft something like that—it looked useful for all my odds and ends.

"I'm a messenger. When school's closed for the summer harvest, I work. Once I graduate, Kyo will hire me to work in the town hall." She put her hands on her waist as though I had challenged her. Her right hand was swathed in a bandage, and I frowned. I didn't remember seeing her with that before. When she noticed me looking, she quickly tucked her hand in her pocket, the look on her face clearly showing she didn't want any more questions.

"I'll let you know if I have anything," I said quickly. "Good luck with your clients!"

She jerked her head in a nod and jogged down the dock, her bag bouncing on her shoulder. Everyone had way more to do than I did.

I stood up, pushing off the bench, and winced as a still-stubbly part of the wood pricked my finger. I'd have to sand it down, but I had something more pressing to do. "Magical repair services," I called loudly. "Need magical repair services?"

A sailor with a slight limp stopped in the middle of the docks with a snort. Unlike the rest of Auteri, usually dressed in blue or gold tunics as luminous as the colorful roof tiles, or the boat workers like Rin, in bottle-green uniforms, this boy and his friends were swathed in gray-black clothes, drab as their constant frowns. My stomach lurched. He was the one who'd been skeptical of my seaweed fix for the ship.

Soma—the pirate.

The scar on his jaw twisted as he smirked, nudging his friend, a girl with long braids that went down to her waist. "Hey, where's the line for the witch?"

My cheeks burned hotter than the early-summer sun.

"I can help with your repair needs," I said, even though I wanted to crawl under my counter.

"I don't need help from a girl without any magic," he snickered. My nails bit into my palms. It felt as if Grottel was sneering in my face and threatening to take away my magic all over again.

His friend shook her head. "What's she doing here anyway? A castoff from the Council, I guess?"

I bit down a retort. I wasn't on a quest to start fights, unlike wizards like Conroy.

Soma stepped closer, with a slight limp that made him even more menacing. "Yeah, her parents probably thought she was useless and kicked her out."

"My parents would never do that." He could say whatever he wanted about me, about my magic, about my sad-looking shop, but *not* about my parents.

He scoffed. "Then why does no one want your help?"

And for that...

For that, I didn't have an answer.

In the gaping silence, with Soma grinning victoriously at me, the line of people waiting for Seafoam Sweets shifted and turned away. Their whispers carried on a sea breeze, harsh on my ears.

A witch with barely any magic.

It's a wonder she could even save the ship yesterday.

Is that why it took so long?

Poor thing. She knows seaweed and rocks don't usually get used in spells, right?

I thought witches flicked their wands and chanted a few words and solved everything.

Then a familiar person stepped next to my counter, facing the pirates with her arms crossed.

"Soma," Rin said, and though she leaned casually against the crates, her narrowed eyes flashed threateningly. "You do know Eva's my ward, don't you?"

Soma spat on the ground. "Yeah, yeah, that stupid quest."

"Do you *want* some magical services?" Rin slowly rolled up the sleeves of her uniform. "Because with what you're saying and how you're staying here, it seems like you *want* Eva to curse you out into the sea."

Perhaps this was the one time it'd be nice if my spells conveniently misfired and sent him into an abyss. Preferably anywhere far, far away. Tension crackled in the air as Soma and Rin stared each other down. "Um, of course, if you need repair services, I can help?" I offered. The last thing I wanted was a fight in front of my stand.

"I've seen witches and wizards like you," Soma snarled, turning toward me. "You all offer to help, but only at a cost."

"If you need help," I said firmly, "I *will* help. I won't charge if someone's in danger. I'm here for you, for the whole town."

His eyes flickered with surprise. "You—*what*? You don't charge?"

"Truly," I said. "Never if someone's life is at stake."

"What if I want you to fix my shirt?" He tugged at the hem of his shirt, the edges ratty and torn as if he'd been attacked by a wild animal.

"Your life isn't at stake over a shirt, is it?" I asked, and he sullenly shrugged. "For that, I'd charge a copper, something small, or teach you how to hem your shirt for free. But if it's something monumental, something that you need desperately... I would help. No charge at all."

"But your Council," he snarled, "they only agree to help when there's gold as a reward."

"What?" I shook my head in confusion. "That doesn't sound like the Council *I* know. On my way here to Auteri, a girl almost fell in the water. My mother saved her from drowning, and she would've never required even a copper coin. The Council is here to *help* the entire realm."

Soma frowned, clenching his jaw. "But—"

"You didn't see her charging for helping during the shipwreck yesterday, did you?" Rin motioned out toward the cliffs. "And on her way to Auteri, Eva saved a passenger with a deep wound, and she *never* asked for a coin in return."

"Well," he spluttered. To my surprise, he seemed shocked. Almost even with a hint of guilt. "Well..."

Rin shrugged nonchalantly. "I rest my case."

Soma opened his mouth, but for once, he seemed flush out of salty retorts. A few of Rin's friends in bottle-green uniforms wandered closer, their eyes keen on Soma and his crew.

"C'mon, let's get some honey cider," one of Soma's friends grumbled. "It's no fun—this witch isn't doing any magic."

"Yeah, cider's better than this," Soma said, but his voice seemed oddly deflated as he and his crew strolled off.

After he disappeared around the corner, I spun to face my guardian. "Rin, you're truly magical!"

She laughed, easing onto the bench. "I'm not sure about *magical*, but I do know a bit about Soma, more than he realizes. So it helps when I have to argue with him."

"What do you mean?"

"After he showed up in town, I wanted to make sure he wouldn't cause issues for my m—" Rin glanced at the town hall. "Ah, anyone in Auteri. To tell the truth, it's a sad tale."

I turned my head, listening.

"Soma's only fifteen, just a few years older than you. True, it's not strange to be working at his age. But some friends from the boats told me that Soma's family owns a farm, and when there wasn't enough food on the table, Soma would tell his parents he was going to work for the carpenter's guild in the capital."

"When he was actually...working as a pirate?" I whispered. "And—and the Council helped the queen stop all pirates on the Rivelle coast just a year or two ago, right?"

"Believe me, most people adore witches and wizards, but...the Council put pirates out of business."

Well. That explained why Soma and his crew had never seemed to like me from the start. Rin's honey-brown eyes darkened in sadness. "His father was too prideful once he found out Soma's real job, even though Soma's three younger brothers *needed* the gold. You see that scar on Soma's face? That's from when his father kicked him out of the house and told him to never come round again. But Soma probably has a chip on his shoulder because he thinks that your Council is in it for the money. Truth be told, they only stepped in once the queen and the merchants' guild offered a big reward. All Soma wanted was to take care of the people who depended on him."

My chest tightened. I glanced back at the corner

where Soma and his crew had slunk into town. He'd—he'd tried everything to help his family, and for that, he had gotten thrown out. It just wasn't right.

"Nothing's fair, is it?" Rin said, as if she knew what I was thinking. "He's doing much better as a sailor, though. He sends a chunk of his pay back home every moon, even if it isn't as much as when he marauded. I heard his father will sometimes even read the letters he sends." Rin cleared her throat and tried to smile at me, as if she wanted to banish the weight of her words. "Other than pirates and stubborn parents, how're you doing, Eva?"

I didn't want to explain to my guardian that no one had stopped by, except for Soma. "Been...busy...Oh! Thank you so much for these crates and the cushions—they're perfect!"

"I'm glad to see them go to a good home." Rin toyed with the tips of her short hair. "Ah, also, one of the sailors said you're looking for ol' Vaud?"

"Vaud?" I echoed.

She plucked the sign up and studied my drawing. "This flamefox—you're looking for his owner, right? The old man whose arm you healed. It's funny, Vaud was asking all around the boat, but he didn't want to wake you."

"I found Ember—I mean, the flamefox—I found him in my knapsack," I said quickly. "I didn't mean to take him, I promise."

Rin grinned, shaking her head. "Believe me, I know. Vaud's brought a few of them in. Each has been more trouble than *I'd* say they're worth. On the ride over, one of them jumped over the railing and the whole boat had to stop or Vaud said *he'd* jump overboard." Rin picked up my charcoal stick and drew a map on the parchment. "Take care, though; he shelters more than just flamefoxes."

She slid the paper over.

"Thank you." I swallowed. I hadn't expected to find Ember's owner so quickly. Then I brightened. "Did you come by to get something fixed?"

Rin shook her head. "Nothing today." I deflated. Then she added wryly, "Unless you have some way for my mother to not be upset again?"

"Er…" Mayor Taira was difficult for *me* to figure out. I couldn't imagine being her daughter. Or a fix for them, either.

Rin took one look at me chewing my lip nervously and laughed, picking up a cloth bag at her feet and pushing it over my counter. "Don't worry, I don't expect you to repair *that*. But here, a few supplies from the grocer; I bought too many emerald onions and coral apples. Let me know if you need any help, okay?"

I needed a lot of help. I didn't know how to get customers to *want* my fixes. More importantly, I still needed to find a way to protect the town from the Culling.

I waved as she made her way down to a skiff, and then I stared at the paper. Ember's face looked up at me, next to the charcoal lines. The map led over the rocky cliffs and through the farmlands.

My heart wrenched in a strange twist. I had to take Ember back to his real home.

CHAPTER 14
A Real Home

The cottage door creaked as I pushed it open and stepped inside, away from the cool evening sea air. I tripped on something and gasped. It looked like a typhoon had ripped through the cottage.

Torn black dresses lay scattered on the floor, bite marks scored book covers, the bed was pockmarked, and my closet door swung on one hinge with telltale scratches on the front.

The flamefox was curled up in the corner of my bed, wrapped in my blanket and fast asleep.

"Ember, what did you do?" I cried.

He woke from the sound of my voice and scrambled out of bed. He started jumping up, his curved claws scratching like paper cuts on my legs.

"Ember, no!" I scolded.

I picked up a piece of bristle lying at my feet. It was disconcertingly familiar. "No, no... The Fiery—"

I strode to the closet and flung the door open. It slammed against the wall, echoing in the tiny cottage. The room shrunk around me as my lungs imploded. The broomstick my mother had given me lay on the floor, with deep bite marks all over. The Fiery Phoenix's magical bristles were a chewed-up stub with broken bits crunching under my feet.

That was the last straw.

My voice was sharp, aimed straight at Ember. "I need the broom to pass my quest." I spun around and glared. "I don't *need* to take care of a flamefox."

Ember stopped wagging his tail and curled it between his legs. He scurried to the bed and hid in the corner of the mattress.

I slumped to the ground, gathering salvageable bristles into a jar. After I'd manifested and first gotten my broomstick, the shopkeeper had told me I could easily fix the broomstick itself, but the magical bristles—the engine of the broom—were difficult to replace. Shoving the jar onto the highest shelf of the kitchen, I boiled a quick dinner of buckwheat noodles, thin and chewy, delicious with the emerald onions from Rin and a bit of salty broth.

Ember got a bit of noodles and a slice of mackerel, even when he didn't deserve anything. He chewed nervously, glancing at me. The mouthwateringly savory noodles couldn't extinguish the fire in my stomach. I didn't want *anything* to do with him.

I'd been planning to spend the next day at the shop, but I wasn't getting any customers anyway. It was time to take Ember home.

Picking up the flamefox, I deposited him on the ground next to my bed. I burrowed under my hole-filled blanket and fumed over the disastrous day as I fell asleep.

෧෨

The sun blazed bright through the morning haze as we climbed through the cliffs behind Auteri. Ember and I puffed out breaths as we trudged up worn tire tracks. It was so steep that it felt like we were walking on stairs up into the sky, and so narrow that there wouldn't have been enough room for us and an automobile. Thankfully, we didn't see any as we walked up the path.

An hour later, with sweat trickling down my back, we hit a plateau. Ember wriggled his curly tail and jumped around, thinking we were just going for a fun walk.

"Oh, we're going places, buddy." I glared. "For a real long hike."

Rin had written the address for a house in the farmlands. I touched my wand to the parchment and traced an arrow mark as I cast a navigation spell I'd made a few moons ago, walking in the forests between my parents' house and Miyada's town square. *"Where to go, where to be, let me know, let me see.*" A red arrow blinked on the paper, pointing straight down the dirt path.

I wished I could use that spell to figure out where my future destination might be. Or where I might be able to find answers to help Auteri.

We walked through low, rolling hills of farmland. To our left, a grove of gnarled trees sagged under branches heavy with dark brown nuts. To our right, the fields burst to the edges with tall cornstalks, the bright green leaves waving in the light breeze. Occasionally, roads wove through the fields and led away to small farmhouses, different crops, or pastures full of grazing animals. From time to time, farmers stopped to wave as we walked by.

"If I had the Fiery Phoenix—*in one piece*—we could've tried flying." I sighed. Ember was having fun, though. He kept darting to the crops and then running back to me making little growls of contentment. "I should find a new name for my broom. Maybe the Bald Phoenix? That would be fitting."

The sun beat down hard overhead by the time we got close to Vaud's house. My canteen was almost empty, and Ember—who had drunk most of my water—began to pant. I checked the map one more time, and the red arrow flickered on the parchment and pointed off the main path, to a tiny blue farmhouse that almost looked like it was afloat in a sea of tasseled cornstalks.

Ember sniffed at the stake marking the driveway. The

sign had recently been covered with a messy splash of white paint, so I couldn't make out the letters.

He tugged at the leash, a bit of red rope Rin had given me so he wouldn't run off. The flamefox wanted to continue down the main road, but I called him back. "Ember...it's here."

We began walking up the gravel path to the farmhouse, past a round, algae-flecked pond. A sleek, sunbathing waterrabbit took one look at us and hopped inside, its round eyes and long, slick-furred ears peeking out of the shallows, tracking our every move and those of the creatures in the pond. In the center, a long, scaly black fin stuck out of the water as a shadow circled under the murky surface. It looked eerily like a dragonshark. I tugged Ember away, and we skirted well around the pond.

As we got closer to the house, a volley of barks rang out. A cloud of dust rose up, moving toward us. The sound of gravel spraying grew louder and louder, and I realized it wasn't a dust storm—but a pack of flamefoxes, much larger and fiercer than Ember.

The flamefoxes' tails flickered with bright orange flames. Their gleaming eyes narrowed in on me, fangs bared.

"Run, Ember!" I shouted, turning around.

But Ember leaped between me and the pack of flamefoxes, snarling, with his hackles raised and teeth bared, though he was just a runt compared to these huge flamefoxes.

"No!" I cried and dove for him, holding his tiny body in my arms and curling into a ball as the flamefoxes rushed toward us.

I shielded Ember in one arm and curled my hand around my wand. My thoughts whirred as the snarling flamefoxes pounced.

"*Deflect and protect!*" I cried, and a flurry of dirt and pebbles rose, swirling from my wand and covering me and Ember in a makeshift barricade.

The flamefoxes slammed into the thin, trembling barrier, their fangs a hair's breadth away from us. They started scratching at the dirt and rocks, growling. Heat from their flaming tails licked at us.

The shield flickered out and the pebbles fell to the ground. "Help!" I cried. The largest flamefox stepped closer, its black eyes glittering, and let out a low snarl that made my hair stand on end. "*Deflect and protect!*"

The shield rose again, wavering but there—for now.

Sweat trickled down my forehead as I struggled to keep the shield up. Magic leached out of me, and my body numbed.

"Ember," I hissed, "if my magic runs out, get away fast." He whimpered, claws scratching as he burrowed closer. "Please."

Then a sharp whistle pierced the air.

"Whoa, whoa!" a voice bellowed from the house. The door flew open and an old man ran out. "Stop!"

Like magic, the pack's hackles lowered, and their growls melted into whimpers of delight. They turned and raced to the old man, prancing around him.

The pebbles fell to the ground around us. I loosened my grip on my wand and collapsed onto my knees, panting heavily. Black spots dotted my vision.

The old man slowed and limped toward me, and the pack parted to let him through. They gazed at him dotingly. It reminded me of how Ember looked when I opened the cottage door and he wagged his tail with his whole body because he was so excited to see me.

"Hey there." It was the man from the boat—Vaud. "Didn't you see the sign at the front of the driveway?"

I shook my head. "It was blank."

Vaud scowled. "Those darn farm kids painted over it again. Nothing else to do in the farmlands, so they think it's a fun idea to scare the living daylights out of the few visitors who walk my way. What'd you come here and risk your neck for?"

Then he saw Ember in my arms. He took off his glasses and wiped them clean. "I was wondering where he went." He put them back on his round nose and stared at us again. "That's why the pack's in a fury. All they see is a flamefox that's intruding on their territory. Don't worry, the pack knows to behave around me."

I set him onto the ground. "It's okay now, Ember."

"You've named him?"

My cheeks burned. "I just needed to call him something other than 'flamefox.'"

"Hmm…" Vaud rubbed his largest flamefox behind its pointed ears. "I asked around at the docks, but I thought the runt had disappeared on one of the earlier stops."

"I'm sorry I held on to Ember—er, the flamefox—for so long," I apologized. "I brought him back as soon as I could."

Vaud's flamefoxes circled us, drool dripping from their jowls. Ember slipped between my legs and poked his head out to growl at them. I hushed him.

Vaud looked at Ember hiding behind me. "Want to come in for a glass of cloudberry lemonade?"

"I'm sorry, I have to head back." The sun was high overhead. I needed to continue fixing up my shop or, at this rate, there was no way I'd be able to protect the town from the Culling.

Vaud let me fill up my canteen at his well, and I wiped sweat from my face with a handkerchief I'd moistened in the cool water. When I slid my canteen into my knapsack, Ember tried to climb in, too, but I tied the top tightly. He clung to my legs, whimpering sharply.

"Troublemaker," I muttered, even as each of his cries scratched at my heart. "You tore up my cottage. Dug holes in my mattress…shredded all my magic tomes…"

Ember sensed something was different, and he was definitely *not* interested in making friends with the other flamefoxes. He kept snapping when they came close to him.

"Well...I have to get going. Thank you for the water, and I'm sorry it took me so long to bring him back."

"Thanks for coming all the way out here." Vaud paused. "Ah, I have something for you—wait just a moment, would you?"

Vaud disappeared into his house and hurried out with a glass jar, waving it proudly. "Watch this."

I stared at the empty jar in confusion. "Is there something—"

"Nothing, right? For now, for now. C'mere, Hina."

The biggest flamefox brushed up against Vaud's legs and sat in front of him, with her red-orange tail waving back and forth.

"May I?" Vaud asked, and at first, I thought he was speaking to me. But Hina moved her muzzle in the slightest of nods. He leaned over and swung the jar through her fiery tail, capturing a flame, and twisted the lid on tight.

"As a thanks for bringing this little one back." He held the jar out.

The flame flickered merrily in the jar. Strangely, the glow seemed to be pulsing brighter.

"For me?" At my side, Ember whined mournfully and

grabbed at his bushy tail, as if that could make it light up. As if having flames might mean he could go back with me.

"It doesn't burn out," Vaud explained. "A flamefox's flame will last as long as it's alive and gives you just the right amount of light that you need, wherever you go. It doesn't burn unless they're real mad."

"Is the jar hot?" I asked.

"Nah, the jar makes it easier to hold, or else it'll go rolling away like a ball of yarn. It's just warm. Like a freshly drawn bath."

I gingerly cupped the jar in my hands. The flaming light circled around the bottom, but the glass was pleasantly warm, like when Ember sat in my lap when I was shivering.

"Oh! Thank you." I tucked the strange jar into my knapsack.

Then, finally, I handed over the red leash to Vaud, who held it tight in his wizened, papery hands.

Ember squealed a sharp puppy sound that wasn't quite a bark. My eyes watered.

"This is your home, Ember," I said sternly. That didn't console him. He strained against the leash. From the front porch, a silver rockcrow with a broken wing cawed uneasily, hopping from side to side at its bowl of dried corn.

Ember whimpered, his eyes wide and confused.

"You belong here." I couldn't delay it anymore. "Vaud's your owner and this is your home."

With one last look at Ember, I turned away.

At the crossroads with the main road, I tapped the sign with my wand and incanted a quick spell to repair it. *"Undo what's done, let it be gone."*

The white paint trickled away and Vaud's warning, BEWARE: VAUD'S WILD-BEAST SHELTER, appeared. A final spell—*"A sign none can paint over, unless you're the owner"*—made it impossible for troublemakers to cover his words. It was the least I could do for Vaud.

I sighed and continued on my path back to Auteri. "Ember's a good-for-nothing fluffball. Eats all the croissants, licks my jars of redbud jam clean, leaves nothing for me."

As I walked down to the main road, I kicked at the rocks on the path. "Remember how the Fiery Phoenix is a *bald* phoenix now? And all my witch's dresses are in shreds?"

My words sounded empty and hollow.

"And I *hate* falling into the holes he chewed in the mattress. Darn Ember."

Even though I trudged farther and farther down the dusty road, Ember's cries seemed to echo in my ears.

I stopped when I got to the cliff that overlooked Auteri. "Darn flamefox. He broke my broom, he—" I pressed my hands to my mouth, barely able to breathe. If I breathed in too fast, I'd break into tears. I couldn't see the path down because my vision blurred.

My jaw clenched up. I didn't miss him. I didn't miss him at all—

Suddenly, shouts rang out from behind me. I turned and my heart wrenched tight.

The old man hitched up his baggy trousers as he ran. His face was splotched red and sweaty, and he chased after something small, a red-gold dot that streaked toward me like a shooting star.

Ember.

The flamefox's eyes zeroed in on me, and he ran faster than I'd ever seen him chase after seagulls around the cottage.

Then Ember was within arm's reach and he didn't stop. He leaped up and my arms opened automatically. I caught him against my chest. *"Ember."*

He whimpered, his body quivering. I realized it wasn't just him. I trembled, too. I slid to the ground, holding him tight.

"I'm sorry." My tears spilled over. "I'm sorry I got mad. I'm sorry. I should have never even thought of leaving you."

Ember narrowed his eyes, reared up on his back legs, and planted his paws on my shoulders. I fell backward onto the ground and caught a glimpse of a brilliantly clear, blue sky. He leaned close.

"I'm really, really sorry, Ember," I whispered.

And then he shoved his warm snout against me. He licked my face with his rough, pink tongue, thoroughly admonishing me. His tongue tickled and I squealed and laughed, but I couldn't push him away. I gathered him closer, back in my arms.

Someone cleared their throat. I sat up, looking around wildly with grass sticking out of my hair, and then realized the old man had caught up to me and Ember. Vaud had his arms crossed with a deep wrinkle carved into his forehead.

I swallowed. "Do you mind if he stays with me?"

Ember barked.

Both of us looked up imploringly at the old man.

"Well, I've been close to running out of space for all my flamefoxes." Vaud's whiskers twitched. "And, you know, I think he's already decided on his home."

I hiccuped. "Truly?"

He grinned, showing the gaps in his teeth. "These little brats, they don't take to people easily. Once they've decided you're theirs, there's little we can do to change their minds. Most times, they're smarter than us humans."

"I think I understand what you mean." The corner of Ember's mouth lifted and his sharp teeth flashed, almost in a laugh.

"I'd give you his leash back, but he sheared it in half to get to you." He showed me his ragged half of the leash.

"Ember!" I scolded, and he wriggled closer, happily.

"How much do I owe you for him?" I asked. Flamefoxes were rare, but right then I'd dive for treasure at the bottom of the Constancia Sea as long as it meant that Ember could stay with me.

The man squinted. "The thing is, I shouldn't have let little Ember here out of my sight in the first place. And he was a rescue anyway. He needs a good home."

"Mister Vaud…"

He cleared his throat. "I guess what I'm saying is… take care of Ember, okay? And if you're ever in the area, stop by and say hi. Deal?"

Still holding Ember to my chest, I scrambled to my feet and took his hand. "Deal."

Ember put his paw on top of our hands. I could almost hear him say *Deal*, too.

Our laughter pealed like bells, making the sky bluer and the sun feel soft and warm on my skin.

CHAPTER 15
Semi-Magical

The next day, after spending the lunchtime rush wishing I could charm customers to stop by and trying to come up with the right spell to protect Auteri from the Culling, I slid the Fiery Phoenix on the counter. Ember had chewed it up well. He sniffed at the broom and curled up.

I sighed.

He opened one eye, staring at me as if to say, *What did I do wrong?*

"Yeah, go on, pretend to be innocent." I glared back, but he'd already gone back to napping. My flamefox let out a suspiciously fake snore.

Mother—or almost any other wizard or witch—could've smoothened out the gnaw marks and mended the magical bristles with a flick of her wand. Since I didn't have her strength, I would have to be clever and use some elbow grease to re-form the misshapen edges.

I rummaged through my jars and pulled out my scrap of sandpaper. As I sanded down the sides, I tried to think of ways to fix up the bristles so it would work as an actual broomstick.

In front of the shop, a little boy called out to his mother. "Mama, Mama, wait for me." His cheeks dimpled as he ran over and threw his arms around her legs.

She ruffled his hair roughly and her voice was stern, but a gentle smile lit her face. "Stay with me, love."

I missed my parents with an ache in my heart I'd never felt before. Whenever Mother was off on her trips, Father and I had always baked breads or worked in the garden, and by the time we'd polished off a batch of sourdough with a wheel of soft cheese, she'd already be back home.

When—or if—I got Mayor Taira's sign-off on my application, the last step would be to fly. All witches and wizards returned to the Council Hall by broomstick.

I peeked at my hourglass. The two glass stars shimmered as sand flowed down to the bottom star, speck by speck. Time was moving quickly. I stopped watching the crowds and focused on my broom with a new fury.

But I didn't know how to fix the magical bristles. My

lips tugged down as I sorted through the broken twigs, trying to think of a solution.

Ember's hot nose nudged my ankle. I turned, my voice sharper than I intended. "What?"

He sat on the dirt, wagging his tail. He had his frayed leash in his mouth.

"It's not time for a walk, Ember."

My flamefox jumped onto the crate next to me. He dropped the leash on my arm and whined.

Ember disappeared under the counter again. He reappeared seconds later, holding something round and golden in his mouth, and set it next to the leash. It was a ball of his fur, from when I had brushed him earlier. He nudged the leash and fur toward me.

Then he bumped his muzzle against my arm and nudged me toward the pile of bristles. *Here*, he seemed to be saying. *Now you can repair them!*

"I can't make bristles out of that."

"Well, I saw you heal a man with a deep cut, so I bet you can manage a few bristles," a familiar, melodic voice rang out.

I jumped. Rin stood in front of the counter in her green uniform. My cheeks flamed. I had been talking to Ember as if he could answer back. "Oh! Rin!"

My guardian broke into a smile. "I didn't mean to surprise you, Eva. I was going to stop by earlier, but you looked lost in your thoughts."

"Oh, you should've said hi—I wasn't busy," I protested. "I—I haven't been getting any customers anyway."

Rin peered at me. "Is something wrong? I'm your guardian—I want to help."

Uncertainty crept into my voice. "I don't think...I don't think I'm doing good for the town, Rin. I barely saved that ship the other day, and I used rocks and *seaweed*, out of all things. After, Soma and his crew came by and made fun of me.... Auteri really lucked out when I decided to stay here, huh? I never seem to do anything right."

Rin settled on the crate across from me and turned her head to the side thoughtfully. "None of us are perfect all the time, Eva," she said finally. "On one of my first boat rides, a passenger yelled at me, and then a different rider threw up on my uniform."

"But...I don't know if"—I couldn't possibly tell Rin that Mayor Taira didn't want me here; I couldn't speak about her own mother like that—"if I'm doing any good, truly."

Rin tapped the edge of the crate. "Still, you're trying, right? Maybe I'm not the best worker on the boat. But people like us, we've got to keep on trying. I'm not going to let one miserable passenger stop me from being out on the sea. Maybe it's not the way the others cast spells, but fates, you *saved* people, Eva. If that's not trying, I don't know what trying is."

I opened my mouth and then closed it. I shifted, fiddling

with my wand, thinking over her words, which had settled around me like a blanket.

Instead of prodding me further, Rin leaned over the counter to examine the broom, and through the layer of sweat and coal, I caught a whiff of her sun-dried laundry, warm and sweet.

"What happened to the broom? It looks, um, different from when I first met you."

"Ember tore it up. He got mad waiting for me and went on a rampage in the cottage. I've learned to never leave this troublemaker alone since."

My flamefox didn't quite seem apologetic as Rin rubbed his head and his sharp teeth flashed in a smile. "Could you use your magic to fix it?"

I tried to think of a charm as her gaze seared into me. Nervously, I grabbed the broken bristles and placed them on top of the fur and leash.

"Go on with what you were doing," she encouraged. I blushed. I still wasn't used to performing magic in front of a captive audience.

Taking a deep breath, I swirled my wand above the bristles. I sang softly, *"Spinner, spinner, spin through the wind; flying together, flying to the end."*

The leash unraveled as the fur braided around the sticks, and magic tugged out of my body. Red light flashed blindingly and my eyes watered.

I blinked until I could see. I had made a handful of

new bristles that were a warm gold color instead of dark sticks. And when I looked closer, strands of the red leash and reddish-gold fur twined around each bristle.

"See? Your magic is working fine now. Try a bit of my uniform next." Rin pulled out the green handkerchief tucked into her shirt pocket and handed it to me.

"Really?" I said, and she nodded. "Thank you."

The orphanage kids had gathered around my counter, their eyes peeking over the edges. Charlotte jogged over, wiping sweat off her forehead, clutching a stack of flyers to her chest. Her right hand was still swathed in a thick bandage that looked stifling in the warm summery air.

"Char, Char, did you see that?" One of the boys, with his hair sticking out in twenty different directions, tugged at her sleeve.

"Ouch! Be careful of my bandage. And see what?" Charlotte asked. She slumped onto the crate next to Rin and grumbled as she moved her messenger bag onto her lap. More papers peeked out of the worn cloth folds. "This errand is never going to end. I mean, pass these out to *all* the stores and every tourist I see? That's everyone! And this job pays a copper compared to my normal three bronze coins."

An old woman stuck her head out the orphanage door. She had short, stiff gray hair and a frown that looked plastered to her face. "Charlotte, I've been waiting for you—it's your turn to prepare supper."

Charlotte groaned. "I'm so sorry. I'll be right inside."

I froze. *I* could do something. From my other side, Rin met my eyes and grinned, as if she knew exactly what I was thinking. My guardian whispered, "You ready to put that magic to use?"

"Absolutely." But I wasn't sure if Charlotte wanted my help.

Rin said louder, winking at me, "I *do* know of someone who might be able to lend you a hand. Someone magical. Someone who's been wanting to help the whole town."

I dipped into a bow. "I'm at your service."

Charlotte stared down her snub nose at me, then glanced at the woman who was sticking her head out the door, huffing impatiently. Finally, her gaze went toward the buildings stretching all the way up to the town hall, crammed into the cliffs. It felt like she was measuring me up, to see if she could really trust me like she seemed to trust Rin and Davy.

"Fine." Charlotte sighed. She dropped the stack of papers on my counter and pulled out a tightly wound scroll and a charcoal stick from one of her belt pouches. "Kyo asked me to pass out flyers for the Festival of Lights to all the shops."

"Oh! I can—"

"And I need the owners to tell me what they're selling at their festival stands."

I breathed sharply with excitement. I'd heard the Festival of Lights was the most beautiful festival in all of the realm, but I truthfully didn't know much about it. "What's the festival like?"

"Lightfish are the best!" cried one of the boys.

"Lightfish?" I echoed. The orphanage kids gasped with horror.

Charlotte's nostrils flared, as if explaining this was a chore. "Once a year, during the Festival of Lights, our sailors bait lightfish with our famous sweet corn, attracting them to the top of our waters. Usually, the lightfish are in the depths, searching for their mates and families before the currents spread them across the sea again. But with the bait, it seems as if the waters are sparkling with light."

The orphanage kids pawed at the flyers. "We wanna go! We wanna see all the sparkly lightfish!"

Charlotte pried off their hands. "The flyers are for the shopkeepers. Or visitors to Auteri. You *live* here. Don't make me send you all inside."

The kids stuck their hands into their pockets, shifting their weight from side to side as they tried their best to listen.

"I'd be more than happy to do that for you!" Maybe I could create a charm to send out the flyers to each of the shops. I started thinking about spells.

Carry on, wind be strong didn't cause my magic to tingle at my fingertips. *Fly again, straight to them* didn't feel quite right, either....

Charlotte wrinkled her forehead. "You know, you need a better sign."

My parchment sign declared EVA, WITCH, which I thought was perfectly functional. But to Charlotte's point, it was barely readable from more than a few feet away.

Rin inclined her head. "Char's right. It's hard to tell if you're a scryer or a weather witch."

I took a deep breath. "Or a semi-magical repair witch?"

Semi-magical. Those words stung, even when *I* said them. It matched me too well. Yet I'd never heard of a witch who did semi-magical work, because there were only witches and wizards or the magicless—nothing in between.

My guardian smiled gently. "Or that."

Charlotte bit her lip. "I'm sort of handy with painting. I can draw up a sign if you can help with the flyers."

"She's more than 'sort of handy' with painting and art and all that. You've seen her paper animals, right?" Rin chimed in.

I sat up straight. Trading jobs was just as good as getting coins. "But don't you have to go make dinner?"

Just then, the old woman stuck her head out the window. *"Charlotte!"*

Charlotte visibly sank. "I'll be back, I—"

"I'll take care of dinner for the little ones, Char." Rin let out a wistful sigh, glancing at the flyers one last time. "Ah, I loved the festival when I was young. My mother and I"—I felt a jolt of shock as I remembered she meant Mayor Taira—"used to go to *all* the stands for the festival foods. Those were the best nights. Back before I started working on the boats."

Rin shook her head, as if that thought had abruptly shaken her out of her nostalgia. She beckoned the kids. "Come on, crew! Listen to your captain—we're getting dinner!"

She peeled the orphanage kids away from my stand and led them inside.

I collected a few leftover planks, and Charlotte asked for red, gold, and white paint. Incanting *The colors that taint, please transform to paint,* I used a sliver of red tomato from my sandwich and magicked it into red paint, plucked bits of honey-colored dried grass for the gold, and crumbled a bit of contomelon roll for white paint.

Charlotte dipped her finger into the red paint and sniffed it gingerly. "It has the scent of freshly picked tomatoes. I almost want to taste it."

"Here, use this." I held out a paintbrush I'd made from a bit of twig and grass and immediately frowned. "Isn't your hand hurt? Do you need my help to paint?"

"It's almost healed." Charlotte grabbed the paint-brush with her unharmed hand. "I'm left-handed any-way. Keep working on a spell for the flyers, Eva."

It was the first time we'd been alone since we'd met. She put the sign on the ground on the other side of the counter, so that all I could see was the tip of her blue hair ribbon, streaming lightly in the wind. She didn't seem to want me to see her painting. For a bit, we didn't say any-thing. Charlotte hummed a gentle, slightly melancholy melody as she painted.

"Why'd you choose to come to Auteri?" Charlotte asked me suddenly. I fumbled the flyers, and they slid all over the counter. I flushed.

"Oh, Auteri? Well, I actually didn't mean to...." I explained to her how my magic worked, how I had been drained of magic after healing Vaud's cut, and before I knew it, Rin had shaken me awake, telling me that Auteri was the last stop.

"Then you could've gone elsewhere."

I looked behind me, where I could see the gold dome of the town hall. "I guess. But...I've been thinking about it....There are so few witches and wizards in the realm. If I moved on, would someone else have come here? Even if it was a series of accidents, I figured I might be able to help Auteri if I stayed."

"Hmm, a series of accidents," Charlotte said. "That's kind of how I came to Auteri, too."

I could only see her crown of braids—she was hidden by the counter. "What do you mean?"

Charlotte stood up, wincing as she stretched out her bandaged hand. "It's a long story."

"I'm not going anywhere. But you don't need to tell me if you don't want to."

"No, it's just that…" She glanced down the docks. "I mean, you can tell from how my hair's paler than most everyone else that I'm not from Auteri. Maybe the Walking Cliffs. Or, even, another realm. Anyway, everyone in Auteri knows, so I've never had to tell my story before."

"I'd love to hear it from you."

She breathed in slowly and then finally spoke. "Mayor Taira was on one of her early-morning walks. When she walked through the docks and past the beach, she saw a blue bundle at the edge of the water and didn't think much of it—until she heard a cry.

"That wet lump of cloth was me.

"Mayor Taira sent out inquiries through the realm. Everyone knew of someone taken away by the sea, but no one had heard of a person being returned by it. There were no witches or wizards in town, so she had no means to figure out where I had come from.

"Mayor Taira started the orphanage to take care of me and the other children of Auteri whose parents were lost to the sea. No one has come to claim me. Someday, I'm going to find out where I'm from."

She stared at me, as if I'd challenge her.

I tore my gaze away, looking out to the frothing, restless sea. I searched for a response, anything to explain the way it felt like her words had stolen the breath from my lungs. "The kids at the orphanage love you," I said, stumbling over my words.

"Well, I'm finished," Charlotte declared, as if she hadn't heard me, and set the sign onto the bench. "It just needs a moment to dry." She smoothed back the strands of hair that had escaped her braid and retied her blue ribbon.

I finally got a good look at her. White paint was smeared onto Charlotte's hair, as if she'd aged seventy years. Dots of gold speckled her right cheek like freckles. To top it all off, she had a splotch of red on her nose. I giggled. "You, um, might need to clean up a bit."

"What?" She hurried over to the orphanage and did a double take when she saw the reflection of her paint-splattered face in the window. I found a handkerchief and tossed it over to her. She caught it with her left hand and began rubbing at her face furiously.

I pointed and called, "Ooh, you missed a spot on your forehead."

Charlotte glared. "Stop looking at me. Look at your sign instead."

I smiled to myself. Only she would do something nice and pretend to be prickly after. I circled around the counter and sucked in my breath with awe. Charlotte's artwork was *beautiful*.

Eva, Semi-Magical Repair Witch twinkled in gold cursive letters against the wood. The words had a faint white outline that made the sign shimmer. On the planks, it looked like the sun rising on the morning sea.

Below my name, she had painted in red: *Sometimes all you need is a pinch of magic.*

When I propped it up on the counter, my storefront sparkled. I breathed out, "Rin said you were good, but this is amazing. Thank you."

"Sure." She shrugged nonchalantly, yet her eyes shone brightly. "And you'll help me with the flyers, right?"

"Charlotte!" the old woman screeched out the window. "I need you to clean up *now*!"

"On my way!" Charlotte called. "Eva, go to the stores around the docks and the town square, okay? I know where the smaller shops off the main street are, so I'll take care of those. Sign up each shopkeeper for their stall, and write down what they're going to sell. And if you see any out-of-towners—you know, the people who don't quite look like they belong?—give flyers to them, too."

I wondered if I looked like an out-of-towner to her. "Got it!" I gathered up the flyers, smoothing out the curling corners. My heart beat faster. I'd been to a few festivals back in Miyada. But Auteri was *famous* for its Festival of Lights.

COME ONE, COME ALL
TO AUTERI'S REALM-FAMOUS,
ONE-AND-ONLY
FESTIVAL OF LIGHTS!

"Oh, Eva?" Charlotte said, pausing.

I looked up. "Yes?"

Her cheeks flushed. "Um, thanks." She spoke so quickly it felt like a breeze on a humid summer day, gone in a flash.

Charlotte disappeared into the orphanage before I could respond.

Something welled up in my chest. Charlotte trusted me to help her. I would do all I could to not let her down. Starting with delivering the flyers to all the shops.

I tapped my wand to the stack of flyers and funneled that strange, ticklish feeling in my chest into my words. *"Deliver to shops with speed. Up, down, around town, for a friend in need."*

The flyers rustled. Slowly, the papers lifted in the air, swirling around me. My hair tickled my neck. I'd never really done a spell like this before.

I snapped my wand toward the town. With a crack, sharp as thunder, the flyers shot across Auteri. The seagulls screeched and swooped away, protesting the strange papers soaring through the sky.

I waited for the flyers to plummet straight into the waters, or fly out to Okayama.

But—I sucked in a breath—the flyers swirled around town, shooting down here and there, as if they were on a mission. As if...as if the spell had worked.

I leaned out to look at Seafoam Sweets. A flyer was stuck on the window, proudly advertising the Festival of Lights.

I sat back on my crate, stunned. I'd done it. Bit by bit, my magic was growing stronger. I was nowhere close to Mother or even Conroy, but in these past few days, I'd taken one step closer to my dreams. Ember jumped onto my lap, filling my heart up with a peculiar warmth. As I blinked, my insides sloshed like the waves.

"Darn water," I muttered. "The spray is making my eyes all damp."

Ember poked me straight on the nose, as if he saw through all my excuses, and curled up tighter on my legs.

Now I had to sign up the shopkeepers for their stalls—and figure out some way to protect Auteri from the Culling. Maybe I could even do both at once, and ask the townspeople for their ideas. After all, they'd know best how to help the town. I gripped my wand and took a deep breath, as magic tingled up my spine.

CHAPTER 16

CORN AND CLOUDBERRIES

The morning fog swirled around me and Ember with every step. I adjusted the straps of my knapsack, full of extra flyers and the festival scroll. Seafoam Sweets hadn't opened yet, and sailors huddled in groups, taking swigs of steaming tea to wake up or slowly loading boats. Once we passed the beach and stepped onto the wood dock, Ember circled around me, crying softly.

"What is it?" I asked. The outline of a man appeared in the mists, standing still as a statue. It was the strange man from before, staring at something in the waters. A parchment flower was sinking, its petals sagging under the weight of the water. The man's sunken eyes followed the blossom as the currents gently pulled it away toward the open sea, until a wave swallowed the paper under. Then the man's gaze set on some point beyond the cliffs I couldn't quite discern.

I shivered and turned, checking over my storefront. Ember jumped onto a crate and poked his nose at the glass jars, probably looking for something to chew.

"Don't you dare even *think* about it." I plucked him away from the jars. "I didn't leave you in the cottage because I knew you'd make a mess, and don't you start here."

He let out a huff and tucked up into a cozy ball.

I sat close to Ember, stealing what warmth I could. I propped up the sign so that Charlotte's painted letters glimmered in the fog: *Eva, Semi-Magical Repair Witch.* Grinning, I threw back my shoulders and straightened up.

And just as quickly, I slumped.

To the right, from where the beach met the wood platform of the docks, a man and a woman walked toward me. I could recognize that stiff, regal walk anywhere.

It was Mayor Taira and her secretary, Kyo, deep in conversation. And they were heading straight toward me.

"I'm…I'm not ready to face her." I grabbed Ember and ducked under my crates, huddling below the counter. I hoped she hadn't noticed me yet. My flamefox squeaked in protest, but I shook my head furiously at him.

"Don't look at me like that," I growled under my breath. "I'm not hiding."

I peeked around the edge of the counter and exhaled. Ember stared. "Okay, I *might* be hiding."

There was a very good reason to avoid the mayor. If she asked me, "What good have you done for my town?" it would be very difficult to come up with an answer. I bet if that happened, Kyo would march me to the next boat out. The mayor's steps drew closer and I didn't dare breathe. Had she seen me?

Then the orphanage steps creaked as she and Kyo climbed up. I sucked in my breath. If she turned around, she'd catch sight of me. She rapped twice at the door and it swung open quickly.

"Welcome, Mayor Taira," Charlotte chirped. She had never sounded that happy to see me. "We're putting on a kettle for your tea."

"Good morning, Charlotte," Mayor Taira responded, her voice smooth and velvety. "Don't worry about the tea, I won't be staying too long. I have a few more inspections along the waterfront."

"Didja bring us toys, ma'am?" a boy's voice asked eagerly. "I cleaned up the main room, like you told me to."

"Hikaru!" snapped Charlotte.

"What?" he said. "All the other kids in town get nice toys for their birthday. We get *blankets*."

An older woman said nervously, "My apologies, Mayor Taira. Hikaru is just…"

The orphanage kids wanted toys. Maybe I could do something for them. I tucked away that idea for later. I strained to hear her reply.

The door groaned as it opened a crack, and my heart pounded in my chest. "Glad to see everything is going well," Mayor Taira said. "Well, shall we go to the town square, Hikaru? I can buy you a corn cake, as long as you help me bring some back for the rest of the orphanage. I'm sorry I didn't bring any toys this time."

My stomach grumbled at the thought of food. I missed my father's croissants.

"I'm ready!" Hikaru piped up. The door flew open.

"Curses!" I breathed out.

If I stayed here, Mayor Taira would definitely see me as she walked down the stairs to leave. I scrambled to my feet, placing Ember on the ground.

"Let's go!" I hissed to my flamefox, who was chasing his bushy tail around.

I snuck around the corner. Ember stood in front of the shop with his head cocked at the man at the edge of the docks, who still stared out at the sea.

"Come on," I begged, waving him over. Finally, he trotted over just as the door swung open. I hissed, "Now, *run!*"

Ember and I darted down the path, zigzagging through the cobblestone side streets. Finally, fifteen or twenty dizzying turns later, when I was absolutely lost, I stopped, rubbing at the stitch in my side, and looked around.

We were in the middle of the main square, with the

town hall looming over us. Around us, three-story-high buildings had balconies at each window, and people hung up lines of colorful shirts to dry in the summer sun. On the ground floor, shops were starting to open up. As I passed by, each store beckoned like a doorway into a new world.

Ember pointed his muzzle down a path where a briny smell wafted from the docks, mingling with the soap-scented laundry. He wanted to go back and sunbathe.

"Not until she's absolutely gone." I planted my feet on the ground.

But while I was in the town square, perhaps I could get started on signing up shopkeepers for the festival. So that if I did meet the mayor, I would have *something* to show for my time here.

"Come on, let's go to the first store," I said, pointing at the grocer's. The man in front was already sweating from the morning rush, his gold tunic damp, and he apologetically tugged his cap tight on his dark curls, asking me to come back later.

I moved on to a store that didn't seem too busy yet. The wood sign on top only said ᴄᴏʀɴ. A specialty store, perhaps? The store next door had a sign with ᴄʟᴏᴜᴅʙᴇʀ-ʀɪᴇꜱ painted in the same red and orange swirling letters. Maybe these were both specialty shops.

I stepped through the doorway, and my mouth dropped open in surprise.

I was in a cornfield. In a store. In the middle of town.

Or, at least, that's what it looked like. Slippery corn silks and husks sheeted the dirt floor. All around me, everything was corn-infused. Shelves were crammed with anything corn-like imaginable. There were even cornstalks growing in the corners of the shop. I ran my hand over a corn-shaped pillow and silk socks woven into the pattern of corn, with each kernel embroidered in gold thread.

Up by the register, steaming golden corn cakes rested on a rack, filling the shop with an irresistibly buttery smell. Ember growled with appreciation.

"What do we have *here*?" A short, thin woman with thick black hair rounded the register. She had a squeaky voice that reminded me of a field mouse, if mice could speak. The apron over her gold tunic was embroidered with corn cobs.

I pulled the festival scroll out of my knapsack. "Would you like to sign up for your stand?"

She snatched the paper out of my hand and mumbled to herself as she read it. "I haven't decided what I want to sell at the festival...."

"If you're not sure, I can come back," I offered, and she nodded. But before I turned to leave, I paused. "Oh, and if you don't mind, I was wondering...The mayor asked for help preparing for the Culling. Is there anything that particularly needs protection?"

"Protection? I hope that Council doesn't think the Culling will hit here." The woman frowned, her thin nose twitching like a mouse. "The last Culling hit Kelpern, and that blizzard caused a lot of water damage even to us. I guess something to waterproof the buildings with that magic those witches and wizards have got." She squinted at me, as if finally noticing my pointed hat. "Are you a witch?"

I heard Mayor Taira's rich, honeyed voice right outside and froze. I glanced at the decadent corn cakes on the counter, and all the blood leached from my face. She and Hikaru, the boy, wanted *corn* cakes. Of course she'd get them from the one store that specialized in corn.

"Curses!" I groaned. I spied a tall, thin door in the wall, probably leading to the shop next door, and I ran over to tug at the knob. "I'm sorry, I have to go."

"Don't you *dare* open that," the shopkeeper said with sudden force.

I stumbled backward, knocking over a stack of corn-scented candles, complete with engraved corn husks. "Okay, okay! But please don't say anything! Pretend I was never here!" I said frantically, piling the candles back onto the shelf.

Mayor Taira stepped inside the shop, and I dove into a patch of stalks, yanking Ember after me.

"What are you—Oh! Mayor Taira!"

"Hello, Trixie," Mayor Taira said, with Hikaru

trailing in her wake, running his hand along the shelves. "How's Trina doing?"

"It's such a pleasure to see you!" The shopkeeper fawned over her. "I assume Trina is her normal *cranky, miserable self.*" She directed those last few words toward the door between the shops, which, I realized, had been nailed shut all along the edges. Someone thumped on the door.

The mayor sighed. "I wish the two of you would get along like you used to."

Ember crawled into my lap, his pink tongue hanging out the side of his mouth, content for a flamefox that had just run circles around town. He started panting, but I quickly shushed him.

"It would've been nice to have a broom so that I could escape," I whispered pointedly, as he wriggled happily. "Now be quiet!"

Hikaru turned and stepped closer.

I didn't dare breathe, but Ember peered back, rustling the stalks.

Hikaru's eyes widened. "It's the witch!"

"What was that?" Mayor Taira called. "You want a corn cake, don't you?"

Please, please, please, I begged Hikaru silently, putting a finger to my lips. He scrunched his nose up, staring at me.

Mayor Taira cleared her throat. "Hikaru?"

His eyes glittered. "Mayor Taira, guess what?"

My stomach plummeted.

"Yes, Hikaru?" she asked, far more patiently than I would have ever expected.

"I…"

I dropped my head and prepared to crawl out.

"I want a *thousand* corn cakes!"

I nearly fell out of the stalks with relief.

◌◌

Some very long minutes later, Mayor Taira and Hikaru headed out, the boy sending me one last wink, with huge bags of corn cakes teetering in their arms.

"I'm gonna eat twenty," Hikaru promised her, his voice fading as they walked into the morning crowds. "All in *one* bite."

The cornstalks shifted and Trixie poked her head in. "So, do you mind explaining why you decided to hop into my display, witch?"

My cheeks burned as I crawled out and plucked corn silk off my skirt. "I, um, I'm not one of Mayor Taira's favorites right now. She doesn't exactly enjoy seeing me."

"Who *are* you?" Trixie frowned.

"Apprentice Eva Evergreen, here to serve Auteri."

"Well, well, the seaweed girl! So that's why you were asking about the Culling, huh?" Trixie crossed her arms, squinting. "Aren't you a little young?"

"I'm on my Novice quest!" I straightened up. After all, her frizzy hair barely reached the top of my witch's hat.

Trixie cackled. "Aren't you a precious one!"

Then someone pounded on that door I'd tried to open earlier.

"I'll be as loud as I want!" Trixie shouted at the door. To me, she asked loudly, "Got any spells to shut up that *pest*?"

Angry footsteps pounded, shaking the ground. Then a silhouette loomed in the front door.

"You there." The newcomer drew her eyebrows into a fierce frown at me. "Tell that human-sized gnat to be *quiet*."

Trixie huffed. "Witch, tell that human-sized *horsefly* to get out of my shop."

"Are you twins?" I looked between the two of them, at their same thick black hair and exact same height. They even had matching gold-colored tunics with pockets on the sides, but Trina had cloudberries embroidered on her apron.

They *had* to be twins.

"Absolutely, definitely not," Trixie said automatically.

"There's no way I'd be related to someone obsessed with *corn* all the time," Trina scoffed.

"How could I be twins with that *pest* who's infatuated with *cloudberries*? It's not like those stupid globs are anything special. Bluebells and honeyberries and saffronberries are all far, far better than cloudberries."

The twins started speaking over each other, extolling the virtues of corn or cloudberries.

An old woman leaned on her cane in the entrance. "Trixie, do you have fresh corn—" She took one look at the arguing twins and hurried away as fast as her wizened legs could take her.

"Wait!" Trixie called, but the old woman had scuttled deep into the crowd. She narrowed her eyes. "I've lost a customer all because of this berrylike *blob*. Isn't there a spell that'll make her behave?"

I froze. "Do you want me to *enchant* the two of you?"

"Whatever it would take to stop this chaos," Trixie snapped, moving her hand somewhere in the vicinity between her and Trina. "I am tired of my corn being disregarded."

Trina blew her lips out. "Pfft. Go ahead, cast magic on us. Even a spell can't make me like these boring stalks. *My* cloudberry concoctions are realm-famous, and corn will never compare."

My eyes widened. If I helped the twins with their relationship, Mayor Taira would love that, wouldn't she? I mean, even the mayor said she wanted them to reconcile. And after I figured out some fix to prepare Auteri for the Culling, she'd definitely have to agree that I was helping out the *whole* town.

As they started talking over each other about who

copied who for their apron designs, an idea better than corn aprons popped into my mind.

I pulled my wand out and fiddled with it. They'd asked for help. My fingers sparked with magic. This was perfect. Even my magic was ready for this fix. Ember wove around my ankles as I thought of the right spell.

"It's her fault that I'm losing customers, being next to this *corn* shop. Who would want *corn*?" Trina sniped.

"Who would want *cloudberries*?" Trixie shouted louder. "No one likes those globs."

"The entire town knows that my cloudberry preserves *always* sell out."

It would have to be a great spell. Something for them to stop shouting over each other. Still, I didn't want to cast anything strange that'd change their personalities. Just a little nudge in the right direction was all they needed.

I cleared my throat. Trixie turned. "What are you doing?"

"Just as the two of you requested. It'll be the perfect fix." I waved my wand around them and chanted, "*Fix and mix, mend a friendship once torn, come together like cloudberries and corn.*"

The shelves rumbled. I frowned.

Trixie and Trina opened their mouths, and—

The door between the shops flew open, and from the other side, I could see thick red cloudberry bushes and racks filled with all sorts of cloudberry goods.

The stalks rattled ominously.

The corn soap floated up into the air, and the socks quickly followed. The shelves shook, and then all noise sucked out of the air.

Uh.

Oh.

Red cloudberry soap flew out of the other shop and into the corn soap with a loud *smack*. The two mashed together, into a red-and-yellow bar.

This was not what I had imagined. The spell was meant to mend Trixie and Trina's friendship. It was *not* supposed to make the corn and cloudberries meld together.

Pop! Pop!

Trixie and Trina gasped, staring at something over my shoulder, and my stomach curdled. I slowly turned around.

The ears of corn burst into clouds of popcorn. Dainty red-orange cloudberries flew into the shop and pelted the freshly popped kernels. It looked like shooting stars arcing across a sunrise of vibrant red and melted-butter yellow, flamefox gold and the palest of pinks. It would've been beautiful if it weren't for—

Pop! Smack! Bang!

All around us, corn and cloudberries fused together. Inside me, too, it felt like thoughts were colliding and falling apart. My magic had never misfired like this before. Mother had been right. Using my powers more and more had increased the amount I could draw upon, but this was more like a magical *wreck* than a proper enchantment.

"I'm so sorry," I cried. "Let me think of a spell to fix this, I think—"

Before I could lift my wand, I felt two pairs of hands on my back shoving me out the front and into a gaping crowd of onlookers, staring up at popcorn streaking over their heads.

"Out, out, out!" Trixie and Trina shouted. "Do not cast a *single* spell!"

I ducked as more kernels flew at us.

Ember frolicked around, chomping at the popcorn raining from the sky.

"*What* is going on?" a deep voice said from behind me. I froze as blood drained from my face. Kyo caught a wayward kernel in his hand and popped it into his mouth.

Mayor Taira's secretary. That meant Mayor Taira would absolutely, positively hear about this. If she questioned me, could I really say, "Oh yes, I blew up their shops, but I promise I was only trying to help them"?

Kyo would probably change his scroll to note *Ruin the town* as my business reason.

Trina and Trixie glared from the doorway. Their frowns were identical, eyebrows furrowing like the slanted signs above them. Even the store names had lumped together into a singular CORNCLOUDBERRIES.

Next to Kyo, Davy opened his mouth and a kernel flew in. "This is the best! Who would've thought that cloudberry popcorn could taste this amazing?"

From Kyo's other side, Charlotte frowned as a kernel landed on her forehead and she quickly brushed it off. She snapped, sounding exactly like Mayor Taira, "What just happened, Eva?"

"She"—the twins pointed at me—"made our shops explode!"

"Trixie, Trina!" Kyo gaped. "The two of you are speaking in sync!"

"We are *not* on speaking terms."

"They asked me for an enchantment." I tried to stand as straight as Mother when she faced Grottel and pushed for information about his investigations into the Culling and rogue magic, but I had to duck as popcorn flew at my face.

"Is this true?" Kyo turned to the twins, who stared anywhere but at each other.

"Maybe." Trina scowled. "But I wanted her to *vanish* that pest."

"Possibly." Trixie crossed her arms. "All I asked for was someone to squash that *gnat*."

"But this isn't what we wanted." They stabbed the air in front of my nose. "This is *her* fault!"

Davy leaned toward me. "I heard they haven't talked in sync since they set up shop. And that's been more than *ten years.*"

Charlotte plucked the festival scroll out of my open knapsack. "Well, Eva, I can take care of the rest of this—"

"Wait, please," I said. "Give me one more chance."

Kyo's mustache twitched as he chewed thoughtfully.

"Please, Kyo, Charlotte, I'm so sorry. I never meant for the shops to fuse."

Charlotte shook her head. "I just don't think an outsider should really be helping us, after all."

"C'mon, Char, give Eva another chance," Davy added. "This popcorn is really tasty, too! Trixie, Trina, want a piece?" He waved a handful of popcorn in front of them, but they turned up their noses.

Trixie said, "Its only redeeming quality is my corn sourced from the Nytta farms, the best in all of Rivelle Realm."

"No, it's because my cloudberries are picked by the cleverest harvesters in the Sakuya Mountains."

Charlotte shot a glance at Kyo, who inclined his head toward me. She took a deep breath and shoved the festival scroll back into my arms. "One last chance. Because Kyo's being nice, and for Rin's sake, since she's sticking her neck out for you."

Davy shot me a sympathetic glance as he chewed on the popcorn. "It's tasty, though!"

I gulped, tucking my arms tightly around the scroll. "Thank you, Charlotte! And Trina and Trixie! If there's anything I can do to fix this, please let me know."

The twins—and Charlotte—stared down at me with matching glares.

I scurried back toward my cottage, the festival scroll safe in my arms, but my heart heavy.

CHAPTER 17
ℬLOSSOM

The next morning, with a good night's rest and Ember's steadfast warmth fortifying me, I loaded the flamefox into my knapsack and pulled out the Fiery Phoenix.

"I'll show the town I'm a witch by flying," I whispered, even as my knees knocked together as I peeked over the edge of the cliff. "I've got to fly, like Mother."

When Mother flew, she soared. She would jump onto our balcony railing and leap off with a whoop. When I ran to the edge, she was already a pinprick in the distance, brighter than any star, and no matter how far I flew, I never seemed to be able to catch up to her.

She'd told me as I wobbled on my broomstick, time and time again, *Evergreen witches don't hide from the sun, heights, or a bit of water.*

"I don't want to hide!" I cried out, but my voice was

lost in the roar of the waves below me. Ember pawed at me through the knapsack, as if trying to pat my shoulder, the way I tried to calm him when he was barking at shadows outside the cottage.

I couldn't do her jumping mount so I sat on the broom and felt it stir with energy, just how it'd flown when I'd trained with Mother. I sat back, tugging the broomstick up, and the winds swirled playfully around me, fluttering my hat.

But just when my heart thumped with joy, the bristles shook like ruffled feathers, dropping me to the ground.

I landed on my backside, Ember neatly hopping out of the knapsack and onto my stomach to stare down, as if admonishing me. The tail of the broomstick drooped. I simply didn't have enough magical bristles, and they were the engine of the broom.

Back in the cottage, I poured the remaining broken bristles out of the jar. I dug through the kitchen shelves and found the cloth Father had wrapped around his latest package of yuzu croissants. Mother had used her magic so the paper bird could carry the package all the way here, so the fabric had a part of her, too. Surely this would work, right?

"*Spinner, spinner, spin through the wind; flying together, flying to the end,*" I incanted, and a burst of light filled the cottage. When my eyesight cleared, I grinned. About a third of the broken bristles had fused with the cloth, gleaming with the same diamond-silver shimmer that marked Mother's Grand Master status. With another spell, I attached the bristles, the tail looking much fuller.

There. Now I could fly. Ember raced next to me out the door, and when I knelt, he leaped into my knapsack.

"I won't hide from the sun, heights, or a bit of water!" I chanted, as if it was a spell, and then I hopped onto my broomstick.

Playful tendrils of wind curled around the broomstick as I kicked off the ground. From my knapsack, Ember let out a yip of glee.

And then the end of the broomstick suddenly dropped down, and I slid off unceremoniously onto the rocky cliffside and into a patch of dusklight flowers.

I rolled onto my back. "I guess I need more bristles," I groaned, as Ember poked his warm, wet nose into my cheek to check on me. Above, the morning light made the clouds gleam like spun sugar.

"Curses! Look at how bright it is! I need to do the festival sign-ups, *now*. We're walking."

Ember and I marched into the town square, ideas for my broomstick swirling in my mind. Maybe I could ask Davy—or even Charlotte—for something to fuse with the bristles? Would Charlotte really give me anything?

But the moment I spied the shadows of Trixie and

Trina arguing in the doorway of their now-combined shop, all thoughts of my broomstick flew out my mind. My hands trembled as I pulled out the festival scroll from my knapsack.

I could figure out how to fix my broomstick anytime before the sand trickled down my hourglass. But I *couldn't* let Charlotte down again.

Since it was early in the morning, the shopkeepers around the square were still setting up before hordes of shoppers and tourists flocked to the grocer's shop, its tables creaking under the weight of barrels of oil and sacks of brown sugar, or the bakery, piping out buttery contomelon rolls and yellow crescent cookies sprinkled with citrusy yuzu peels.

Head ducked, I hurried to the closest shop at the corner, the florist's stand, breathing in the cane-sugar scent of dusklight flowers. The glass vases lining the counter were heavy with dusklight stems, the velvety purple buds closed tight. The stand was a thick wood, unlike my flimsy crates, in front of a small room. A silhouette moved inside the door that was slightly propped open.

I knocked on the doorframe.

"Come in," a light, delicate voice called.

I pushed open the door and something rustled above me. I stiffened, tightening my hand around my wand. Ember jolted backward. We both peered up.

Flowers lined the ceiling. It was like I'd wandered into a new world.

Blossoms of every shape and size and color smothered the walls, the ceiling...every spare space other than a few winding paths and the windows, filled with light.

A young woman in a wheelchair looked up from where she was trimming a stem and turned her head to the side. "Hello there." Her voice was gentle, like wind rustling through grass.

There was something so peaceful about her and this tiny, filled-to-the-brim shop. It was like the fields back home, when I'd lain on the side of the hill with my parents and pretended to scry the future in the sky. And every time I saw a cloud, I believed it was in the shape of a witch's hat, or an Elite license, or something that meant I, too, could become a witch. I smiled hesitantly. "I'm Apprentice Eva Evergreen, helping out Auteri for my Novice quest. I'm here to sign up all the shopkeepers for the Festival of Lights."

"I'm Ami, the town florist. Sign me up for flower crowns." Then she paused, nodded at my birch wand. "You're a repair witch, right? I heard about you from Rin."

"At your service." I bobbed into a quick bow, curiosity tugging at me. My heart thumped. Did she have a repair job?

She brushed her short black hair behind her ear. "Ah,

then, if you have a moment—do you mind taking a look at the ceiling pipes?"

"Pipes?" I echoed. All I saw were lush flowers.

She gestured above us. "Many years ago, a weather witch charmed pipes onto the ceiling to water my plants. But over time, some of my vines have wrapped around them, wearing the copper through, and they've been leaking over the walls."

When I looked closely, glimpses of copper pipes and sprinkler heads peeked out from behind the vines and flowers swathing the ceiling. And some of the plants around the broken pipes looked faintly limp, as if they weren't getting quite enough water.

"The local metalworker said she wouldn't be able to fix the pipes without having to snip out vines." Ami cast a soft look at her plants. "And cutting them feels wrong when they don't need pruning. All they're missing is their proper dose of water."

I paced, trying to think of a spell. How could I fix the pipes without harming the plants? *Mend what's within...* Maybe something like—

Knock, knock.

I spun around, breaking my concentration.

"Ami," a familiar voice called. "Mind if I come in?"

Strangely, Ami turned red, darker than the peonies in her arms. "Oh! Of course, come in."

My stomach flipped as Kyo stepped inside. He swung a paper bag in his hand and stopped abruptly as he saw me. "Hello, Eva."

Curses. Hopefully, Mayor Taira wasn't with him.

"H-hello." I inched toward the door, Ember at my heels, straining to see if Mayor Taira was nearby. "Am I in the way? I can come back later."

Ami smiled. "It's all right, Kyo just stops by with breakfast every once in a while. Not often enough."

To my surprise, the steely guard turned pink at her words, and shuffled his feet. "Well, I...if you ever need breakfast, just let me know. I can drop it off anytime."

My shoulders loosened. He was alone.

"Oh, thank you. But you treat me so much already, I couldn't possibly ask for more."

"Well, your tea is the best in town," Kyo replied. "I'd climb mountains for it."

They glanced bashfully at each other out of the side of their eyes, and probably would've stayed like that forever. I wondered if Ember and I could silently tiptoe out without them noticing.

But my boot squeaked on the tiles, and Kyo stumbled backward, nearly smashing a pot of white moonlilies.

"Ah, right!" Kyo's face burned crimson. "Have a contomelon roll, Eva. You too, little flamefox." He pushed the bag at me.

"Would you like some tea?" Ami asked.

"Not today," Kyo said, checking his wristwatch. "I'm late as it is." He tipped his hat at us and hurried out.

The sweet, sugary scent of the freshly baked rolls made my stomach grumble. I offered the bag toward Ami. "Want a roll?"

"Hmm?" Lost in thought, the florist was watching Kyo slip through the crowds. Then she brightened, turning to me. "Right! Contomelon rolls."

After Ami, Ember, and I gobbled down steaming-hot contomelon rolls with cups of Ami's blooming flower tea, I started investigating the leaks.

Sure enough, using a small ladder from under one of Ami's shelves, I found the spots where vines had eroded the copper and plants hung limply from lack of water.

How could I fix this? I searched for a spell, glancing around for any ideas. My heart jumped when I realized that the morning crowd in front of the bakery, waiting in line for breakfast, peered inquisitively through the shop's open doors and windows.

"Look, it's the witch!" one of the townspeople said.

"Who uses *seaweed* for a spell?" someone else grumbled loudly. "What'll she use today, potatoes?"

I had enough sense not to use *potatoes* for a spell. Unless I could eat the spell afterward.

Still, I bit down a retort and flexed my fingers for magic. A sluggish feeling stirred up and down my arms. I definitely had more blood than magic. Gritting my teeth, I took a deep breath and chanted, "*Close the metal, gentle on petals.*"

A faint white light zapped along the copper. It still looked like there were holes, but maybe the spell had magically sealed them.

"You can turn on the water over there, when you're ready." Ami pointed at a knob by the door.

I twisted the small metal wheel. Water slowly trickled out of the sprinkler heads and not the holes, spraying a faint, gentle mist.

Excitement sparked inside my chest. It hadn't leaked through at all. I grinned, spinning the wheel to turn it up, and peered up at the pipes. "It worked!"

The crowd shifted closer—

And water gushed straight through the biggest hole, directly above me, splashing down on my hat and all over my blouse. Ami shot backward, the water barely missing her.

I spluttered, wiping my face as I cranked off the water. Some of the crowd snickered, and I shot a glare at them. They were sailors in gray, likely Soma's crew.

"Looks like Soma was right." One of the sailors smirked. Ember growled, but I quickly shook my head at him. Soma *was* right. I wasn't much of a witch.

I willed myself to melt away like the water droplets. "That—that—should've worked," I stammered. "My magic's low from yesterday." I wrung out my hat. The pointed tip drooped to the side, as if it, too, wasn't so certain that my spells would work.

"Ah, don't worry. There's nothing to be sorry for." Somehow, Ami's gentleness hurt more than if she had yelled like Trixie or Trina. I wilted as she handed me a towel.

A man stepped up to Ami's counter. "Er, is now a bad time? I'd like a bouquet of dusklight flowers."

"Well—stay as long as you need," Ami said to me. "Let me know if you want more tea." I nodded faintly as she headed to her counter.

From outside, I could hear the whispers of the crowd. One of the sailors snorted. "I've never heard of a witch or wizard that's run out of magic." A few people nodded along with him. Beads of sweat tickled my neck.

Even if they didn't realize it, there were limits for all witches and wizards. That's why there were ranks within the Council, with higher levels able to go on more difficult quests. Still, I'd never heard of another witch or wizard who had fainted from overusing their magic.

There was something else I had in mind, but it wasn't quite a charm or a spell. I opened up my knapsack, and my hands slid over my jars of odds and ends, searching for anything that would help. Parchment, no. Sand, no. Candle wax? That might plug up some of the holes.

"Ami, do you mind a semi-magical fix?" My heart felt slightly sore at the words.

"Not at all," Ami called back.

Instead of casting a charm, I molded the wax onto the pipes. Warming up my hands, I rolled the wax into thin layers and then pressed them onto the holes. My arms burned as I worked, and the crowd buzzed, wondering what I was doing.

Their whispers sank deep into my heart, burning with every word.

Such a strange thing for a witch to try.

That isn't magic, is it?

It wasn't *pure* magic. But semi-magical repairs were the best I could do.

I melded the last wax sheet into one of the corner pipes. "Just about done."

Raising my wand, my voice cracked with nervousness. *"Wax hold water true, together through and through."* The wax sheets flashed with a coppery light, melding into the pipes, and a ripple of surprise went through the crowd.

Glancing toward the onlookers, I spoke louder. "I'll test it out now."

Twisting the small metal wheel, I turned it eagerly. Instead of starting with a trickle, the sprinkler heads roared as water spouted out.

"Eep!" I yelped, tottering backward. The pressure was likely too high after weeks—if not months or years—of broken holes.

Ami rushed inside. The sprinklers rained down on her, and she backed up, out of the shop. "Oh! Eva, are you all right?"

"Yes!" Even though it felt more like a *no*. I had to fix this. I summoned up my magic. *"Sprinkle the flowers, lighten your powers!"*

The tip of my wand flashed, and the water lessened, turning into a gentle mist. The plants seemed brighter in the spray, as the leaves drank in moisture. I stared up, examining the pipes and sprinkler heads. They were *working*.

"Oh, this is wonderful, Eva!" Ami clasped her hands with delight. "I haven't seen it like this in years!"

I cranked the knob shut, and the mist faded away. A fragile smile crept over my lips, like a delicate flower pushing up through early-spring frost, as the crowd moved closer, peeking in at the shop with surprise.

"Oh, curses." I clapped my hand over my mouth.

"What's the matter?"

I gestured faintly at her dress, which was now splotched with water.

Ami waved her hand at me with a gentle smile. "It's all right. This happens all the time in a florist's shop, and a little water never hurt anyone." She glanced out toward the sea with a sad smile. "It's when there's a lot of water that it's trouble."

I swallowed as my hat dripped onto my face. A

shudder ran down my cold, wet skin at the thought of the Culling. "Well," I said, waving my hand at the pipes faintly. "It's fixed."

"See, when I heard about you, I knew you'd do good for our town." Ami smiled. "Thank you, Eva."

I turned to look at the bright green plants and the vibrant flowers all around. Even if I hadn't fixed it with pure magic, maybe I *could* do something good. Perhaps— just maybe, I could figure out a way to protect Auteri from the Culling.

That night, by the light of the merrily flickering flamefox jar, I cracked open *Potions of Possibilities* for the first time. Like spells, the instructions provided vague suggestions instead of an exact recipe.

A waterproofing elixir would help the whole town prepare in case of hail, snow, or floods, being so close to the water as it was. If I was going to pass my quest, I needed to help Auteri withstand the unpredictable rage of the Culling. Like Trixie had recommended—before she'd banned me from her shop. And it'd be useful for Ami, too.

HOW TO MAKE A WATERPROOFING POTION:
Use warm things, think warm thoughts, mix together, and hope for a drought.

WARM THINGS INCLUDE BUT ARE NOT
LIMITED TO: flickering candles, campfires,
and snug socks.

I shook my head at the so-called instructions. I
stirred the ingredients the tome suggested—shavings of
wax candles, burnt wood, and bits of wool—in my frying pan with my wand. *"Stay dry and warm, let it stay
together...."*

The frying pan flashed a strange green-brown color,
and I jumped back. The charm hadn't rhymed at all, and
I was pretty sure the potion wasn't supposed to turn into
a burnt brown sludge with smoke pouring out of the pan.

Peering in suspiciously, I caught the faint scent of
chimney smoke. It didn't look explosive, at least. I coated
slivers of parchment in the smoking mixture and dunked
them into water.

The paper was soaked.

Something wet nudged my ankle. Ember gazed up with
one of the books I'd summoned, *Magical Adventures*, in
his mouth. "Oh, thank you for bringing that over," I said
absentmindedly. "Wait...*why do you have that?*"

Ember deposited it at my feet.

"I was *not* looking for more paper," I cried, holding
up the yellow cover. "Especially not just the cover!" The
rest of the book lay in the corner, the broken spine peeling away from the thin pages.

He wagged his tail, eyes begging for mackerel as a reward.

"None for you, troublemaker!" I groaned and threw myself on my bed, pressing my face into my pillow. Wrapping myself in my thin sheet, I swore that tomorrow would go better.

CHAPTER 18
SWEETER THAN SUGAR

A gurgle rumbled loudly, and I rubbed my stomach. It was lunchtime, but I'd forgotten to bring Father's latest package from the cottage.

"Hungry?"

I jumped. A woman leaned on the counter. She had a long face with a wolfish grin, and her hair was tied back into two braids, reddish-black curls sneaking out. In her hand, she dangled a paper bag. The mouthwatering scent of freshly baked bread wafted toward me. I swallowed.

"I'm Yuri, the shop manager from next door." She hooked her thumb toward Seafoam Sweets. "I've been meaning to introduce myself."

I shook her hand. "I'm Eva, the owner of this, um, semi-magical repair shop."

"So it's true?" she asked. "You're really a witch?"

I nodded. "I'm on my quest to become a Novice Witch."

The woman grinned. "Well, Edmund sent me over to ask. He didn't believe that a witch had come to Auteri, even with your hat and all the stories. I guess I win!" She spun around and laughed—a face peeked around the corner.

Edmund had dark, sun-warmed skin and tightly curled hair mostly covered by his chef's hat. Although he wasn't plump, his broad shoulders blocked the sun from my face, and he smiled shyly at me.

"So there are two of you in the shop?"

"Four of us—Mister Rydern, he's the owner, and his son. Mister Rydern's the most talented artist in the realm. He makes the sugar sculptures in our window displays." Yuri peeked over her shoulder. "Him."

It was the man I had bumped into on one of my first days in Auteri. He stared out at the water as if he was frozen in time. The dockworkers hefting crates over their shoulders always steered clear of him, as if he was a familiar statue they knew to skirt around.

"What is he looking at?" I asked.

"His wife was a captain," Yuri said softly. "A few years ago, she sailed out on her ship, the *Maiden of Auteri*, right before the fourth Culling hit. None of us expected the earthquake. Nor the tsunami in its aftermath. Worst of all, none of us expected—"

A familiar voice cut in from behind them, speaking quietly but with a heaviness that hung from each word. "That my mother would disappear without a trace."

They froze.

I peered around Edmund and saw Davy. His hands curled into trembling fists as he met my gaze and continued, "It's almost as if she was magicked away, as if she never existed."

Yuri's face burned red.

And, finally, I understood why the man's eyes stayed glued to the waters for something he'd never find. Because hope was a cruel sorcery of its own; the power of hope was always tainted with the sharp sorrow of unfulfillment.

Davy stepped next to Yuri and Edmund and leaned on the counter. His smile was forced. I remembered the way Kyo had carefully asked about Davy's father. And how Charlotte had spoken with a strange fierceness about the sea taking away lives. It'd been about Davy's mother.

A bell rang through the docks, making me jump. "Boat comin' in!"

The workers looked up, put down their crates and barrels, and beelined toward the skiffs, heading out to pick up passengers.

"Another ship, already?" Edmund said and shuffled back into the store, but Yuri and Davy stayed. Yuri glanced over at Davy's father.

"I'll bring him in," Davy said.

Yuri called, "I'm sorry, Davy."

He stopped and turned in the middle of the walkway, the crowd milling around him. A sad smile flickered on his face. "For what, Yuri? You have nothing to be sorry for."

Davy walked to the edge of the dock, next to Mister Rydern, and knelt down, pulling something out of his many pockets. He placed it gently into the sea and watched as it floated away.

"What was that?" I whispered.

"Davy folds paper flowers and offers them to the Constancia Sea every day. He says that maybe his mother will follow the trail of flowers back here." Yuri's forehead creased. "When Edmund and I first arrived in Auteri, the Ryderns treated us like family. And now, to see them like this…"

For a few seconds, Davy and his father continued to stare out at the sea. Finally, Davy dragged his gaze away. "It's time, Pa."

His father spoke, his voice gravelly from lack of use. "She's a'coming, she's a'coming."

The hair on the back of my neck stood up.

Davy shook his head. "No, Pa… She's not… She's…" His voice cracked. "Pa, it's me."

Mister Rydern blinked, staring at his son. "Ah… Davy."

Taking his father by the arm, Davy guided him back

into the shop. His father craned his head over his shoulder, eyes glued to the endless sea, until the shop's door rang shut behind them.

Mister Rydern's words crawled over my skin. *She's a'coming.*

I turned to Yuri. "Is he—is he always like that?"

"After his wife disappeared, he's become particular about the waters. Says strange stuff no one understands about her still being alive. But when he's away from the water, he's more coherent, less wrapped up in his grief. It's like the waters enchant him. Maybe...maybe it's that the water's all he has to remember her by." Yuri's voice wavered. Then she lifted up the paper bag abruptly, and her eyes pleaded for me to talk about something else. "Take these, won't you? The bakery delivered an extra meal, and I thought it was due time to meet our new neighbor. We've been sorely remiss in greeting you."

I opened the crinkling paper and breathed in the aroma of the freshly made sandwiches, with pure white cheese cut in slivers like the moon, slices of tomatoes and bright green herbs between thick-crusted bread, dusty with flour and the crust shaped in whorls, like a seashell. On the side, two powdery ginger chews were wrapped in wax paper.

My stomach gurgled and a smile broke out on Yuri's face. "Sounds like they're going to a good home. Come by for more candies, too. Those ginger chews are spicy, but my absolute favorite."

"Thank you, Yuri." I waved at her before she disappeared into the store. "Come over if you need any repairs."

I stared out at the water, Mister Rydern's words echoing in my ears. *She's a'coming.*

I spent the next few days properly signing up shopkeepers for the festival, without a single catastrophe. My hourglass showed that I'd already been in Auteri for two weeks; the days had passed so quickly. When I had a chance, I stopped by my counters. I'd left a sheet asking anyone to write down if they wanted me to help them, but the parchment remained empty.

But my counter wasn't empty. Each day, a dusklight flower waited for me, lushly fragrant, and I smiled toward the florist's shop in the town square, murmuring under my breath, "Thank you, Ami."

Even though I hadn't gotten jobs lined up...those I'd helped did appreciate my work.

Ember and I plopped onto the bench just as Rin stopped by with a brown paper bag, dropping it onto the counter. "Morning, Eva. What've you been up to?"

"I got a repair job from Ami," I said, tucking the fragrant dusklight blossom behind my ear. I decided to leave out the part about me blowing up Trixie's and Trina's stores.

Rin's lips split into a grin. "And how was that?"

"Well..." I paused. "I was able to fix Ami's copper pipes. After a few tries." I fiddled with my wand thoughtfully, then I sat up. "Is there something I can help you with, Rin?"

"Do you have time for a fix?"

My heart jumped in my chest. A repair job!

She nudged the bag of cloudberry cookie drops toward me. "That's for you." Then she rummaged in her uniform pocket and slid over a rose-gold compass. "And this, too. It needs a fix. It was a gift from my father just before he passed away. The needle seems to point a little more east every time I use it."

I picked up the rose-gold compass, examining the delicate leaflike engravings. "I'll get this repaired." But then I remembered what I'd done with the corn and cloudberries, and the excitement drained out of me. What if I messed up something so precious to Rin?

"Is everything else all right?" she asked, peering at me.

"I've done something terrible," I blurted out, and explained the mess with Trixie and Trina, and how I was never, ever going to their stores again.

Rin bit down a smile. "Kyo told me the popcorn was pretty tasty."

"But—but—I made their stores *explode*."

"You made Trixie and Trina talk to each other, didn't you? And in sync, nonetheless. Back when they set up shop, they couldn't decide whether they should stock cloudberries or corn. So instead of sharing, they split the store down the middle, and they hadn't talked since."

"Davy mentioned something about that...."

As if he'd heard his name, Davy poked his head out of Seafoam Sweets. "Hey, Eva, could you help me with something?"

"Me?" Me, the semi-magical witch whose charms could turn into a complete disaster, like with Trixie and Trina, or a semi-disaster, like with Ami?

Rin stretched her arms. "Time to head back to the ship. I'm on the evening route back to Okayama. No rush on the compass. Take a look whenever you've got a moment."

But I clutched the compass in my hand and didn't move toward the shop.

"You helped Ami. And even if they won't admit it, you've helped Trixie and Trina." Rin leaned over, with a knowing look in her eyes, and whispered, "Go on. You're *our* town witch, Eva. And even though I doubt it'll hit us, I know you'll figure out something to help us with the Culling, too."

I filled my lungs with a deep breath, as if trying to draw in Rin's words before they floated away on the salty breeze. I motioned for Ember to wait, and he happily curled up on the counter to bask in the sun.

Rin waved at me as she jumped into a skiff, calling, "Good luck!"

Squaring my shoulders, I jerkily walked to the end of the line of customers, clutching my wand in my sweaty hand. I'd never been inside, though I'd been saving my coins to buy my parents something sweet at the end of the moon.

Yuri pulled me inside. "Oh, Davy asked you for a repair, didn't he? No need to wait."

When I stepped into Seafoam Sweets, I was hit with a blast of sugary air and the excited voices of the shoppers milling around the displays. The white stone walls held shelves with big glass jars of all different shapes filled with cheerfully bright candies.

"Here, Eva," Yuri said, offering up a tin mug filled to the brim with a familiar tan drink. She drew a stool up to the wood counter and patted it. "Take a seat, Davy's getting something from his room."

"Ooh, barley tea!" I took a sip and the chilled brew tasted like home, like picking sun-warmed tomatoes in the garden with Mother and Father and then cooling down in the shade.

Beyond the counter, Edmund turned a clear blob on a stick, carefully cutting and twisting it.

"Is that *sugar*?"

He smiled shyly as he snipped a corner and curled it outward, forming a petal. "It's a dusklight flower, but yes, made of sugar."

"It's beautiful," I whispered.

Yuri picked up another pair of scissors and cut a glob

of clear sugar off a hunk, warmed on top of a stove, and nodded at a corner crowded by tourists. "Take a look at *that*."

I drained the tea to its last dregs and headed over to the display, but there were too many people blocking my view. Finally, a shopper moved away, clutching a jar of pale orange-red gumdrops, the warm color of an Auteri sunrise, to her chest as she breathed out, "Absolutely breathtaking."

Sparkling in the light streaming through the window, the whole town of Auteri was made in sugar. Each building was spun out of golden sugar strands, down to the curtains on the windows and the cobblestones in the street. In the glowing afternoon rays streaming down, the sugary town was radiant.

Spun in sugar, Mayor Taira and Rin walked hand-in-hand with a much younger Charlotte along the docks. The sugar version of Charlotte looked up at both of them with pure adoration. Children sat on the orphanage steps, pointing at skiffs flitting on the foaming waves. Kyo swept down the steps of the magnificent town hall, a bag tucked under his arm and seemingly on his way to Ami's florist shop. I even spotted Trixie and Trina, side by side, but looking like they were about to shout at each other.

A small card was propped up in front of the sugar-spun town.

> **NAME:** Auteri, Home of the Festival of Lights
> **ARTIST:** Toru Rydern
> Five hundred gold coins.

My jaw dropped.

There were more sugar-spun creations. On a small shelf, a forbiddingly tall tower somehow radiated with cold, smothered in vines and deep in a thick forest.

On a different table, tiny sugar flamefoxes danced around the figurine of a portly old man—Vaud.

As the tourists inched along, drinking in the sights of the beautiful sculptures, I caught glimpses of more and more pieces, revealing Auteri's glorious landmarks, even Queen Alliana's magnificent crystal castle in Okayama. It felt like I was zipping over the Sakuya Mountains and traveling all around the realm.

"Davy, can you handle the register?" Yuri called, as a woman stepped up to the counter, cradling a handful of sugary dusklight flowers. "Just a minute, ma'am."

A curtain separated the showroom from the back, and feet rattled down a set of stairs before Davy popped out and grinned. "Ah, great, you're here!" He cradled something in his hands and set it on the counter as he rang up the customer. "One silver, please."

"I traveled all the way from the western coast for these." The woman happily handed over a silver coin. "I can't afford one of the big sculptures, but these will help me remember this beautiful town."

"From the west? The Walking Cliffs?" Davy squeaked.

"Oh, no, the mainland," she said quickly. "I daren't go by the cliffs. My sister's been. Says it's frightening— but beautiful. The bit she *can* remember from her trip."

Davy bowed as she headed out, a dreamy look in his eyes. "The *Walking* Cliffs. I'd love to go there...."

"Did you have something for me?" I prompted him, but Davy stilled as footsteps shuffled inside and Mister Rydern moved behind the counter.

"Hello, Pa," Davy said, but his father only grunted.

Edmund cut a chunk of sugar and handed it over to Davy's father. He slowly picked up a pair of scissors and started snipping away at it. In mere minutes, he turned a clear globe of sugar into a waterfall cascading down miniature rocks, with fish swimming under the frothing spray.

"Can you fix this?" Davy asked me quietly, when Mister Rydern shuffled away to a shelf in the corner, filled with tubes of food paint.

Davy held out a sculpture of three people, standing together: two parents, holding the hands of their son, who stood in the middle. The mother and father were smiling down at the boy, whose face was lit up with a mischievous look that I could recognize anywhere, even though the details had faded.

My throat went dry.

"Wh-wh..." But I didn't need to ask. Even in sugar, Davy's crooked grin glimmered.

Mister Rydern turned, as if he could sense the sculpture, and growled, "Why do you have that?"

I winced as Davy deflated.

"This is special." Davy held it tightly to his chest.

"Pah," Mister Rydern said, his eyes dark. "No, nothing. That's nothing."

Davy stubbornly slid the sculpture over the counter and repeated, louder, "This is special to me."

Yuri and Edmund exchanged worried glances. "Would you like to come back later to work on the sugar?" Yuri asked Mister Rydern hesitantly.

"Going to the water." He tossed the pair of scissors onto the counter, leaving it spinning in circles.

"It's melting." Davy's eyes stayed glued to the sculpture as his father moved out from behind the counter. "I can't...I can't see the details anymore. I know Ma used to have a smile brighter than the moon. I know her eyes shone like water dancing with sunlight. But I can't *see* it anymore. And I can't forget her. I can't. Then it's like she's gone forever."

My heart ached, like it was shredding into pieces, falling apart bit by bit. I thought of Mother and her bright smile, always believing in me. Or Father, with his comforting presence, that constant warmth steady as his favorite baking oven. Just like Davy, I would be willing to search to the ends of the realm—even all seven realms—if my parents were lost. I wished, wished, *wished* I knew how to create an enchantment to bring his mother home. But I didn't dare try it. What if it went terribly wrong, like when I'd summoned a thunderstorm instead of banishing clouds, or my "fix" for the twins?

I couldn't find Davy's mother. But...if I couldn't do that, I had to do something for this sculpture.

"*Arms from above, together with love,*" I whispered, clutching my hands around my wand. The tip of my wand glowed with a yellow-gold light.

The statue shifted. I rubbed my eyes.

The spun sugar woman knelt down and gathered the small boy in her hands. The father turned and laid his arms around her shoulders.

The figures slowed, like molasses trickling, and solidified, locked in a warm embrace.

A sob burst out from Davy. "She...she used to hug me like that. At least, I think she did."

A subdued, sad voice whispered, "Of course, of course she did."

Davy's father stood frozen in the center of the shop, with tears rolling down his cheeks. Mister Rydern reached out, slowly, like he was made of stiff sugar, too. He clasped his son in his arms, like the statue. Davy's shoulders loosened, trembling softly.

"It's terrible to have her gone. I wish I could trade places with her, every day." Mister Rydern's voice creaked, as if nearly rusted over. "Even though I miss your mother so much, I'm still glad she left you with me. I would be nothing without you."

Yuri and Edmund slowly guided the customers out, whispering, "So sorry, but we're closing the shop for the day."

"You can relocate to my counter," I volunteered.

Yuri shot me a grateful smile. I crept out of the store, with Yuri and Edmund gathering armfuls of yellow contomelon candies, powdery ginger chews, and sugar dusklight flowers to sell. Before we left, I placed a paper sign in the window, with an arrow pointing to my stand next door.

I spent the rest of the afternoon with Yuri and Edmund, selling their candies and meeting the tourists who gasped with delight upon seeing the delicate sugar flowers.

"It's more beautiful than what I've heard!" cried one man, spinning the blossom in his hand.

"Look at the way the petals catch the light." His friend brushed his fingers against it. "Now I understand why Auteri's the hometown of the Festival of Lights."

"Ah, and you should come to our festival." Yuri winked at me.

I passed over a flyer and grinned. "Yes, come to our one-and-only Festival of Lights!"

The tourists nodded excitedly. "Why, it's only a few weeks away. Maybe we can sail back for this."

Yuri, Edmund, and I shot one another wide smiles as we sold the candies and kept handing out flyers.

Occasionally, we glanced at the store. The scent of bubbling sugar and faint voices drifted out the windows, but we didn't strain to hear. I didn't want to intrude on Davy's time with his father.

Ember licked my sugarcoated hand and snuggled into my lap. I smiled. I'd thought Rin might be the only friend I'd make on my quest, but then I'd realized I had Ember at my side, too. And Davy, now.

I glanced out at the horizon and my heart jolted as a dark cloud lingered in the sky, as if watching me. I stared back, blood pounding in my veins, until the cloud drifted north. But the uneasy feeling in my stomach stayed.

I'd have to do all I could to protect my friends and their town.

CHAPTER 19

SHELTER FROM THE SUN

The midday sun beat down as I sat behind my counter, examining Rin's compass and occasionally calling out for clients. "Repair services!"

Then, breathing in deep, I added, "Semi-magical fixes, too!"

After all, I *was* semi-magical. With the fix for the boat and even for Ami's watering pipes, I'd relied half on magic and half on my cobbled-together inventions to solve the problem.

I didn't know if being semi-magical was enough to pass a Novice Witch quest, though. Or protect Auteri from the Culling.

As I was testing out another spell to fix the compass, Davy hollered from down the docks, "Eva! Our town witch!" He and Charlotte propped a roll of tarp against my crates with a sigh of relief. Charlotte moved as if to stride away, but Davy looped one arm over her shoulder. "One of the folks down the harbor had some supplies lying around, and so I asked if there were extra for you. I thought you could use some sun cover."

"But—"

Davy's eyes were gentle, as if he knew my doubts. "After all, you're Auteri's special witch, and we have to take care of you."

According to the mayor, though, I was barely a witch.

Charlotte raised her eyebrow, as if she knew exactly what I was thinking. "Even though we were expecting at *least* an Elite witch, like Mayor Taira had requested."

Her words felt like a punch to my stomach. It seemed that Charlotte was still a bit unhappy that I'd created a mess of the corn and cloudberries, even if I'd sort of reconciled Trixie and Trina.

Davy smiled. "Don't blame Mayor Taira, Eva. She only wants the best for Auteri. And you helped a lot with the *Hyodo*, and me and Pa. We'll just have to show her that you're the best for our town."

Even if Mayor Taira didn't believe in me, I wanted to believe in myself. I stood up. "I do want to convince her."

"That's right. But you don't just *want* to convince her." He grinned. "You *will* convince her."

His words were an elixir pouring strength back into me.

Charlotte crossed her arms. If I couldn't convince her, I'd never be able to convince Mayor Taira. I met her gray eyes evenly. *I can become the witch that Auteri's always needed. I'll find a way to help with the Culling, I promise.*

She turned her nose up and looked away.

Davy glanced between me and Charlotte. "Er, well, let's put up the tarp, then." He nudged Charlotte with his elbow.

I put away the compass, and then they held up the tarp as I tried to charm a few extra planks to stand firmly in the ground. My first spell somehow made them burst with flowers and, red-faced, I quickly reworded it so they'd simply stand, not *sprout*.

Davy eyed my wand. "Can I use that?"

"Well...magicless can't use magic."

"Do you think I have magic?" Davy asked, turning his arms over as if he'd see WIZARD stamped on the crook of his elbow.

"No one ever knows if children have magic until they manifest," I explained, and he pulled out a small, tattered notepad from one of the pockets of his overalls. "For me, it was when my father was on the roof of our cottage, fixing the tiles, and he slipped off. In that moment, I reached my hand out, wishing more than *anything* for the power to save him, blurting out a few words that almost sounded like a spell: *Slow down, sky-fall.* And that wild, unexpected magic slowed him midair, just enough to save him."

Davy's eyes were wide as saucers as he scribbled away. "So if someone needs saving, I might get magic?"

"No one knows. But for most witches and wizards, it happens before they're five years old." I grimaced, thinking of Conroy, who loved to remind me how he'd manifested on the day he was born. "They show a spark of magic doing something like unintentionally animating a toy to play with them. It's rare to manifest so late, like me."

"I'm curious..." He jotted down a few more notes. "Is there a way to test for magic?"

"None approved by the Council; they consider it bordering on rogue magic," I said. "I manifested almost too late to go on my Novice quest."

"Late or not, we're lucky to have you," Davy said, and my heart warmed just a bit.

"According to Mayor Taira—and a few others— Auteri isn't so lucky." I sighed. "Sometimes I'm not even sure it's possible for me to become a Novice."

He shook his head resolutely. "There's got to be a way. Absolutely. It's like my inventions for my future adventures." He held up his watch, this time coated in something that looked strangely like sugar. "Each time, I try something new. Even if I fail or mess up, each attempt is one step closer toward my dream of a perfect, water-proof watch. Each one is a step closer to adventure."

Under the new shade, he and I chatted about how to convince Mayor Taira, while Charlotte fiddled with a piece of paper.

"I think magicking the blue and gold rooftops of Auteri to flash with lights all day would *definitely* help attract visitors and make Mayor Taira proud," Davy said.

I was certain that his idea would only get me kicked out of Auteri.

"Want to hear about the time my mother helped the queen trick her evil stepmother?" I said instead.

Davy raised his eyebrow. "You know I can't resist a good adventure story."

For a bit, he helped me forget about my failures as a witch as I explained how my mother had helped Queen Alliana sneak out of her miserable life as the servant at her stepmother's house and enter the realm's academy for potential princesses and princes. Even Charlotte seemed interested in my stories—"She charmed a *pigeon* into a *nightdragon* to fly away from her evil stepmother? Well, I guess flying away on a flamethrowing dragon as big as the town hall makes it certain no one would follow her"—as she folded parchment into different shapes.

When she noticed me watching, Charlotte said, "Rin showed me how to make this."

Charlotte had a bandage on her palm, yet her fingers flew deftly over the paper. Her hands turned the paper in and out as she made a tiny dolphin and a turtle with a round shell.

"You made all that in the time it would've taken me to *start* a bird."

"I make these to amuse the other kids at the orphanage. Davy gives us stacks of old scrolls from Kyo. So at least these toys are free." She studied my face, as if searching to see if I'd pity her.

"I think that's wonderful," I said softly.

Charlotte widened her eyes, and her blue hair ribbon flashed as she turned quickly away, toward the water.

Davy bumped me with his elbow and drew my attention to him as he wondered aloud about ways to make his watch waterproof—short of using magic—and telling me about the other adventures he had in mind. "Someday, I figure, I can be the first captain to voyage to the other six realms around us. Constancia's got the abyss blocking us off and they've closed their ports, but I'd find a way in. I'll even go beyond the seven realms we know about. And, Char, if you had magic, what would—"

"Um, I have to go pick up the molasses cookies I ordered earlier," Charlotte cut in, the tips of her ears suddenly turning pink, and she hurried down the street.

"Someday, Char will stop being so secretive and tell me what she's *really* dreaming about. More than just working in the town hall." Davy shook his head, as if trying to clear his thoughts, and turned to me. "Speaking of secrets…Char's not the best at making friends, but you know, she tried to save you."

"What?"

"Remember when you…" he said delicately, "fainted?"

I wished I could forget that. I cringed. "At the *Hyodo*?" I glanced at the tall, black cliffs and the trading ships moored in between the two massive walls of rock.

"You almost hit your head when you fainted." Davy fiddled with his watchband. "Char dove and caught you."

I blinked. "I thought it was Rin."

He shook his head. "Rin was on the boat. Char stopped your fall. Did you see her bandage? That's from when she hit her hand on the rocks."

"Oh," I breathed out. I had told myself I hadn't needed Charlotte to like me whenever she flounced past me sitting alone at my counter.

Pass the quest, pass the quest… That was all I was here for.

But the way that Rin had vouched for me, without a second thought…and Davy's steadfast confidence in me…

And Charlotte's willingness to save me—even though she had hurt herself…

Davy grinned. "I know she's stubborn, and after seeing how you wouldn't give up on us, I think you're stubborn, too." He quirked his lips to the side. "But I think the two of you could be really amazing as friends."

Friends. That word fluttered against my heart.

Back home, I had spent every free hour trying to get my magic to manifest. Conroy, when he'd lived with us, had always been too busy creating his own spells to spend time with a magicless girl, unless he was teasing me for his own amusement. After my powers had woken, I'd been consumed with preparing for this journey.

Before coming to Auteri, my parents had been all I needed. I'd never had a true friend. The other kids in Miyada had never cared about being a witch like I did, and they got bored with me trying and trying to cast enchantments. I'd never been surrounded by real friends before.

When Charlotte returned with a paper bag of cookies, she peered suspiciously at me and Davy. "What? What's with that weird look on your faces?"

"Ah, nothing." Davy winked. "I gotta go help out. I'll see you later, though. I've got something I need to ask you." He loped away, bypassing the crowd to sneak inside the shop. I glared at his retreating back.

Charlotte scooped her paper art into one of her pouches and turned toward the orphanage.

"Oh, Charlotte, wait!" I leaned over the counter. "Do you mind if I try magicking some of your paper art?"

"My animals?"

"Please? I'll trade you some redbud jam in return."

She bit her lip, but she gave me a paper dolphin, dog, and turtle. I squinted. The dog sort of looked like Ember.

I thought of Hikaru, who had begged for a toy from Mayor Taira. I couldn't create a toy out of thin air, but there was a chance I could do something with her animals. "Thank you, Charlotte. I'll bring the jam over tomorrow."

"Um, sure," she muttered. "Redbud jam would be nice, I guess." Then she darted into the orphanage.

I shook my head after she disappeared. If only I could create a spell to understand her.

As the sun dipped toward the cliffs, scents of roasting meats and freshly baked bread drifted through the air, making my stomach grumble. A quick dinner of a day-old roll and hard cheese waited for me in the cottage, leftovers from when Rin had dropped by. Then I perked up. I still had a few yuzu cookies from my parents' latest letter.

One look at my star-shaped hourglass told me what I already knew: less than half my time was remaining. I needed to work on my potions so that I had *something* to show Mayor Taira soon.

When the dinner bell rang, Davy guided his father back inside the shop, gently pulling him through the evening crowd. Then Davy poked his head out of the shop. "Eva?"

I looked up from reading *Potions of Possibilities*, turning the page as steam curled out of an illustration of a particularly noxious-looking potion. "Hmm?"

"Want to join us for dinner? Edmund's made his famous roasted-squab skewers."

My stomach protested as I motioned to the still-steaming tome in my lap and the half-fixed compass on the counter. I'd polished up the rose gold, but the needle continued pointing aimlessly, searching for something I couldn't quite figure out. "I should really head back to work."

Davy didn't disappear back into the shop. Instead, he shuffled closer to the front of my counter and peeked out from under his dark, messy hair. "I don't have much to pay with, but...can you help me with something?"

I put down my tome instantly. "What is it?"

"Come for dinner first," he said, almost pleadingly. At that, my stomach growled and Ember's belly echoed mine. Davy laughed, but there was a hint of sadness that chewed at me.

"I hope you have enough food for this bottomless pit," I said, gesturing at my protesting stomach, and he finally cracked a true smile.

A small kitchen was tucked behind the stairs that went up to the bedrooms above Seafoam Sweets. The kitchen was a tidy, cheery corner, like the pristine shop, with sky-blue walls and thick herbs in planters on the windowsill. There, Yuri, Edmund, Davy, and I gathered around the rickety nettlewood table, and Edmund even set a plate on the floor for Ember. After Davy brought out some food for Mister Rydern, we tucked in to the feast, though Yuri and Edmund rushed back to the store whenever anyone rang the bell at the counter. Mayor Taira had mandated that all shops close at dinnertime, but since Seafoam was next to the docks, they had special permission to stay open late for any tourists searching for the perfect last-minute souvenir.

Over juicy squab stuffed between folds of pillowy-soft bread drizzled with melted butter, Yuri told me stories about how she and Edmund had met as bakers in Lunea, the realm north of Rivelle, and regaled me with tales of fallen soufflés and meals they had cooked up for the queen of Lunea. But when I shot a glance at Davy, his eyes were foggy with thoughts, and for Yuri's jokes, his laughter rang a touch late.

Edmund shyly nodded along with Yuri's stories, and his dark cheeks reddened when she exalted his cooking skills. On their honeymoon, they'd journeyed through Lunea and crossed the border into Rivelle. And when they'd seen a single spun-sugar dusklight flower displayed in Seafoam Sweets' window, they knew they weren't going back to Lunea.

My stomach groaned with fullness when I pushed

away from the nettlewood table. The bell rang insistently, and Edmund and Yuri returned to attending to customers.

Davy and I washed the dishes in a quiet silence that stretched out. Finally, I cleared my throat. "The fix— what did you need?"

He dropped his dish into the basin, and a wave of soapy water splashed onto his shirt. "Well...it may be a lot to ask."

I nudged him with my elbow. "I'm here to help Auteri. What can I do for you? Need help with your water-repellent watch? I'm working on a potion to repel water."

Davy glanced at the front of the shop and lowered his voice. "It's for my mother."

My stomach dropped. This was more than a simple fix.

"Pa's trances get worse when he's by the water, and especially worse if the Culling is close. I...I know this sounds impossible, but what if Ma's out there? What if she's waiting for us?"

My chest ached with a strange loneliness. Something in his face mirrored the frothing, restless waters in the bay.

"How...how can I help you?" I asked, setting the last dish to dry on the rack. I slowly dried my hands as Davy poured out a tin cup of warm barley tea for me.

He jerkily set it on the table and tea sloshed over the sides. Grabbing a towel, Davy dabbed at the spill absently. He looked up at me, a faint gleam of hope in his eyes. "You wouldn't have a charm for finding people, would you?"

I spoke carefully. "I'm not practiced in those enchantments."

"But you fixed my sculpture. That was amazing, Eva."

My heart twisted into knots. His mother had disappeared while at sea, years ago, without a word since.

I sat down at the table, my heavy stomach churning uneasily.

I couldn't let him down, and yet—

What if I summoned her and ended up with nothing?

Or, even worse, a pile of sun-bleached bones?

"Davy, I'm not strong enough," I whispered. "Mayor Taira's expecting me to prepare Auteri for the Culling, but I haven't got the slightest clue of how to help. I'm not strong enough for this, and I'll bet that the Council will swoop in and take my magic after...after all this."

Davy furrowed his forehead. "I think you're stronger than you realize, Eva."

I didn't want him to pile on sympathy for me. He was the one asking for help. So I needed to find a solution, even if it wasn't through one of my enchantments. "Maybe my mother would be able to create a finding spell. There's some magic that witches and wizards can't dabble in, though. Blood magic or anything related to rogue magic is absolutely banned."

"I'd give any amount of blood to have Ma back." Davy's hands curled, his eyes clouded.

My fingers twitched for my wand. Just like with that woman in Mayor Taira's office, I longed to vanish the shadows to his eyes and blast them away with a charm for infinite joy. I wanted to promise him that I could help find his mother, but there were still limits to magic. "I'll discuss this with my mother, as soon as I see her. If there's a way to find your mother without blood or rogue magic or anything like that, she'll know."

He dried his hands on a towel and leaned down to rub Ember behind his pointed ears. My flamefox smiled his foxlike smile, leaning into Davy's hand. "Thanks, Eva. You're a true friend. Well, I gotta go meet my sailor friends. They've been moaning about how Soma's crew is beating them at ferrying in the most crates, so I said I'd help."

Ember jumped into my lap, and I tightened my arms around him.

Davy glanced at me one more time, his brown eyes searching for answers I wasn't sure that I could give him. He set his hands on the table and leaned forward, looking intently at me.

"Eva..." Davy's breath caught in his throat and he said thickly, "You say you're only semi-magical. That you're not sure if you can become a Novice Witch. But I've seen what you did for my sculpture. You have real magic."

As Ember and I walked out of Seafoam Sweets, a new sculpture in the window caught my eye. It was a globe of clear sugar, shaped like a teardrop. Suspended inside were three fish made of honey-gold sugar, glowing brightly as they swam. The fish stuck close together, like they never wanted to be apart.

> **NAME:** Family
> **ARTISTS:** Toru and Davy Rydern
> Not for sale.

My heart beat in my chest, pounding louder and louder in my ears. My pale face reflected in the window and my dark eyes stared back, challenging me.

I felt like a girl who was not that tall, not that strong, not that magical.

But I had helped Davy and his father. The passengers and sailors that I had saved from the *Hyodo* tipped their hats at me when I saw them in town. Rin and Davy always made time for me. I'd helped Ami with her shop, and even Charlotte with the flyers. And Ember wanted to stay with me, instead of being part of Vaud's pack of flamefoxes.

I wasn't my mother.

But I still had magic.

There were people who *did* believe in me.

A fierce wind blew up from the waters, and the building creaked. I shuddered, touching the cool, white stone walls of Seafoam Sweets. Rin had said that some of the buildings had gotten knocked down during the Culling. What if I reinforced them?

Well, I didn't want to try out my idea by knocking down houses. I needed to test it first. Ember took one look at me pulling my wand out and skittered away to chase a hissing cat down the street.

I raced to my counter and rummaged through the jars for a piece of parchment. Setting it on the crate, I gripped my wand as I thought of a charm. Could a building withstand the force of a storm tearing down the coast? I shivered.

I wanted a spell that wove in words about strength and protection. An enchantment that would help Auteri stay the way it was, with its beauty.

The words I had used on the boat—*Stand up, stand tall, this boat will stay strong and protect all*—had strengthened the hull when the walls had threatened to collapse. My skin prickled, imagining the coast battered by a storm or the buildings crumbling from an earthquake. Maybe if I used that enchantment and tweaked it just a bit...

Pressing my wand to the paper, I said, "*Stand up, stand tall, this town will stay strong and protect all.*"

The parchment flashed with a yellow glow. I reached

out slowly and tapped it. It had hardened like a shell. A prickle ran up my spine.

Maybe—*maybe*—this could work.

Ember padded over and sat, watching.

"If this works out, I can pass my quest." My heart pounded in my chest. There was still a chance for me to become a Novice Witch.

Most of all, I still had a chance at helping Auteri.

I turned toward the orphanage. The windows were flung open, breathing in the sea air, but the children were likely at dinner, getting fussed over by Charlotte.

I pressed the tip of my wand to the wall. Bits of stone crumbled down from my touch. I poured hope into each and every word, so that the spell would last through the end of the year. I needed to protect Auteri—and most of all I needed to protect the people who were coming to mean so much to me. *"Stand up, stand tall, this town will stay strong and protect all."*

My vision wavered, as magic leached from my blood. The building pulsed with a faint pearly-white glow.

"Did it work?" I gasped. I brushed my fingers against the stone and rubbed them together.

This time, the grains of stone didn't come off. It had to be doing *something*. I peeked up and down the docks, but no one had noticed the spell. Very quickly, I snatched up a pebble and tried scratching at the wall.

When I took my hand away, I stared. It hadn't made a mark.

I breathed out. I could—I could do something.

A man came out of Seafoam Sweets, hoisting a big bag of candies onto his arm, and furrowed his brow. I quickly turned away, hiding my wand in my pocket. If someone noticed my wandwork, rumors might spread, and the townspeople might expect the impossible. I wasn't sure if it would be enough, but...

Closing my eyes, I imagined Mayor Taira's sharp eyes as I presented my paperwork to her.

Once I was sure this could work, I would reveal the charm on all the buildings, spelled to stand up to the Culling, and show her how the sharpest of rocks didn't leave a mark.

That would change her mind.

Then she'd *have* to sign my paperwork. And I'd get to keep my powers.

If the cursed Culling hit Auteri, the buildings that I charmed would still stand through an earthquake or blizzard or anything that the Culling tried on the town, and she would acknowledge my work, far and wide.

A lightning bolt of fierce, wild hope shot through me, stronger than any waves that slammed against the shores.

I turned toward the center of town. My lungs pressed in sharply.

Hundreds—if not thousands—of buildings stretched from the edge of the water to the path leading up to the farmlands. I'd have to work every morning and every night to cover even a tenth of the town.

Mother had said that practicing magic was the only way to get better. Sometimes I liked to pretend that the only reason why Conroy was stronger was because he had been an Apprentice for years and years. I had thousands of charms, ready and waiting for me.

I gripped my wand and walked to the next building.

I had a sliver of a chance, but I'd take it.

CHAPTER 20
A Pinch of Magic

I woke early with magic zipping through my veins. A peek at my hourglass told me what I already knew, as if the sands of time coursed through my blood. I'd been in Auteri for more than three weeks, and less than ten days remained.

Ember and I had started roaming the town early in the mornings so I could cast spells on the buildings before the workers woke. Today, each step I took felt infused with hope, that this would be the way I could protect Auteri from the Culling.

"Eva Evergreen, your town's semi-magical witch, on the go!" I called, walking through the morning fog, even though only Ember was around to hear me.

I tapped my wand against the walls and chanted,

"*Stand up, stand tall, this town will stay strong and protect all.*"

While I faced the wall of a house and prodded my wand at the stones, a sleepy-eyed worker stumbled out his front door and rubbed his eyes. I pretended I had been talking to Ember.

"Stand tall, Ember!" I said quickly.

Ember glared as if saying, *Of course, blame the flamefox.* And then he squatted, narrowed his eyes at me, and relieved himself. The worker gawked and hurried down to the docks, throwing one last suspicious look over his shoulder.

My face burned brighter than the sunrise.

◌◌◌

It was a muggy day, and I diligently went from store to store, recruiting shopkeepers for the Festival of Lights.

I signed up the grocer for gold and blue necklaces he'd ordered from a witch in the farmlands, who had charmed the beads to glow in the dark, and mediated a debate when two bakers both wanted to make lightfish-shaped yeast rolls. I convinced one baker to make contomelon rolls formed like the town hall, and the other to make flaky croissants with petals shaped like delicate dusklight flowers.

Slowly, slowly, I was becoming more than the "seaweed witch" to the town.

As I wended up the cliffside, I heard an insistent tapping on glass. I grinned when I turned the corner to my cottage. A paper bird hopped along the windowsill. As my footsteps crunched on gravel, it perked up, fluttering over to my hand. The paper bird slid a small, cloth-wrapped package into my palm. When I undid the blue cloth, I gasped with delight.

Father had sent along cakes in the shape of tiny, elegant phoenixes, one of my favorite creatures in the entire realm. Each pastry phoenix had bright sesame eyes, and its intricate, whorled dough feathers were baked to a delightful golden-brown color. Ember's eyes glinted as if he was ready to pounce, but I held them out of his reach, breathing in the mellow vanilla scent.

"Let the seal be broken, let this letter open," I whispered, and the paper bird unfolded. My parents sent letters—and Father's baked creations—almost daily, but this letter was different. Mother's handwriting, usually elegant, was cramped and jagged.

> *Dearest Eva,*
>
> *I should've told you more about the Culling before you left, but we were busy trying spells and going on flying lessons for your quest. . . .*
>
> *I should've told you more.*
>
> *It was a secret within the Inner Council, but Kaya Ikko was—is—a scrying witch. When I went to meet her for tea, Kaya*

never showed up. And her rooms behind the bookstore look as if she's just left it for a walk, everything still intact. Yet all my letters come back unopened, as if my spells can't find her. She's vanished.

Kaya created the strongest enchantments to scry the Culling. I don't like where this is heading. If the Council didn't ban others from interfering in Novice quests, I'd be with you in Auteri. I don't like this at all.

The Inner Council has forbidden me from telling the public— or even the queen—that Kaya's missing.

I have suspicions about what might've happened, but it'll have to wait for your return. I fear our letters may get intercepted if it truly is rogue magic at work. But you'll be done soon—just around ten days now, isn't it?—and I can't wait to see you. Stay safe. I'm worried that you're out there alone. Protect your town, Eva. Do good.

With all my love,
Mother

My skin chilled as a sea breeze ruffled my hair. Kaya— missing? And one of the best scryers in the realm? What if the Culling hit before the Council could send out a warning?

I looked over at Auteri, at the beautiful lights flickering in the glass windows. Where Davy was likely chomping down his dinner as he took care of his father. Charlotte was probably stopping Hikaru and the orphanage kids from fighting over another paper animal. Somewhere, Mayor Taira was surely drawing up plans for the next day, figuring out how to manage the townspeople's requests.

I couldn't cast a spell to shield Auteri like Mother or the other witches and wizards. But if I managed to strengthen enough buildings and get my waterproofing potion just right, I could help them all, even after I left.

I had to perfect my potion.

That night, though I was bone-weary, I mixed concoction after concoction. Time kept ticking in my hourglass, sand gathering in the bottom star and filling each curved glass point.

I knew I was missing *something*. I stared at the lumpy sock and candle stub.

The magic leached from me and into the frying pan, as I mumbled, half-asleep, "*Stay dry and warm, let it stay together and stay...and stay...*" The potion exploded, spraying black, sulfurous slime all over my face and hair.

"No!" I jumped up with a cry, and Ember tumbled off my lap with a shriek. My hair stuck to his fur. I carefully peeled the slime off and he shook his coat, looking at me indignantly.

"Curses! I'm sorry, Ember." I grabbed an empty vial from the table and shoved in my concoction. "If this potion is the exact opposite—sticky rather than water-repellant—maybe..."

Time for an experiment. I peeled another blob off my

hair and onto the edge of a book cover that Ember had sheared off.

I aligned the cover onto the spine and pushed down. The blob stuck, but the cover flopped around.

I poured three drops of water onto the slime, and it fizzled and turned stone-gray.

When I turned the cover, it finally stayed on the book spine. This potion was definitely not what I'd been trying to make, but it made an amazing glue. Ember sniffed the book, his shiny black nose wriggling with interest.

"Don't you dare try to chew it off again, trouble-maker." I shoved the tome and sticky potion on the highest kitchen shelf—far, far away from my mischievous flamefox.

CHAPTER 21

A Whisper of Warmth

Despite being midsummer, the clouds gathered thicker than usual, hiding the sun. Down at the docks, a family hurriedly carted rolling trunks from an inn to their waiting automobile. The father grumbled, "I thought Auteri was supposta be nice this time o' year! For all that I've heard, it's as gloomy as an autumn day."

His son, a few years older than me, shuddered. "But I want to stay for the festival."

The father squared his shoulders. "It'll be better to go home, away from the coast. I've got a feeling in my bones this quiet won't last for long. Festival or not, a storm's going to hit. I'll bet all my gold on it."

I stopped and stared out at the sky. A storm—like the Culling? No, it couldn't be the Culling. It was at least five moons too soon.

Along the docks, half-finished stands lined the street. Workers buzzed to and fro, carrying crates like the ones that made up my counter, and hammering in posts to hold signs.

By the water, a few of the workers had gathered for swigs of tea before finishing up a stand. One of them, with her hands wrapped around her tin canteen, scrutinized the red sky. She sipped at her hot tea, the steam curling mysteriously around her face as if she was a scrying witch. "Red sky at night, sailors' delight. Red sky in the morning, sailors take warning."

A strong gust blew in from the sea, and I shivered.

The worker next to her chugged down his tea. "Too early. I'll eat my hat if it's the Culling. We haven't heard anything from our region's Advisor, and the Council would've announced something. It's just a spot of summer rain."

That had to be all. But if it wasn't... The Council's scryers could only see the pattern hours before because each attempt got blocked—by something, or someone. I shuddered. And now they'd lost Kaya, their best scryer.

But I was sure that Mother or the Council would notify me as soon as they heard—though I hoped I'd be home and licensed as a Novice Witch by then.

I greeted Davy's father—even if he didn't respond—and made my way to my shop.

I was about to pick up the festival scroll from under

my counter when a window swung open at the orphanage and a girl shouted, "Sky's red! Toldja so!"

"Fine, fine, you're right," her friend grumbled, rubbing the sleep from his eyes.

"It better not ruin the festival. I wanna see *all* the stands."

"But it's not like we have even a bronze coin to spare anyway."

They sighed together, heads propped up on their hands as they stared at the fiery clouds.

Instead of my scroll, my fingers curled around the paper toys in my pocket. I wanted to do something nice for them. I wanted to charm Charlotte's art into toys that the other kids in town would be jealous of.

The toys had to be just slightly magical. Nothing that would cause trouble, but enough to make them special.

Turning the dolphin around in my hands, I pondered ways to charm the paper animals. When I'd made my way into Auteri, dolphins had danced next to the skiff. Maybe I could do that, too.

I took a huge breath. *"Jump higher than a bump."* A faint blue spark quivered at the tip of my wand and floated onto the paper. The dolphin leaped up, spinning in a circle, and then landed neatly in my palm.

"Oh!" I said, stunned. "It worked!" I slid it into a glass jar and screwed the lid on tight so it wouldn't leap away.

Then I picked up the parchment dog. It was the size of my palm, with a sharply pointed nose and curled tail. The little dog reminded me of Ember, so I whispered, *"A friend by your side, no need to hide."*

It grew and grew, until it stood on the counter, as tall as Ember. To my surprise, it even wagged its tail when I petted its head. My magic was still doing more—and less—than I expected. A girl ran past my shop, calling to her friends, "I want cloudberries!" and I winced.

Trixie and Trina had yet to sign up for their festival stands, and after remembering the way the corn and cloudberries had splatted together after my misadventurous spell, I didn't blame them for staying away.

Ember jumped onto the counter and prodded the folded dog curiously. Then he butted his head against the paper and nudged it off the counter.

I caught the toy dog before it fell onto the dirt, placed it carefully on the shelf below the counter, and scowled at Ember. "Don't be jealous. That's for the orphanage."

He turned away to stretch and shake out his red-gold fur. It flickered like flames.

"How beautiful!" gasped a sailor, as Ember fluffed up his tail and preened under his compliments.

My flamefox turned smugly. *See? They like me instantly,* he seemed to say.

I rolled my eyes and tickled his belly. He capered out of my reach, his eyes laughing. As I stared past Mister

Rydern, and out to the frothing, choppy waters, my hour-glass warmed up.

I pulled it out of my blouse. About a fifth of the sand remained. I had less than one week in Auteri until I'd have to appeal to Mayor Taira for her signature on my application. As I watched, the white grains trickled away.

"Whatcha doing?" a familiar voice chirped. Davy clambered onto the bench, and I slipped my hourglass back under my shirt. He unloaded his bag, teeming with steaming-hot contomelon rolls that beckoned at me, onto my counter. The sugar-glazed crust sparkled like the sea, even in the hazy morning light. "Want breakfast, Eva?"

I bit into a roll and sighed with delight. "Contomelon rolls are the best!"

Charlotte trailed behind him, breaking off the corner of a purple honeyberry cookie and popping it into her mouth. She slipped the bag into her pouch. I waved at Charlotte, inviting her to sit.

"Have you got the scroll ready?" she asked.

I winced. Maybe Charlotte would be able to sign up the missing shopkeepers, but I'd have to *tell* her first. And I'd far rather fight a nightdragon than explain that I'd missed two important shops.

"Well…" I didn't know how to break the news.

Someone plopped a waxed box on my counter, and I blinked. Familiar fluffy popcorn peeked out, the kernels coated with a pinkish glaze.

Trixie and Trina nudged each other to talk, not quite meeting my eyes. Had I charmed them to appear?

"We're here to sign up for our stand," the twins said.

Charlotte stared, wide-eyed, as I hurriedly unfurled the scroll and poised my charcoal stick above the parchment. "Stand names, please?"

"Corn and Cloudberries," they said. "One stand."

I slid down into my seat. Charlotte took a look at my face and grabbed the charcoal out of my wobbling hand. "What're you selling?"

"Iced corn-and-cloudberry tea," Trina said, and then eyed the sky. "Or hot tea if it's chilly."

"Got it."

"Oh," they said, exchanging a glance. "And, ah, cloudberry popcorn."

I froze. "Excuse me?"

They grinned sheepishly in unison.

"Some days, I can't believe we're talking again," Trixie replied.

"Some days, I wish we were never talking again," Trina retorted.

They glared at each other, then let out loud, honking laughs. "Most days, we thank you, Eva."

"Oh." I could barely speak past the lump in my throat. I had never, ever imagined they'd be grateful to me. Ember jumped into my lap, warming me up. "Of course, at your service."

"We have to go make a few more batches," they said. "See you at the festival!"

Our wide-open jaws swung in the wind as Trixie and Trina strolled up the main street side by side, bickering as they went.

"Well," Charlotte said quietly. "That was a surprise."

Davy nodded. "I think you worked some real magic there."

I shook my head in disbelief. Picking up a piece of popcorn, I chewed on it methodically. It crackled satisfyingly and then burst with flavor, as if they'd somehow bottled the softest of clouds in the sky with swirls of tangy-sweet cloudberries. Ember pawed me for a taste.

"Wow," I whispered. Charlotte and Davy popped handfuls in their mouths and nodded in agreement. Then I glanced down, remembering my duty. "We've got all the sign-ups now." I offered the scroll to Charlotte.

A thoughtful look flashed on Davy's face as he finished chewing his mouthful. "I'll bring it over to Kyo. I have to go meet my sailor friends soon anyway." He snatched the scroll out of my hand and slipped away before I could protest, throwing one last wink over his shoulder at me, nodding his head toward Charlotte.

"Thank you for helping with the festival." Charlotte slid off the crate, tugging at a strand of hair that had slipped out of her braid. She turned to go inside.

I blurted out, "Wait, I want to give you one of your animals back."

"Animals?"

Placing the dolphin in Charlotte's hand, I nervously fiddled with my wand as I waited for her reaction.

She stared at the folded paper, turning it from side to side. "It looks exactly the same...."

"I charmed—"

"Oh!" she said, as the paper dolphin jumped. "How did you...?" A tiny smile tugged at her lips, and joy bubbled inside me.

"The enchantment will last until the next full moon, I think. I...I hope the kids will like it."

From the orphanage, the door squeaked on its hinges. Charlotte looked over her shoulder and sighed. "Come over, you troublemakers."

The door swung open and five younger kids tumbled out, two girls and three boys, all around five to seven years old. I recognized a few of them, including tousle-haired Hikaru, the one who had asked Mayor Taira for toys.

"Be careful, Charlotte!" one of the boys squeaked. I froze. Were the orphanage kids scared of my magic?

She swung her head to stare at him. "What?"

"You called her an evil witch when she got here!" one of the girls piped up. "'Cause she's Rin and Davy's new friend!"

Charlotte's ears burned red. "I did *not*." I stifled a laugh as her eyes shot daggers at them. "Come here. Eva's got something special for you."

At those words, the kids jumped down the stairs, two at a time, pushing one another. They hovered behind Charlotte, wide-eyed and staring at her palm.

The dolphin quivered and jumped in a full circle, arcing up above Charlotte's hand. She caught it neatly.

They all gaped in awe. "It's amazing," one of the girls whispered reverently.

"For us?" Hikaru held his hands close to him, as if he didn't dare reach out. "Do you charge?"

"Charge?" I spluttered. For the toys?

"Just name your price." He folded his arms. "I'm a very wealthy man, you know."

A pigtailed girl jabbed him with her elbow. "Wealthy with what? Stinky shirts?"

"I am too wealthy!" he insisted. "I just haven't found my treasure yet. And my shirts smell like honeyberries, thank you very much!"

Charlotte groaned. "You've been listening to too many of Davy's stories, obviously. There is *no* hidden treasure in the Walking Cliffs, no matter how many theories he pulls up."

I studied the boy, with his face full of pride. Then I scanned the faces of the others. They had grown up like Charlotte and knew that nothing came free.

"Okay." I breathed out a big, overly weary sigh, trying hard to hide my smile. "I've been having trouble with one of my spells."

A boy jumped backward, ready to scuttle up the steps. "I don't want to be turned into a frog!"

"I'm not going to be doing any magic on you." There was a very good chance that if I tried charming the smudges off his shirt or something like that, I'd end up turning him into a pile of dirt. I didn't trust my magic *that* much. "But I will be asking for something from each of you."

The second girl tightened her grip around her pig-tailed friend's hand, and they gawked at each other. "Will we have to sign in blood? Davy says witches use blood!"

Charlotte and I exchanged a glance, and she snorted under her breath. "I am absolutely going to tell Davy that he is *forbidden* to tell a single story after this."

I leaned close. "In order to receive this charmed animal, you'll have to give me an ingredient for one of my potions."

They hissed. "Not my blood!" yelped one of the boys.

"No blood, I promise." I tried to keep a straight face. Raising my eyebrows, I met their eyes in turn. "Even more important. I need *warmth* from you."

"Warmth?" One of the boys narrowed his eyes, wrapping his arms around his shoulders.

"I'm working on a waterproofing potion." I spun my wand in one hand. Their eyes followed my wand with fascination. "And I need ideas of warmth, the opposite of cold water."

The kids turned to one another. "Is this for the Culling? The witch is supposed to help us fight the Culling, right?"

"We'd be helping the town, too!" Hikaru puffed out his chest.

"But it has to be something special, not just candles or fire. It has to make you feel warm *inside*," I explained.

They huddled, their heads nearly touching as they discussed my offer. Finally, they broke up and nodded solemnly.

"We're ready," the pigtailed girl declared. One by one, they bent over the counter, cupped their hands around their mouths, and whispered their secrets to me:

Warmth is that tickly-good feeling when Charlotte tucks us into bed.

I think of warmth when we're sitting on the front steps together eating corn on the cob, freshly roasted in the oven.

I'm warmest when we're all playing in the water, and then we get out to dig our feet in the hot sand.

My favorite kind of warmth is when my friend holds my hand, even if we're just walking to school.

Finally, it was Hikaru's turn. He inched toward me and leaned forward:

I feel warm from fires and fuzzy sweaters and fighting

pirates with friends. And I feel warm when I know we've got a witch protecting the town.

He shuffled his feet and eyed me, strangely quiet. "Will that help the potion?"

I nodded solemnly. "I'll try tonight and let you know."

"All right," Charlotte said, "Eva's got to work now."

"C'mon," one of the girls said. "Let's go down to that boat on the beach and play pirates!"

The other kids nodded eagerly, just as the dolphin flipped again. Hikaru plucked the dolphin out of the air and pounded down the dock, roaring, "First one to the ship is the captain! The rest of you are gonna be my crew!"

"You all better share that, or none of you will be able to play with it!" Charlotte hollered after them, shaking her head.

"Oh! Charlotte, I have one more ready." I pulled out the second paper toy.

The paper dog pranced on top of the crates, wagging its tail. Charlotte widened her eyes. "That's clever, Eva. Can we really have it? I've—I've always wanted a dog."

I nodded. "Keep this one. I can make more for the other kids."

We grinned at each other.

"This is really nice of you." Charlotte paused, and the tips of her ears burned slightly pink, as if she realized that she was *actually* smiling. She jolted, mumbled something about having to take care of the kids in the house, snatched up the dog, and spun on her heel to hurry back into the orphanage.

Some days—most days—I didn't understand her. But the corners of my lips tugged up. When we did understand each other, it felt like a special kind of magic.

I tinkered with my broomstick for the rest of the day, to prepare it for flight. The bristles infused with the cloth from my parents had helped, but I needed *more*. But how? I scrubbed at Ember's gnaw marks with my handkerchief as I tried to think of a fix.

When the dinner bell rang, the five kids abandoned the boat and returned to their house. They stopped at the foot of the steps, nudging one another and whispering under their breath.

I glanced at them curiously, and Ember sat up to look at them. Hikaru chewed on his lip. "Thanks, Eva. This is way better than any store-bought toy."

"Oh." Strange tingles ran up my skin. I smiled, tugging the rim of my hat. "Of course. After all, I'm Auteri's witch, at your service."

∽

That evening, Ember and I walked up to the cottage slowly. The winds had picked up, so I leaned into the gusts and held on to my hat so it wouldn't flutter away. It had been almost four weeks since I'd come to Auteri, and between mornings of charming the buildings, days of tweaking the compass and figuring out how to fix my broomstick, and nights of potion-making, I was using every bit of my magic. Mother had been right. Slowly, I'd been able to cast six spells a day to prepare the town for the Culling. Then seven, then eleven. I was just about at forty-seven spells now.

Sand kept trickling; the Culling would be hitting the realm by the end of the year. When I held the star-shaped hourglass to my ear, I could hear time slipping away. In less than a week, I'd either be receiving my license as a Novice Witch or...

I'd rather venture into the abyss at the Constancia border and fight nightdragons than consider other options.

I focused on dinner instead. Even though I didn't have any appetite, I needed to keep up my strength for the enchantments I'd cast tonight. I scarfed down a quick meal of the last of my buckwheat noodles, swirled with slivers of emerald onions and cubes of roasted squab that Rin had given me earlier in the day. She had even set aside a hunk for Ember, who nearly inhaled it all in one mouthful. He didn't have any issues with appetite, as my increasingly bare cupboards revealed. I took a deep breath as I cleared the table and set out my potion-making supplies.

My potions worked better these days, but they weren't good enough to withstand a flood. The mixtures worked for a few seconds, and then water leached into the paper and it got soggy.

Tonight...tonight had to be different. I had a special kind of enchantment, with words heavy with power.

I consulted *Potions of Possibilities* one more time. The quick-fix guide stated, "*Think of potions like spells. Simple and sweet is better than long-winded, meaningless babble.*"

But...the spell had to mean something to me. After all, magic came from my blood. What were the absolute warmest things I could find?

I filled the frying pan with everything I had been using before: shavings of wax candles, burnt wood, and bits of wool. Then I tapped the edge of the table, thinking about what else to add.

This wasn't going to work. I turned over the pan and dumped everything out.

Instead I added things that made *me* feel warm: shreds of parchment from my parents' letters, the corner of my trusty blanket, and dust bunnies made of Ember's fur. I added in a snippet of a sweater from the bottom of my knapsack and a leftover sliver of emerald onion from Rin and picked up my wand.

I began stirring in circles, keeping all the orphanage kids' stories in mind, as if I could fill the pan with those thoughts.

There were some ingredients that I could touch and see. But other things—like the way my chest had squeezed tight from hearing the orphanage kids' stories—couldn't be counted or touched, and the power of those memories rested in their words.

The warmth of a fuzzy sweater. The warmth of love. The warmth of a good meal. The warmth of a perfect day. The warmth of a friend.

I thought of everything Auteri had done for me. The town felt less foreign than when I had first arrived. Rin always stopped for a chat, bearing food, and when I passed by the town square, Ami never let me disappear without tucking a flower behind my ear.

With those thoughts in mind, I murmured, *"Stay dry and warm to weather the storm."*

The frying pan glowed as the ingredients melted into a shimmering liquid, better than any of my smoking elixirs from before.

I fished out Charlotte's last paper animal from my pocket—it was a tiny turtle. When I dipped it into the frying pan, the paper pulsated a bright blue. Ember jumped into my lap and watched as I dribbled water from my canteen onto the turtle.

The droplets rolled off the shell and the paper stayed dry.

I clutched the tiny turtle in my trembling hands.

It felt like I'd cast a spell on myself. A rush of excitement tingled the tips of my fingers down to my toes. The potion repelled *water*.

Finally, *finally*—I had a potion to help Auteri fight the Culling.

PART THREE

PAPER
VS.
WATER

CHAPTER 22
CLOUDS

Ember poked my leg with his wet nose, startling me awake. I jolted up, rubbing my forehead. My face had been pressed into the crack of my potion book. I'd been trying all night to make gallons of potions to bring to the mayor when I appealed for her signature, but batch after batch had failed. I had a panful of elixir—my first batch—and that was it.

Something was different. When I had been stirring another batch of waterproofing potion, it had been pitch-black outside, and I'd taken out my jar of flamefox fire to ward away the darkness. But reddish-orange rays of light trickled in through the window.

It was already morning.

"Curses!" The sun was well over the horizon, though it was covered by gray-tinted clouds. I had missed my time to walk around town and enchant the buildings. My shoulders drooped. There was still so much of the town left. But there was something else....

"It's the day of the festival!" I yelped. Ember, having done his work to wake me up, snoozed as I darted around the cottage to get ready.

This was an official appearance as Auteri's one and only witch, so I dressed in the closest thing I had to a witch's outfit: a dark gray blouse, my black witch's skirt, a pair of black tights, and black boots.

"I could've worn one of my proper witch's dresses if you hadn't torn them all up." I sighed, glancing at Ember, who simply burrowed deeper in the blankets as if he hadn't been responsible.

Mother and Father hadn't sent me a letter in the past few days, so I dashed off a quick note—*The Festival of Lights is today! Will bring back souvenirs.*

The wind whipped at my skirt as I hurried down the cliff with my flamefox at my heels. From the path, I could see shopkeepers putting finishing touches on their stands and laying out their goods.

I wasn't looking at the trail—which was always empty—when I turned the corner.

Suddenly, a flurry of gray flew at me, and I stumbled backward with a yelp of surprise, tripping over a rock.

Ember squeaked as he darted forward, tugging the top of my boot to pull me away from the edge. Pebbles skittered out from underneath us and dropped off into the churning sea below. I clutched the cliff and caught my breath.

"What was that?" I gasped, gathering Ember in my arms, my heart pounding, as I stuck close to the wall of rocks. All around, tiny torn pieces of ashy, burnt paper fluttered like snow.

That couldn't possibly be a letter from my parents—could it? If it *was*, what had it said?

I studied the dirt, but I couldn't see any footprints other than my boots or Ember's paws. Still, a sense of foreboding twisted through me as shreds of paper swirled in the wind and made their way into the sea, disappearing in the frothing foam.

◎

In town, there was a strange quietness that didn't quite feel like the day of the festival. The dockworkers tasked with setting up stands kept peering over their shoulders at the gray waters. The tide was high, too, adding to the unease. Tourists kept coming out to the stands to check on the progress and scuttling back into their inns for warm mugs of barley tea.

I met Charlotte and Davy in front of the orphanage.

"Have you seen anyone on the path to my cottage?" I asked, lowering my voice.

They frowned, and Davy shook his head. "No, why?"

"There was a bunch of torn-up, burnt paper. Almost like a letter, like the ones my parents send me."

"Someone stole your letter?" Charlotte looked around indignantly, as if we'd discover the thief and she could give them a piece of her mind.

"I'm not sure. But that path only leads to my cottage," I mused. "And it *looked* like a letter. The scraps were too small to read, though."

Charlotte and Davy frowned again, worry flitting across their faces like the heavy clouds overhead.

Then Davy nodded toward the sky, his forehead smoothening. "Maybe someone used old papers to light their fireplace and scraps blew up toward your cottage? After all, there's a storm coming in."

"I suppose," I said, but Charlotte met my eyes. She didn't think that was likely, either.

At the edge of the waters, Mister Rydern reached out to the dark horizon and then fiddled with his gold watch. He muttered under his breath, but a gust carried away his words. Davy sighed and looked longingly at the stands setting up. "The winds *are* getting stronger. I'm worried Mayor Taira will cancel the festival."

"I'm more worried about what'll happen if she *doesn't*," Charlotte said darkly.

"But this is the best day of the year," Davy groaned. "Sky-high sweets, marvels to be seen. And the lights display! I've been counting down the days, hours, *minutes* until Mayor Taira opens up the festival. I saved all my coins since last year, just waiting for this night!"

"This might be a big storm, though," Charlotte replied, and the hairs on my neck prickled.

"By the way," I said, peering at the cliffs. "It's called the Festival of Lights, right?"

"You've been passing out flyers for the past two weeks and you don't know the name?" Charlotte said, appalled.

"I know there's lightfish, of course. Are there fireworks?"

I pointed at the cliffs behind the town hall. Davy and Charlotte spun around.

A burning globe of light slowly floated down to somewhere in the farmlands. A trail of smoke followed it, pale against the thick clouds.

Charlotte spoke, her voice scratchy. "That's not part of the festival."

"That's a flare," Davy added. "Signaling for help."

CHAPTER 23

ANTS AND AUTOMOBILES

I drew my broomstick out from under the counter as my heart pounded. The scratched-up, dull handle was now a glossy pale wood that gleamed like moonlight. Only a faint trace of Ember's teeth reflected in the light birchwood. I had attached the bristles infused with mementos from Ember, Rin, and my parents. There had been a few bare patches, so I'd filled them up with the bristlelike brush on the path between Auteri and the cottage. Those weren't magical, but hopefully it would be enough for a quick ride.

"Eva, what're you doing?" Charlotte asked.

I met her gray eyes. "I'll go. It'll take too long for anyone else."

"But—"

"I'm Auteri's witch, aren't I?"

Davy nudged Charlotte, and she swallowed. "Fly safe."

The sky was overcast and the sea churned an ominous gray. A light mist coated my skin. I shook my head. Maybe I was imagining things because I was scared to fly.

I walked to the edge of the dock, past Davy's father, where the waves crashed against the wood.

"I hear her," Mister Rydern mumbled. "She's there, she's waiting...."

A bead of sweat trickled down my back.

I stepped away from the frothing sea. Ember whined, pawing at my boots. I took a deep, shuddering breath.

My mother had always told me that Evergreen witches didn't hide from the sun, heights, or a bit of water.

"I just need to remember I'm an Evergreen. I've flown before. Not amazingly, but I've flown. And I can fly again," I told Ember. "This'll be good practice for my trip to the Council Hall."

My fingertips prickled as the broomstick stirred awake. I gripped the broom tightly and then tugged it up. A gust rustled my hair as I rose above the docks. I was *flying*.

The broom bucked and I clung on. My stomach lurched. *No.* I'd tried fixing it. And I *needed* it to work right now.

Ember barked, jumping up and trying to grab at my boots. Davy and Charlotte gasped.

"It's okay. I...I think the broom's getting used to flying again, just like me." I flashed them a grin, and Ember sat down roughly on his curled tail and glowered, as if saying, *You better be right about that. And I'm going with you next time.*

"Fly safe!" Davy and Charlotte called. The dockworkers looked up, waving, too.

Below me, Auteri sparkled. The blue and gold rooftops glimmered in the faint morning light, and the white buildings looked like delicate sugar cubes. Over my shoulder, the moored trading ships bobbed in the choppy water, pulling slightly toward the open sea, like they ached to adventure to new lands.

Shoppers in the town square waved at me as I flew above the path toward the farmlands. The wind pushed stronger when I was up in the air. The broom shuddered strangely, and I held on tight, too scared to wave back.

I jetted toward the tall peaks, climbing the wind currents faster than a boat in water, and my stomach leaped. I was starting to understand why Davy loved sailing.

The broom kept veering right, and I had to push it forward. I rose above the farmlands, searching for the flare, until the trees were small pinpricks below me.

Finally, I glimpsed the faint trace of smoke and followed it with my eyes to a silver automobile, farther up the road.

I shot forward. Suddenly, the broom bucked. I clung on to the broomstick, my nails clawing into the wood. I hovered down to the tree-lined road slowly, begging the broom not to kick me off.

My broom jumped again and my teeth clashed painfully. I cried out as the broom shot out from under me and I fell straight down, screaming.

I tumbled through a tree, hitting branch after branch, each one raking me without any end in sight.

When I felt I was nothing more than a bag of rattled, bruised bones, I finally hit the ground. I groaned, picking myself up.

The broom shot up into the sky and then torpedoed down, straight at me.

My heart pounded in my chest.

"Whoa, stop!" I screamed, rolling over just before it slammed into the dirt, right where my head had been, piercing the soil.

The broom twitched when I pulled it out of the ground. "Don't worry, I'm definitely not riding anymore," I gasped, trying to catch my breath.

I turned the broom over in my hands, examining it. It hadn't been the wind. My colorful infused bristles were firmly stuck in, but the cliffside brush had fallen out, and the bare patches stuck out like a sore thumb.

When I touched the brush, the broom jumped out of my hands and fell to the ground. I glared at it. That was why it had veered off course—and kicked me off.

The remaining bristles were tucked away in the cottage. There was no way I'd be able to summon them from here.

I groaned. "Guess I'm walking."

I hurried toward the silver car on foot. The clouds were rolling in thicker than ever. If I was going to make it back before it started raining, I'd have to rush.

As I turned the corner around the sunflower fields, I saw the automobile stopped half on the dirt and half on the grassy slopes that lined the side of the road.

A woman scrambled like a frantic ant trying to avoid getting eaten by a bird. She ran from side to side and stopped on the right to look under the body.

"Excuse me?" I peered around the car.

The woman straightened, smoothing out her simple periwinkle gown. She towered over me, radiating a sense of power. I had a strange urge to curtsy. For some reason, she seemed familiar, even though I could've sworn I'd never seen her before.

"Hello, I'm Eva Evergreen, Auteri's witch." I drew myself up as tall as I could. "At your service."

"My name's Stella and thank goodness you came by." She spoke rapidly, grabbing my hand with a firm shake, and pointed to the right wheel in the front. "I was driving fast, hit a rut and some rocks and, well, the wheel's busted. I don't know why there was such a rut in the road to begin with. Please, can you fly me to town?"

"My broom's broken." I gestured at the end. "A few bristles are missing and I can't fly without them."

"Ah, that's unfortunate." Stella tapped her chin. "Would you be able to help with my tire, then?"

I ran my hands over the tire and winced. It was solid rubber, but the rubber was punctured and slashed into ribbons.

"This car isn't fit for long distances." Her fiery dark brown eyes looked out through the mist, toward the sea. "Nonetheless, I didn't have a choice. I need to get to Auteri—now. And at this rate, magic is the only thing that'll help me." She turned, focusing her gaze on me. "Can I ask you to help me, Miss Evergreen?"

"Please, call me Eva." I rolled up my sleeves. "And of course I'll help."

It turned out the reason why my parents always took their automobile to the repair shop was because cars were *complicated*. Not only was the tire busted, but the axle and the alignment and the parts of the car that I didn't even have names for weren't working.

Stella's heels crunched on gravel as she paced, and sweat dampened my blouse. I needed to get this fix done fast.

Less than half an hour later, I was slightly faint as I finished magicking Stella's car back into one piece. Just as I cast my last spell, the clouds rumbled and rain started pouring.

Stella curtsied with grace. "Thank you, Eva."

I dipped into a much less graceful curtsy and resisted the urge to fall face-first into the dirt road and curl up for a nap. "My pleasure, ma'am."

She dug into her pocket and handed me a gold coin. "Here, take this for repairing my automobile. I would've been stranded for hours without you."

"For me?" I grinned, despite my weariness. It was my first coin for a repair job, and it felt heavy in my hand. "Thank you, ma'am."

"I do have one more request, though," she said. "Can you please go with me to Mayor Taira? I have urgent business with her, and it involves you, too."

"Me?" Had something happened to Mother? Had the Council sent Stella to discuss my magic? But why would the mayor be part of it, too? Because if not Mother or my magic... My stomach dropped.

The corner of Stella's lips tugged down as she followed my gaze toward the dark horizon. "Unfortunately, I don't bear good news. Ready to ride?"

I closed my mouth and nodded numbly. I nearly collapsed onto the leather seat, my mind spinning and my hands sweating as I clutched my broomstick. She couldn't possibly mean...Stella took a fast turn, and my stomach dropped further.

Was it the—no, *no*, it...it couldn't be. It was too early for the Culling.

I stretched my fingertips. Unlike the little bubbles of magic that usually fizzed inside, I felt only the tiniest flickers of magic, like a dying fire. I swallowed, turning to look out the window at the darkening sky.

With Stella's speedy driving and her eyes glued to the muddy road, we whipped through the farmlands. At the edge of the peak overlooking the town, she grimaced and slowed the car. "Are you buckled in?"

I nodded, patting the leather belt strapping me to the seat. "Secure."

"This is a fate-blasted hill. All the water means no traction." She pulled a lever and gears ground as they shifted.

Dense mist had rolled in, burying the buildings in thick gray clouds. I shuddered. It looked like Auteri was underwater. I wondered if the festival stands might float out to sea. Yet again, I hadn't done enough to help my town.

We rattled down the muddy hill, cutting through the fog and rain, and Stella's knuckles whitened as she strained over the wheel to see through the sheets of water gushing down. "The rain's making it slippery," Stella muttered under her breath. "I *told* Mayor Taira to pave it."

Finally, the automobile rolled onto the cobblestone streets of Auteri. She yanked at a lever with a quick shake of her head. "Lost too much time there. Hold tight, Eva."

Stella pressed on a pedal, and the car shot forward with a screech that echoed through the metal frame. We wove past the buildings in a flash and slid to a stop in front of the town hall, spraying the puddles of rainwater in arcs.

"I don't think we can park here," I said, as we got out. "Mayor Taira might get upset."

"Ordinarily, I wouldn't, either." Stella smiled, rummaging in the trunk. She drew out a thin circlet and slipped it onto her head. "But in times of need, anyone should be able to, including princesses."

My jaw dropped. The circlet glimmered with diamonds and sapphires, with thin gold vines braided into a delicate circle. Stella—*Princess* Stella—was the Queen's Advisor for Auteri and the surrounding region. No wonder she seemed familiar; there was a portrait of her in one of the corridors of the town hall.

She smoothed down her wrinkled, dripping dress. "You wouldn't have a spell for ironing out clothes, would you? No, never mind. We haven't got a second to waste."

I trailed behind her in stunned silence as she strode up the stairs. *What is happening? It can't be....*

The princess knew exactly where to go. She pushed

open the doors to Kyo's receiving room. Townspeople waiting to talk to him murmured in surprise.

Kyo startled and shoved his chair back quickly to bow. He rapped on the gilded door behind him and pushed it open, calling, "Announcing Princess Stella."

The crowd broke into a clamor.

"I *knew* she looked like a princess—didn't I say so?" A merchant crossed his arms and nodded knowingly.

"Isn't she the princess who races automobiles? Didn't she try to fly an airplane or something, too?" a sailor said, craning to catch a glimpse of her.

Deep in the adjacent office, Mayor Taira looked up in the middle of her conversation with a sailor. Her hands shook when she saw the princess.

"Princess Stella, honored Advisor to our region." Mayor Taira dipped into a curtsy.

Stella bowed in return. "Thank you for seeing me so suddenly, Mayor Taira of Auteri."

Mayor Taira noticed me over Stella's shoulder. Her thin eyebrows lifted and my stomach curdled. "To what do we owe the pleasure of this visit? You've traveled a long way from Okayama, haven't you?"

"With my speed, it was a short drive—until my tire busted on a rock. Nevertheless, I'm here now." Then she took a deep breath and raised her voice. "I've brought news for the town of Auteri." Her voice rang against the walls as the townspeople hushed. "As the Queen's Advisor for this region, I came here as soon as the Council warned me...." She swallowed, scanning the crowd, as if she was searching for her next words.

"No...no..." Mayor Taira's pale hands curled into her dress, crushing her skirts in her fists.

Princess Stella creased her forehead, like lines in sand. "As soon as we found it was brewing, the weather witches and wizards worked for hours on end trying to scry its path—and once I heard the news, I came here straightaway."

She faced the receiving room; her circlet sparkled as bright as her fierce eyes as she spoke to us. "The Council's scryers foresee a typhoon will hit the coast by Okayama."

The townspeople buzzed. Okayama was hours away by boat—it was far enough that—

"Citizens of Auteri, this is not just another storm. After Okayama, it's going to change paths...." Stella turned, her gaze locking with Mayor Taira's. "The Culling is aimed straight for Auteri."

CHAPTER 24
ᲢHE ᲫTORM

The door rattled as Kyo rushed in, pushing through the crowd gathered in the main hallway. His gray hair was plastered to his face. "Mayor Taira." He bowed low, but she quickly motioned for him to speak.

"How does it look, Kyo?"

"The water's rising like nothing I've ever seen before. The Culling is definitely on its way." His eyes were dark. "The fog is getting thicker, too."

Lines etched into the mayor's forehead. An attendant handed Kyo a towel, and he wiped at his dripping hair. "Most of the festival stands have washed away."

The crowd let out a sad, disappointed cry, but Mayor Taira held up her hand. They hushed, waiting for more news.

"And the ships?" she asked.

"I told the traders to send their goods in. The skiffs are anchored up at the docks, as safe as they can be. Most of the captains are choosing to try to outrace the Culling. It worked for some of the ships during the past tsunami. If they can make it into Constancia's territory, they might have a chance."

"Constancia?" Princess Stella croaked. "Is that any better than the storm?"

He swallowed, bowing his head. "They understand the risks."

Mayor Taira turned to Princess Stella, lips thin. "How much time do we have?"

"Only a few hours," Princess Stella said. "The Culling will hit Okayama around sunset. The typhoon will make its way down the coast by midnight. And the storm surge will hit soon after."

Hours. Auteri had only hours before the storm would hit.

I tried to speak, tried to find some words to ask more, but my throat sealed up. My breath still felt shallow, as if I hadn't been able to properly breathe from the moment Princess Stella had announced the Culling. Inside me, a cyclone of doubts raged. *I haven't finished fortifying the buildings. I need more time.*

The crowd swelled into an uproar of voices, strong as the waves hitting the shores.

"Here? Now?" shouted a dockworker.

"Can't the witch fix it? Zap the clouds away?" a shopkeeper asked.

"We're all likely to die before she can help us," one of the gray-clothed sailors snickered, from where Soma and his friends leaned against a wall. "She's too weak. Doesn't deserve magic."

I narrowed my eyes at Soma and his friends, but Soma's forehead was puckered as he stared down at the ground, as if deep in thought. I wanted to accuse the pirates of meddling with my letters. Out of anyone, they were the most likely to want to cause me trouble. But they were right—I was drained after getting Princess Stella here. The walls spun around me at the thought of stopping a typhoon.

Stella shook her head. "When the Culling first happened, one weather wizard tried to stop it. Magicking the earthquake caused the abyss in the land and weather patterns, making it more volatile. That's the year it destroyed half the capital. We need a shield like the kind Grand Master Evergreen creates, or the barriers at the Constancia border."

As I had learned, one of the scariest parts of the Culling was that the Council had tried, year after year, to scry it before the onset. Each time, the Council's attempts had been blocked—by something, or someone—until hours before the Culling. Or, sometimes, when it was too late.

"We can do something, right, Eva?" A whisper came

from my side. Davy ran his hand through his wildly tousled hair, trying vainly to tame it.

I pinched my lips together, my stomach sinking.

It felt like a storm was growing inside me, too. Filling me with doubt, with certainty that I wouldn't be able to help Auteri.

On Davy's other side, Charlotte crossed her arms, listening intently. She had her messenger bag slung over her shoulder and her belt heavy with pouches tied around her waist. It looked like she'd stopped midway during her work.

Charlotte was focused on Mayor Taira and Stella, her eyes flicking between the two of them as they talked. If Charlotte had been the witch instead of me, I bet she would've found a way to save the town instantly. I bet she would've had more than a pinch of magic. I stared at the ground, my eyes burning like seawater had sprayed into my face.

Then a thought occurred to me, draining my worries and replacing them with a new horror. "Where's Ember?"

"At your cottage," Davy said, his face pale. "I thought he'd be safer there; everyone was running about trying to disassemble and bring in the stands for the festival."

Oh no. My flamefox probably thought I'd left him to face the storm alone.

"Keep your head up." Charlotte nudged me. "The Culling's just beginning."

Davy and Charlotte slipped closer, and I followed

them. "Would it be safer for the townsfolk to go up to the farmlands?" Mayor Taira asked Kyo and Stella.

Mayor Taira spotted me behind Charlotte and Davy, and she crooked one long finger, beckoning me forward. "Evalithimus."

I dreaded every step toward her. I curtsied, with a slight tremble, in front of Princess Stella and Mayor Taira. "At your service."

"Witch of Auteri," Mayor Taira declared, and I suppressed my urge to wince as her sharp voice echoed through the hall. "We need your magic *now*."

My legs buckled under me, but Davy and—to my surprise—Charlotte were at my side, holding me up.

"I...I'm not strong enough to enchant a protection shield out of thin air. But...I've been spelling the walls of the buildings ever since I got here, so those will hold strong—I think."

The stares of the townsfolk focused on me, and I ducked my head.

"There's nothing else you can do?" Mayor Taira asked. Her cold eyes pierced me, as if she saw who I actually was—a shadow of a true witch. "Nothing, when the water spills over the docks?"

"I have a waterproofing potion," I said, and one steely eyebrow rose.

"Oh?" She finally sounded interested. "And is this potion enough to cover the entire town?"

I was too ashamed to speak. If I explained that I only had a frying pan filled with my potion, sitting on my stove, Soma would laugh and laugh, and if Auteri somehow managed to survive, I'd never hear the end of it.

Slowly, I bowed my head. "I'm sorry," I whispered.

The mayor turned away.

Stella threw me a sympathetic look, yet she too turned to talk with Kyo and Mayor Taira.

I stumbled backward, letting the crowd push past as they tried to catch word of what was happening. Some of them shook their heads as they passed me.

Princess Stella, Mayor Taira, and Kyo murmured to one another rapidly and broke apart minutes later with a plan.

Kyo would lead the townsfolk who could make it over the cliffs to the farmlands on foot—before the typhoon and torrential rainstorms hit the coast. Princess Stella and I had made it back to Auteri just before the pass had turned too muddy and dangerous for automobiles.

Kyo looked around the town hall. "Pack lightly and spread the word—I'll lead us up. We'll go as soon as possible."

Mayor Taira stepped up next to him and nodded. "Anyone who can't make it up the cliff will stay here. And we'll need a few volunteers who'll help us board up the windows and set up sandbags. That'll be our plan."

My hands fell at my sides helplessly. I wasn't part of their plan because no one—not even me—could count on my pinch of magic.

"We'll stay," Charlotte said to Davy, and then they caught a glimpse of my face and looked guilty. Even Charlotte and Davy were making plans without me. I tucked my head down. I couldn't look into their pitying eyes.

When Soma pushed off the wall and opened his mouth to speak, I couldn't take it—he'd just laugh and laugh at how weak I was. I was really no better than a seaweed witch.

Tears stung as I turned away and pushed past them, out into the rain.

CHAPTER 25
ONLY ME

Rain lashed against my skin as I slipped out of the town hall. I couldn't see the edge of the bay or the cliffs that were supposed to protect us from the brunt of the waves. I shuddered. The storm was only going to get worse.

I peered up at the cliff. My cottage was hidden by the rain, but Ember waited there for me. My heart twisted. "I'll get you after I help secure the town," I promised, even if he couldn't hear me. I had let Ember down, too.

Boarding up each building felt like nailing Auteri into a coffin. The glimmering town was slowly turning into an ugly mess of brown. Even if I didn't have enough magic to do anything helpful, I would use every remaining bit of my energy to help board up the windows.

Through the rain, a trail of townspeople holding

lanterns made their way up the slippery cliff. In the farmlands, they would be protected from the brunt of the typhoon's waves, if not from the torrential rains that pounded down.

I hammered down nail after nail, the rain soaking through my clothes, making me feel like I'd never be dry or warm again. I boarded up the windows of Corn and Cloudberries and Ami's flower stand. The town looked abandoned without the usual bustle and the smiling shopkeepers to invite me inside.

"Ouch!" I cried out. I'd hammered my finger. A thought bubbled up in my mind. I hastily tucked the hammer into my belt loop and ran to the town hall.

More than a hundred townspeople swarmed around inside—those who couldn't make it up the cliff in the limited time remaining, like Ami, or those set on staying in Auteri to help in whatever way they could, like Mayor Taira.

Princess Stella was one of those who had stayed. She was hammering boards over windows on the town hall. I cleared my throat. "Excuse me, Princess Stella?"

"Ah, our witch." Those words burned. She added gently, "Yes, Eva?"

I lowered my lashes. "Will anyone from the Council come here?" My heart buzzed with hope. Maybe, just maybe, since I couldn't do anything, a *real* witch or wizard could.

A shadow flickered on her face. "The realm has too few witches and wizards as it is. We don't have enough to spare."

I knew too well that magic was hard to come by. "Did you happen to meet a witch named Nelalithimus Evergreen?"

"She's up north, protecting Okayama. Since our weather witch said that the typhoon will first hit our coast up there, she's one of seven witches and wizards creating a shield. The capital city has ten times the population of any town within the realm. Still, we couldn't find enough of you to protect it in time." Stella paused. "Your last name—Evergreen—are you related to her?"

"She's my mother."

"Ah, she mentioned that Auteri was in good hands—I didn't realize the two of you were related."

My heart plummeted and lifted at the same time. "That sounds like her."

"Then you must be strong."

I hung my head. "I'm just a girl trying to pass my Novice Witch quest. And I only have a pinch of magic compared to her. That's...that's why my magic ran out."

The faint scent of roasted tea and jasmine wafted from Stella. Her warm finger lifted my chin and her gaze locked onto mine. "And I'm only a princess, I'm no queen."

I swallowed.

She held me by my shoulders and spun me around to

face the town. I spied Davy, Charlotte, and a handful of shopkeepers hammering in boards or piling up sandbags to do anything they could to save Auteri.

"Look. Look at your fellow townspeople. They're trying to survive, like me and you. And they trust you, too."

"But...I can't put up a shield. I...I don't have enough magic to do that."

"And I'm only a princess. I couldn't do anything in Okayama, but I could drive fast—short of my car breaking—as a messenger. The Council had sent letters, but I had a bad feeling that they might not make it through the storm, and I was right. I did what I could with what little power I have. And I know you're doing the same, too."

My heart beat quicker, louder than the rain drumming against the cobblestone streets. The reason I had chosen to stay in Auteri wasn't because I was trying to help in the way that Mother or other witches or wizards could.

I didn't have their magic. But I was clever and resourceful. I would help by doing whatever *I* could—whether magical or not.

I raised my chin. "I'll do anything I can."

CHAPTER 26
A Tiny Hope

Charlotte and Davy were lugging sandbags from the beach to Seafoam Sweets, skirting around Davy's father, who was standing at the end of the dock. They nodded at me, wiping away the rain and sweat dripping down their faces.

I grabbed a sandbag from Charlotte and helped by piling it against the edges of the shop door. In the window, the sugar-spun boat sliced through the translucent, cresting waves. Behind me, real waves rumbled and water crashed into the docks.

"I'll have to drag him in soon." Davy looked bleakly at his father. "It's going to be tough."

A piece of paper dropped out of my pocket and into a puddle—it was the turtle I had waterproofed. Charlotte picked it up, brushing off the water droplets.

"There has to be something else we can do," I said. "Something. Anything."

Charlotte stared down at the small turtle in her hand and tugged the shell back into shape. "We're magicless. You're the witch. You can't make a shield?"

"I would've done that if I could. I won't be able to make a shield to last through the storm." I swallowed. "I...I'm not strong enough."

The paper crinkled in her fists. My blood pulsed so fast that my heartbeat drummed in my ears.

"You're plenty strong with what you have," Charlotte said, her voice cracking slightly. "Even if you say you've got just a bit of magic, you've done a lot for the town already. For me, even. Think of all you've done."

Seaweed and rocks. Corn and cloudberries. Fixes that, without a clever idea and a pinch of magic, would've never worked....

Yet—yet they *had* worked.

An idea unfurled in my mind. The turtle's shell was round and solid...kind of like an umbrella, or maybe even a shield.... *What if we made a lot of these?* I grabbed Charlotte's hand and uncurled her shaking fingers. "I might have an idea...."

And I knew a fearless adventurer, too, someone who had told me stories about his childhood climbing all over the cliffs....

I brushed my fingers against the turtle cupped in

Charlotte's hand. It was still dry to the touch, even though it had fallen into the puddle. The waterproofing potion had worked well. My heart started beating faster and faster.

"What if...what if you folded parchment into shields, like the shell of a turtle? We could link the shields together."

Davy turned his head to the side with curiosity. "How'll the paper withstand the water?"

"My waterproofing potion. And it'll take a simple spell to stick them to the entrance of the bay so they lock in place. I'll use one more spell to expand Charlotte's paper chain and make them gigantic and strong, and they'll be high enough to stop the brunt of the Culling. I don't have the magic to turn tides or create a shield out of nothing. But I might be able to do something like this."

His eyes widened and he nodded slowly. "It...it might work."

"I'm not going to be able to make enough to cover the whole coast," Charlotte whispered. Yet she pulled a new square of parchment out of her pocket, and her fingers whirled as she started folding a new piece, this time into a shield.

Davy's eyes sparkled. "We have a whole town that wants to help." He gestured his thumb at the town hall. "All we need is parchment and instructions. Char, show us how to make the shield and we'll ask around. We'll get these finished in no time."

Charlotte, Davy, and I sprinted to the town hall. First, I found Rin, and explained the idea to her.

"I always knew you'd think of something." My guardian's hand on my shoulder, full of belief in me, felt just like Mother's touch before I'd boarded the ship, and my heart swelled with hope.

Rin waved over Ami, who introduced us to a handful of her friends, including a few older shopkeepers whose legs were too weak to walk up the slope, some of the dockworkers who had rowed me in to Auteri, and their families. The kids squealed and grabbed at the parchment with relish.

"This is perfect. They were about to crawl up the walls with boredom," one of the dockworkers said, shaking his head at his three kids.

"And this feels like I'm doing something more than waiting and listening for the typhoon to hit our shores," added Ami, rubbing her arms for warmth.

Charlotte waved over some of the younger orphanage kids who couldn't make the climb up. Hikaru still clutched the dolphin, holding it close to him like a good-luck charm. One of Davy's sailor friends limped over, looking like a soggy scarecrow with a shock of black hair covering his scarred face.

Charlotte showed us how to make the shields, and we began piling the finished shields into her messenger bag. Some of ours—Davy's in particular and, well, maybe a few of mine—looked more like lumps than shields.

Charlotte's fingers whizzed over our papers and teased out the uneven corners, and Ami gave her spools of bright blue thread and a needle to link the shields together.

The townsfolk took to folding the parchment with ease. Before long, they began chatting and telling tall tales as their fingers crafted shields. Even so, their eyes darted to the door each time it creaked open.

"Checking in," one of the sailors called, the rain roaring as he slipped inside. He hurried up the stairway to Mayor Taira's office.

Hikaru snuck after him and returned a few minutes later, reciting his report: "He said, 'Water's flooding well over the docks, Mayor Taira.' Is that bad?" He looked around.

Davy's father was still out at the docks. Yuri and Edmund rushed out to pull him to safety.

Charlotte handed Hikaru another piece of parchment, her voice wobbling slightly. "It's okay. If we fold these papers, it's the best chance we've got to save the town."

Sweat beaded on my neck. The sea roared outside, creeping closer. What if our idea didn't work?

Charlotte, Davy, and I stared at one another, trying to hide our unease from the other townsfolk.

"I need to make a run to my cottage." I breathed in quickly, my lungs feeling strained. "The waterproofing potion's up there."

"We just need a few more shields." Charlotte's forehead creased as she glanced at me. "We can do this, Eva."

Davy nodded, yet even he looked pale.

As more townsfolk filtered into the town hall, we handed them a stack of parchment squares and set them to work. Before long, the burlap bag was plump and nearly spilling over.

I nodded tersely at Charlotte. "This'll have to do. I'll get the potion and Ember and—"

Charlotte looked at something behind me and dropped her shield. A prickle ran down my spine.

"See, Mayor Taira," a girl's voice cut in. "The witch is having them all fold paper."

I spun around. The pirates—Soma and his friends— had brought the mayor to us. I glared at Soma, whose eyes slid away as soon as he caught sight of me, and the girl with long braids leading the pack. Soma opened his mouth. "Crew, we should—"

"What are you doing?" Mayor Taira's voice rang through the hall. "We're supposed to be protecting our town, not toying with paper crafts like children."

Ami hid her parchment in the folds of her blanket. A shopkeeper gathered her grandchildren to her side. One of Davy's sailor friends palmed his parchment, making it disappear up his sleeve. The townsfolk dropped their heads, like they had been caught in a daydream.

Soma's friends leered at me. Rin frowned, stepping forward, the tilt of her head showing that they would have to go through her first if they were going to try anything.

"Yes, they're right," I said slowly, and Rin—and everyone else in the hall—turned to me in surprise. "We're folding paper."

The group of pirates smirked, preening under the guise of being right. I narrowed my eyes at them.

But I wasn't the same girl as when they'd called me a seaweed witch, or when they'd stopped by my counter to laugh at me.

This time, I was determined to win.

"However, I've learned a lot in my almost-one-moon in Auteri." I curled my fingers around my wand. "I've learned that sometimes it takes time to make friends, but those friendships"—I glanced at Charlotte and Davy—"feel stronger than anything I've found in the realm. I've learned that magic takes so many forms, and sometimes"—I turned to look at Rin and then Hikaru and the orphanage kids—"spells are best when I work alongside the entire town."

"And?" Mayor Taira asked, impatiently tapping her foot against the cold stone.

I put my wand back in my pocket and pulled the carefully folded turtle out. "And maybe paper, which wouldn't ordinarily stand up to rain, might have a chance—as long as there's a witch like me around."

The sneers on the pirates' faces froze. From the back, Soma sucked in a huge breath, his scar paling.

They could try to get me in trouble. To make fun of me, to try intercepting my messages. But I was stronger than their cruel words.

And I was no longer going to fall for their tricks.

I looked beyond them, at the mayor, and swept into a deep bow. "Mayor Taira, I have a plan to help Auteri."

She steepled her hands and stared. "I thought you were out of magic."

At her side, Princess Stella's fiery brown eyes studied me, her face indiscernible.

"I may have only a pinch of magic." I swallowed. "But...well...that might be enough."

I explained our idea to Mayor Taira and Princess Stella. I showed her the waterproof turtle and tapped it with my wand. "*Stand—*"

"That's ridiculous," one of the pirates protested, and his friends nodded. "That girl's basically magicless, she's—"

"Let her speak," said a voice from the back, and everyone spun on their heels to stare at Soma.

He crossed his arms. "If she's going to save the town, that means *us*, too. Because we're stuck here just as much as her or anyone else in Auteri." From across the hall, Soma's eyes burned with fear, with worry, but most of all, with hope.

Rin's words echoed in my mind: *All Soma wanted was to take care of the people who depended on him.*

At my side, Davy's jaw dropped. I couldn't speak, either, but only for a moment. Because I—and the town—didn't have any time to lose.

"Thank you," I mouthed, and he jerked his head in the slightest of nods as the rest of the pirates continued to stare at him in shock. Then I raised my voice. "This is more than just paper."

Magic prickled at my fingertips. I snapped my wand and chanted, *"Stand up, stand tall, stay strong and protect all."*

The crowd gasped as the turtle inflated up to the ceiling, towering over us.

"I'll make these shields bigger, too." Now it was my turn to cross my arms, as if daring the pirates to say another word. From behind them, Soma cracked a tiny smile.

"Go on." Davy nudged me and handed over a tin mug filled with water. "Show them what you've got, Eva."

I turned to Mayor Taira. "And they'll hold up to the rain. Look." I tipped the mug over the waterproofed paper. Mayor Taira narrowed her eyes as droplets slid off the shell.

"Paper." She stared flatly. "We're going to entrust the fate of our town to a pile of paper."

"Paper can *fight* water," I said. "This is a shield for Auteri."

She shook her head dismissively. "I won't let you endanger the lives of our townspeople for this foolish plan."

"Mother—Mayor Taira, we don't have any other options," Rin said. "This is our only chance at saving Auteri."

"Please," I said. "I'll leave this town afterward and never bother you again. I won't ask you to sign my Novice Witch application. Anything you want. Please let me try to help Auteri, one last time."

Mayor Taira raised her chin, and I stiffened my shoulders, staying steady even as I wanted to sink into the ground. If she turned me down now, I wouldn't be able to do anything to help Auteri. "The risk—"

Then someone stepped next to me. It was Rin, silently staring at her mother, hands clasped in front of her, with a small paper shield in her hand.

Around me, the townspeople held up their tiny paper shields.

Ami, Trixie, Trina…Hikaru, the kids from the orphanage…the shopkeepers from all around town…

At the back of the hall, Soma lifted up a shield, and the rest of his crew scrambled to grab the tiny folded pieces of paper.

From next to me, Davy, even Charlotte…

And from the mayor's side, Princess Stella turned to Mayor Taira, too.

We—me, Princess Stella, Rin, Charlotte, Davy, and all the people of Auteri—gazed at Mayor Taira.

The mayor closed her eyes briefly, and in that second I realized how worried she was, how she had done her best to take care of the people of Auteri with all of her heart and will.

She cleared her throat. "Our people are the most important part of Auteri. We can build new buildings and repave roads. But our people are irreplaceable. If the people of Auteri believe in Eva, well"—she turned to Rin and picked up the tiny paper shield from her hand—"I will believe in Eva, too."

The townspeople roared, shaking the walls more than the storm. "Eva! Eva! Eva!"

A shout echoed through the cheers. Soma pushed his way to me, with Rin watchfully tailing him. When he got to my side, the boy glanced down, staring at the floor as if it was mesmerizing, and then finally coughed out, "You're… I…I believe in you, too. I'm sorry for everything, before. I never met anyone like you from the Council. The whole town—the whole *realm* is lucky to have a witch like you."

I felt like I was flying.

Charlotte and Davy's faces gleamed.

"Let's go," Davy whooped, racing out the front door. Charlotte and I scrambled after him.

I could hear Rin cheering us on from behind. "Go on, Char, Davy! We believe in you, Eva!"

CHAPTER 27
FLYING FREE

We dashed through the torrential rain up the path to my cottage, passing dusklight flowers crushed in the storm. We still needed the waterproofing potion. Davy clutched the burlap bag to his chest to keep it dry, and I carried my broom with me. Even if it was acting up, I needed my broomstick for my plan.

We ducked inside. My bed was a mess, a halo of blankets and my lumpy pillow, with Ember nestled in the middle, shivering as rain and wind lashed at the walls.

He squeaked and jumped off the bed, circling around me. I knelt down and he leaped into my arms.

I buried my face in his warm fur. "I'm glad you're safe."

Ember made a content half-growling noise that made me smile. I looked up at Charlotte and Davy. "I have to take him to the town hall. I can't leave him here."

Davy rubbed his head, his curls splaying all over as he thought quickly. "I have to make sure my father is safe. Char and I will take Ember, too."

I grabbed the vial of sticky potion and tucked it into my pocket. Then I scooped up the flamefox jar and handed it to him.

"What're you doing?" Davy yelped. Then his face filled with wonder as he turned the jar around.

Charlotte brushed her fingers against the glass. "It's not hot. But it's so bright."

"Just don't open the jar," I warned. "Use it to light your way."

Then I lifted up the frying pan full of waterproofing potion. "Can you open up the bag?"

Charlotte looked at the pan strangely. "Where's your cauldron?"

"Witches don't use cauldrons. That's a myth. I simply need a vessel. After all, I don't have warts or a crooked nose, do I?"

Charlotte ran her eyes over my face, and I glared at her.

"That was a *joke*."

Davy and Charlotte held the burlap bag open as I tipped the pan and drizzled the shimmering, opalescent liquid over the shields. We shook the bag, coating the thread and each shield. The bag pulsed a brilliant blue.

"You did it!" Davy said.

But we all stared out the window, and even Davy looked pale under his tanned skin. "There's still so much to do."

"Let's go." I grabbed my troublemaker broom—it seemed to try to tug out of my grip—and we tumbled out the door. The rain poured down in buckets, thunder shook the sky, and jagged lightning streaked through the black clouds.

Davy gulped. He reached down to brush Ember's head. "Ready to run fast, buddy?"

"Please watch over him. I don't want him to slip out." *Especially if I can't make it back.*

Charlotte's hand snaked out and tugged the sleeve of my shirt. "Wait—what's your plan?"

"I'm going to seal one end of the chain to the far side of the cliffs," I said. Maybe that sticky potion would come in handy, after all. "And then I'll fly the chain across the bay, enchanting the shields to grow and strengthen." *For as long as my magic lasts.*

"Alone?" she asked.

I nodded. "I'm Auteri's one and only witch, after all." My face felt like it had become colder than rainwater.

I mounted my broom slowly. Under my breath, I begged for the broom to fly.

Even if I flew just this once, even if I never flew again, I would be fine as long as I could fly far enough to help Auteri.

Davy leaned over to examine the broomstick. "Afterward, you have to show me how this works."

"After? Of course." My voice cracked. *If there's an after.*

I tensed my legs and pushed off. My nails dug into the rain-slicked wood. "Please let me stay on," I whispered. The broomstick jumped as if it could hear me but wasn't quite interested in listening. "Please."

I went higher, clutching the burlap bag with one hand and the broom in the other. From below, Ember whimpered nervously, but then a gust of wind shoved me.

The broomstick kicked furiously. "No, *please*, no."

My insides rattled as it yanked me from side to side. My hands slipped just as it sharply lurched to the right. I screamed as I tumbled out of the air, straight down toward the cliff.

"*Eva!*" Charlotte shrieked.

I desperately tried to think of a simple, quick spell that could help me, and it came to mind when I was a hairsbreadth from crashing into Charlotte. "*Slow down, sky-fall!*"

I decelerated enough for Charlotte to grab my arms, and Davy lunged for the bag of shields. The vial of sticky potion tumbled out of my pocket, and Ember leaped to catch it. Charlotte stumbled under my weight, dragging me away from the edge of the cliff. We sank to the ground; my legs were too weak to stand. My whole body trembled.

"A-are you okay, Eva?" Davy clutched the burlap bag in his shaking hands. His face was paler than the clouds. "You...you fell so fast. I couldn't do anything."

"I'm okay." I breathed out slowly. Charlotte and I untangled from each other, and I sat on the muddy ground, shivering.

Ember jumped into my arms, his small body warming me. He gently deposited the vial in my lap. He quivered, too.

"Evalithimus." Charlotte glared at me. "You'd better explain what just happened."

"I, uh, didn't quite finish fixing up my broom."

"What d'you mean?" Her eyes widened. "I thought all witches could fly from birth or something."

"Apprentices get a magical broom from their mentors as a final gift. I know how to fly a little bit, so this should've been just a matter of practicing...until I left it out and Ember tore it all up, including the magical bristles."

Ember had the grace to look a little ashamed.

I showed her the brush tip. "See, here're the ones I melded with Ember's fur and his first leash. Rin gave me her bottle-green handkerchief, and I used a bit of a cloth from my parents to create the silvery ones. It's still a few short and...magical bristles can't be replaced with ordinary brush."

"So you thought you would try flying anyway?"

"A bumpy ride was the least of my worries." I glanced out at the thick clouds, ominously creeping toward the gap in the cliffs. "We need to help *Auteri*."

Davy rummaged in his pocket and extracted a watch-band. "How about this?"

"For me?" My heart warmed, even as I shivered from the cold.

He nodded. "It's one of my favorite wristbands, the first model I ever made. That way, at least part of me will go on every adventure with you."

"Thank you," I whispered.

Charlotte and Davy exchanged a glance, and then he held up the steadily glowing glass jar. "After I check on my father, I'll go to the other end of the bay, so you know where to fly."

I protested. "It's too dangerous—"

"And it isn't for you?" Charlotte narrowed her eyes. "The mist is too thick. You won't be able to see where you're going."

"Only if you'll turn back if it gets too dangerous, okay?" I met Davy's eyes.

He pressed his lips together. Finally, he inclined his head in a nod. "Only if."

Then Charlotte pulled her blue ribbon loose, and her thick waves tumbled down around her shoulders. She held out the strip of silk. "Here."

"But that's your ribbon. I've never seen you without it."

"And that's why it'll work. It has to be something that really matters, right? From a friend?"

"We're friends?" I echoed.

"I would've let you fall if I didn't care," she muttered, her ears turning pink at the tips. "But there's one condition." She stared straight at me and a tingle ran down my spine. "Take me with you."

Davy started. "Charlotte, you just saw Eva fall off her broom—"

Her gray eyes were full of something I'd only seen flickers of before...almost like *trust*. "I know I've been acting rotten ever since you came here. Still, I'm not scared of heights or tumbling off your broomstick."

I opened my mouth. "But—"

"I'm more scared of us failing." Her words seemed to meld with the wind and rain, prickling my skin. "Auteri is going to go underwater without your magic—and I'll do anything to help you. If I hold on to the shields, you can focus on flying through the storm." She pressed the ribbon into my hand. "Take it, please."

I chanted a spell to bind my last bits of bristle to Davy's wristband and Charlotte's ribbon. Their gifts stuck fast, faster than any of the other times I had tried to spell together the bristles.

I charmed the bristles on and, finally, it looked like a

real witch's broomstick. But that spell had taken its toll on me—a shudder ran over my skin as magic drained from my blood.

I clambered on, patting the potion in my pocket to check on it.

"Wait." Charlotte untied her belt, heavy with pouches, and lashed it around my waist. She plucked the vial and slipped it into the smallest pouch, tying it tightly shut. "There. Now you can focus on flying."

I pushed up until my feet barely grazed the ground. I hovered and hovered and it twitched—but it didn't throw me off. "It's...it's working." I whispered under my breath, "Thank you, Fiery Phoenix."

And I could've sworn the broom shook its bristles at me in response.

Charlotte grinned. "Not to say I told you so and all, but...don't doubt us and don't doubt yourself, Eva."

Davy clapped his hand on my shoulder. "Fly fast. This rain is bad enough, and it won't be long before the real typhoon rolls in."

He called for Ember to join him. Ember took one step forward and then circled back, his eyes glued to me.

"Go on, follow him, Ember." I leaned down and cupped his muzzle. "I'll be back for you, I promise."

"C'mon, let's see who's faster, you ol' flamefox!" Davy and Ember sprinted down the cliff, Davy shining the flamefox jar to light their way through the storm.

Charlotte slid onto the broom behind me, one hand circling around my waist and her other hand holding tight to the shields. "Go on," she said. The determination in her voice echoed the feeling pounding through my heart, burning in my blood. "Let's fly, witch-girl."

CHAPTER 28

Ꝉooking for Ꝉight

The wind battered my skin as we lifted off, but I breathed a sigh of relief—the broom stayed steady. *Figures that it would only work for what might be my very last ride.*

"Hold on," I shouted over the wind, and Charlotte tightened her grip around my waist. We soared straight down the side of the cliff, hugging the rocks, then I pulled the broomstick up to hover above the roaring waves. Davy and Ember were two dots sprinting down the side of the cliff.

Down by the docks, I saw Yuri and Edmund straining to pull Davy's father away from the waves. He was yanking against their grip and trying to walk closer to the edge of the docks. The water frothed at their feet as it spilled over the ground. I swallowed and turned to look out at the bay that we would have to cross.

Through the downpour, I couldn't even see the entrance to the bay. I shouted over my shoulder at Charlotte. "Hang on!"

We propelled forward in a burst of speed and the wind screamed in my ears. We dodged the crashing waves. Still, our clothes dripped from the rain and spray of the salty seawater.

About halfway over, a swell of wind screamed in my ears, shoving my broom back. Charlotte's grip on my waist anchored me as I maneuvered the broom through the gust. I stared down at the choppy waves a long way below us and shuddered. I didn't want to fall.

"There it is!" Charlotte shouted, pointing straight ahead. The cliff loomed in front of us, a dark outline in the mist.

Finally, we touched down on one of the paths that crisscrossed along the side of the rocks, and Charlotte slid off the end of my broom. We were on one of the ledges on the inside of the bay, so we hurried to the mostly dry shelter of an overhang, the waves roaring just below us.

Across the water, the other side was shrouded in waves and mist, and we pressed against the cliff, breathing hard, peering for a sign of the flare. Without Davy's light, I wouldn't know if I was heading toward the open sea or to the other side. But he wasn't in place yet. The rain pounded down, and the gusts tore at my skin, growing stronger and stronger.

CHAPTER 29
THE MEANING OF MAGIC

Look!" Charlotte cried, pointing. Bright orange-red light flickered in the thick fog and mist. Davy was waiting for me. I breathed out in relief.

"I'm going to fly over." The wind yanked away my voice, howling in our faces. We had to shout into each other's ears to be heard.

She huddled next to me, shivering. Her hair was plastered to her skin, and her gray eyes were as dark as the churning waves. "But the wind's getting worse."

I bit down on my lip.

Charlotte grabbed my hand. "Eva, please, don't look like that. It's not because I don't believe in you or our plan. I'm...I'm scared for you, Eva."

She squeezed my hand and her warmth brought some feeling back to my fingertips. Charlotte helped me hold the end of the thread to the rocks. I pulled the tube of slime out of my pouch and poured out half the potion.

It fizzled and hardened instantly in the rain, sealing the thread to the cliff. I corked the vial and slipped it back into its pouch.

"There. Now you can head back to the town hall."

Charlotte shook her head grimly. "I'll wait here till you're done, Eva."

"It's not safe. You should go back."

"It's not any safer for you, is it?" she said. "At least if I'm here, I'll walk with you back to the town hall—because if it's like last time with the boat, you're going to need some help."

"I'll be back soon, then."

If I make it back.

I swallowed, casting a look out at the stormy sea. There was only one place to go.

Winding the other side of the chain around my hand, I mounted my broomstick. There was a break in the wind, and I pushed the broomstick forward to surge toward Davy. The chain of shields fluttered behind me, unfurling.

"Fly strong, Eva!" Charlotte's shout barely carried over the winds.

The shields looked small and pathetic, like specks of dust against the roaring sea.

Freezing wind pushed me into the waves below. The

gusts were growing fiercer—the Culling was heading our way. And I was still so far from Davy.

A wave roared at my side and I screamed. I plunged into the tunnel of crashing water. The salt spray burned my eyes, and I barely shot out in time. The wave collapsed behind me.

The flare flickered brighter—I was closer. I dove around another wave, but I wasn't flying fast enough. A wall of water crashed into me, shoving me underwater as I gasped for air. The string cut into my palm, yet I couldn't let it or the broom go.

Water burned in my lungs as I swam up to the surface. I swiped the water from my face, looking around for the flare. The gray-black waves rose around me, blocking my vision. My heart ricocheted. The sea battered me as I spun left and right, desperate to see Davy's flame.

Where was the flare? Where was Davy?

When I saw it glowing to my right, I nearly cried out in relief. I mounted my broom and shot out of the water and into the piercingly cold rain.

I looped over and around and through crashing waves, pushing closer toward Davy's light. It flickered, just out of reach.

Suddenly, the tall cliff appeared through the mists, and I barely braked in time to stop from slamming into the rocks. I tumbled down, into the waves, and threw my hand out to scrape my nails at a ledge.

Davy's hand grasped my wrist and dragged me out of the water before the tide pulled me away. My drenched clothes stuck to my skin and my boots sloshed.

I lay out on the ledge, soaking wet and coughing up seawater, my chest heaving. Davy knelt down and unraveled the thread from my hand. "I'll hold it, Eva."

The chain stretched taut across the bay. It was barely long enough. He quickly wound the thread around his hand and held on tightly, wincing as it bit into his hand. "Do your magic."

I pulled myself onto my knees and swallowed, drawing out my wand and touching it to the chain. My magic stirred sluggishly.

Davy leaned over, shaking my shoulder gently. "Are you okay?"

My magic was draining too fast, but I nodded. "Just needed to catch my breath. *Stand up, stand tall, this shield will stay strong and protect all.*"

The parchment shield shivered and glowed a pale blue. It grew and grew, like a sapling shooting up toward the sky, until it rose to twice the height of the town hall.

Davy yelped. He tried to hold on, but the wind picked up the shield like a kite and pulled him toward the water.

I grabbed onto the thread with him, digging in my heels. Pressing the strand to the rock, I poured out the rest of the slime. It sizzled and hardened quickly.

Still, the water pulled and tugged at the fluttering

shields. I needed another spell, fast. A spell that would make the shield stay in place...

"*Stay here, stay near. Auteri is your home, and there's no need to roam.*"

The shield creaked and settled down, pressing against the rock. Waves gushed around the paper, but it locked into the cliff and all the way to the bottom of the bay.

"One shield done." Staying on the ledge as long as I could, I chanted the spells and pointed my wand out at the shields. Davy cheered as each shield grew and locked into place with the others. Too soon, the shields were out of my reach.

The other side of the bay was hidden by the heavy rain and turbulent waves. We were separated from Charlotte by hundreds of shields. "Wish me the best, Davy."

Davy nodded. "Do what you can, Eva. Just come back to us."

The rest was all up to me.

I mounted my broomstick and jetted over the water, hiding from the waves behind the gigantic shields as I cast my spells.

My magic was trickling away so quickly.

Spots of darkness spun around me, and I struggled to keep my eyes open. I focused on the bright blue thread that led to Charlotte.

One shield, two. Three shields, four.

My magic flickered.

A gust shoved me into the closest giant shield, and I ricocheted off, spinning dizzyingly, and my hands slipped on my broom.

I leaned down, hugging the wood, and looked around. I couldn't see the thread or the shields.

I was lost in the thick fog.

CHAPTER 30
A Flicker of Light

Rain poured on me as I turned and turned, trying to catch sight of the shields, the cliffs—anything. The wind picked up, shrieking in my ears like screams of the wounded and dying.

No, no, the storm howled, forming into humanlike voices. *You can't make it, you nothing-of-a-girl, you fake witch.*

You are nothing.

The murky mists surrounded me, pressing the breath out of my lungs. Where was the coast? Was Charlotte in front of me or behind me?

I couldn't fly anywhere. If I went the wrong way, I might end up in the middle of the sea, far from the seven realms.

If I cast my compass spell—the words were on the tip

of my tongue—I knew I wouldn't have enough magic for the rest of the shields. I might not even have enough energy to fly back. I was already bone-cold from the magic's drain.

A sob racked my chest. I had failed.

My broom spiraled downward, toward the choppy waters.

The town doesn't need a witch like you, the voices in the storm shrieked. *You are useless. You are unneeded.*

If I drifted into a deep sleep...If I slipped into the dark waters...

No one will remember you when you're gone.

Through the darkness, a bright red-gold light flickered faintly.

A long, mournful wail carried over the wind, stabbing me deeper than the ice-cold rain.

It—it couldn't be—

Like an answering call, light glowed behind me, from the brush of my broomstick. I stifled a cry with my trembling hand. The twigs that had been fused with Ember's leash and fur *glowed*, radiating light that illuminated the churning waves below me—and the edge of the half-finished chain of shields.

The faintest of shouts carried across the bay, guiding me forward. "Eva!" Charlotte's voice cut through the rain and thundering waves. "Eva, where are you?"

Ember echoed her words with a fierce shriek. How—how was my flamefox there? The wind stung my eyes.

Knowing his stubborn streak, he'd likely broken out of the town hall the instant he knew I wasn't going to be there, too. Ember—and Charlotte—were fighting alongside me, reminding me that I wasn't alone.

A gust pushed me back, trying to fill my ears with its haunting sounds, but with Ember's howls and Charlotte's words, I remembered why I would do anything—whether as a witch or magicless girl—to save Auteri.

I saw Rin's honey-brown eyes crinkling at the corners as she invited me to stay in Auteri.

I tasted sweet cloudberry popcorn from Trixie and Trina.

I breathed in the scent of Yuri's sandwiches, warm as the afternoon sun, carefully packed with her favorite ginger chews.

I smelled the sweet dusklight buds that Ami tucked behind my ear, the petals soft against my skin.

I recalled Davy's squared shoulders, melting as his father reached out to him.

I heard Ember's sharp cry as he sprinted to me, out of Vaud's grasp.

I felt Charlotte's arms around me, with her words sharp but her actions pure-hearted.

I sensed the townspeople of Auteri standing with me, each holding out a shield to Mayor Taira.

If these were my last spells ever, in my clumsy, semi-magical attempt to save Auteri—even if these enchantments drained me of every last drop of magic—I would make peace with being magicless.

If I could do this last bit of good for Auteri, if I could save them, it would be worth *all* my magic.

I propelled the broom toward the shields, fighting through the wind and soaring out of reach of the waves. My heart pounded against my ribs. I could fly. I *had* to make it.

Finally, I reached the edge of the chain and stared down at the tiny shields waiting for my spells.

Staring fiercely, I pointed my wand at the shield. *"Stand up, stand tall, stay strong and protect all."*

Chanting slowly, I inched my broom forward as the shields grew and latched into place. Wind shoved me around, and I trembled with shivers as I clung to my broom, but I kept flying onward, shield by shield, bit by bit, with Charlotte's voice and Ember's blazing light drawing me forward.

Charlotte cried out, "Just a little more!"

Ember howled, long and sharp.

Charlotte and Ember were so close, beckoning me to the ground, just as a swell crested and slammed into the rocks. Seawater poured down on the overhang and they disappeared from sight. My hands nearly slipped off my broomstick. *Please, no.*

I scanned the lower path, my breath caught in my throat. I couldn't see them.

"Charlotte! Ember!" I cried, jetting forward. I tumbled

off the broom and clung to the wall, slipping down the slick footpath.

Seconds later, water streamed off the ledge and they reappeared, drenched yet safe.

"Eva!" Charlotte rushed up the path and slid to a stop in front of me. Her hands reached out, trembling, as if she wanted to grab me, but she lowered them as if unsure of how to help. Ember curved around my legs, whimpering as my cold skin met his warm fur. His tail was ablaze with light.

"Ember!" I cried out in surprise, my heart swelling. "Your tail lit!"

My flamefox gave me a pointed look as if to say, *Of course. You're my witch. No storm's allowed to take you away.*

Then, from behind me, water crashed against the shield. My heartbeat skittered as I turned around.

One last shield remained unspelled, creating a gap that waves poured through. Charlotte and I stared at the shield and then at each other.

"C'mon," she said. "Just that one. A single shield. Then you can rest, and I'll feed you porridge and hot tea. You're almost done."

I wanted to shoot back a retort, but I was so tired.... *Curses, Char, must you always push my buttons?*

One more shield... *"Stand up..."* My legs trembled, threatening to give out from under me.

"Lean on me, witch-girl." Charlotte took a step forward. "Don't you dare give up."

I pressed into her side, breathing heavily.

My arm shook as I pointed my wand at the shield. *"Stand tall…"*

She held my hand steady.

"This shield will stay strong and protect all."

A blue-and-gold shimmering light shot from my wand and straight at the shield, and it blossomed like a flower, shooting up into the sky. But it wasn't locked into the other shields; we ducked as another wave crashed through the cracks.

"One more spell," I croaked.

Charlotte's eyes gleamed. "You can do it." Ember circled around us.

I took a deep, huge breath and then I whispered, *"Stay here…stay near. Auteri is your home…and there's no need to roam."*

With a glow of blue-gold light, the shields shifted slightly. Finally, the chain of shields locked in.

Charlotte and I stared up at the colossal shields that towered over us, higher than the cliffs and tougher than the rocks.

Outside the bay, waves crested and thundered as they crashed against the papers.

The shields stayed straight and tall.

Inside the chain, the water was still choppy, yet it was

slowly quieting. The water level was still high, lapping at the edge of the path.

"We did it!" Charlotte shouted. Ember yipped and reared on his hind legs as he let out a howl of joy.

Charlotte's eyes blazed bright as a cloudless sky, and she grabbed me in a hug. I stared over her shoulder at the shields in disbelief.

It had worked.

"C'mon, let's get back to the town hall." Charlotte slung her arm over my shoulder, her cheeks pink. "They'll want to know. Can you imagine Mayor Taira's face? She'll be so proud, Eva."

I tried to follow her to the path that led back toward town, my feet dragging, and I tripped. I held my hand out to lean against the shield. Seawater gushed over my feet, soaking into my boots.

"Ember? Char?" I mumbled. Spots of darkness pricked my vision, and the waves roared in my ears. I took one more step forward as my legs buckled under me. My breath slowed. The rain and storm were cold, but my limbs felt frozen. My magic had truly run out.

"Eva, no, no. Grab my hand!" Charlotte's sharp scream and Ember's cry pierced the air as I tumbled into the water.

Charlotte scrambled toward me, but she was so far away....

As I fell, her hand grabbed at me, nails scratching my

skin, and the magic in my blood sparked one last time. I heard Mother's voice, or maybe it was Charlotte.

We're here for you now. You've done good for Auteri, Eva.

I was too weak, too weary.

I sank down into the murky sea, until I was surrounded by darkness.

PART FOUR

Fly
On,
Witch

CHAPTER 31
ᑭORRIDGE

My vision swam in front of me. I blinked. I was covered with piles of blankets on a cot in the crowded town hall, lit by flickering lanterns. Some of the townspeople napped and others gathered in small circles, murmuring to one another.

My freezing-cold body burned with scrapes and bruises. Still, I was in one piece. But my breath caught—I couldn't feel a spark of magic in me. I was drained dry.

A booming sound shook the hall, like two buildings slamming into each other. I jolted and looked around. The townsfolk didn't seem to notice—they kept talking to one another.

Ember rested on top of me, keeping me warm. The flame in his tail had burned out. When he peered into my open eyes, he waved his tail so fast that I swore it flashed with bits of fire.

I tugged at the sleeve of the person closest to me, a sailor. "Excuse me?" I mumbled. Darkness flickered at the corner of my vision. I could barely speak. But I needed to know if the shield had worked.

"She's awake!" It was Soma. His eyes relaxed with relief as he smiled at me, seemingly not noticing how Ember growled at him from my lap. "I'm glad you're back safe. I—we were all so worried."

The townspeople gathered next to my cot, babbling loudly, and Soma gave me one last nod before slipping away. My flamefox pranced around my legs, yapping cheerily.

Charlotte and Davy pushed their way to my side, wearing dry clothes far too big for them, their wet hair dripping on my blankets.

"What's that sound?" I whispered, as the *boom* echoed through the town hall again.

Charlotte grinned at me. "That noise? That's the waves and wind hitting the shields." She put her hand on my shoulder, and through the blanket, I felt her blazing warmth. "The shields worked, Eva."

Davy's eyes danced, and he flung his arms around the both of us. "You have more than a pinch of magic. Your idea—your *magic*—was just as strong as any witch or wizard in the whole realm."

My heart swelled. The saltiness of their damp hair

tickled my nose as I pulled them into a hug. At the same time, we all breathed out a huge sigh of relief and then looked at one another and laughed.

"Still, you owe me one. Ember tried jumping in the water after you." Charlotte's eyes flashed darkly. "I had to dive into the water and drag your flamefox and your half-drowning body out. I thought we'd lost you."

I had thought I was a goner, too.

"It was the oddest thing, though—I swear, the waves calmed enough for me to dive down and grab you." She shook her head, trying to make sense of it. "Anyway, Rin and I made you porridge. Eat up. You need to regain your strength."

"But—my parents, I need to send them a message." I tried to swing my legs over the edge of the cot, but I was so drained that I couldn't move an inch.

Rin leaned over, brushing the hair out of my eyes. "As your guardian, I'll write to them so they'll know we're taking good care of you."

"You'll be a pile of porridge if you don't rest up. Go back to sleep." Charlotte pushed me back into bed.

My arms felt tired; my whole body hurt. The bed felt like the best kind of hug from my parents, pulling me in warmly.

Charlotte smirked. "See? Porridge."

"I'm not porridge," I muttered crossly, as I sank back into my pillow. But she was right—I didn't feel any tickles

of magic fizzing at my fingertips. The shields had drained
me dry.

I hoped my magic would return.

Charlotte picked up a steaming bowl and nudged me.
"Want some of my amazing cooking?"

I nodded, and she fed me by the spoonful. Salty with
just a pinch of pickled flameplums, the warmth of the
rice porridge spread throughout my body, and my eyelids
drooped lower and lower.

This time, I let the darkness claim me.

CHAPTER 32

ℳISADVENTURE ℳAGIC

*C*reak. *Creak.*

The shutters shifted as balmy summer air swirled through the town hall. The storm had broken its hold on Auteri.

I pulled the chain from my neck and peered at the hourglass. Time had stopped trickling. I had finished a full moon in Auteri.

In theory, it was time to get my application signed.

Around me, the town hall was deserted, with just a few empty cots piled in corners. Ember was curled in a tight circle next to me, radiating gentle heat. In the doorway, a woman leaned against the frame, facing the sea as she sipped at a mug. Was that Rin?

I blinked at the dark hair, locks as inky as mine, cascading down slightly past her shoulders. A diamond-like

shimmer laced into her black witch's dress. Strength reso-
nated from the set of her shoulders as she looked out on
the town, as if she knew everyone she met would listen to
every word she'd say.

My voice cracked. "Mother?"

Mother spun around, the tin mug clattering at her
feet. She didn't bother with a spell to clean it up. My
mother strode across the hall, eyes blazing, her hair swirling in her wake.

"Eva," she breathed out, and crushed me in a hug.
"Eva. It's been a terrible three days since the Culling, seeing you so worn out."

I swallowed, stunned. I'd been asleep for *three days*?

"I'm sorry I worried you," I whispered.

Mother frowned, drawing away to peer into my face.
"Sorry? Sorry for what?"

"For...for getting drained of magic every time I cast
spells. And how you have to clean up things after me."

"Oh, Eva. This town didn't need my help at all. *I* simply wanted to check in on you, as your mother." Mother
smiled down at me. "You are far, far more powerful than
you realize. You may have an affinity for repairs. Even
so, I have a better name for your magic—misadventure
magic." She leaned over and tweaked me on the nose.
"Even if you have just a pinch of magic, your magic flour-
ishes when you're saving people, when you're doing good.

You're fulfilling the Council's work, Eva. You've become an amazing witch."

My heart leaped as a spark seemed to kindle within me. Magic rushed through my blood, echoing those words with a tingle that went from my toes to the tips of my hair. My powers were nothing more than a faint whisper, but I still had *my* pinch of magic. I couldn't wait to feel the ticklish feeling of magic bubbling at my fingertips again.

Slowly, tentatively, a smile tugged at my lips until I was grinning back.

Rin peered through the front door. "Oh, you're awake!" Charlotte and Davy were right at her heels.

"Grand Master Evergreen was right!" Davy stared between me and my mother. "She *knew* you'd wake today!"

Mother smiled. "Just a bit of motherly intuition. No magic for that."

I grinned. "Mother, Rin is my guardian, and these are my friends, Charlotte and Davy."

"We met earlier, when I flew in from Kelpern," Mother said. "I hated waiting, but I came as soon as I could."

I turned to her. "How did you know—"

"I wanted to be sure that Hayato wouldn't have a thing to complain about." She lifted up something dangling at her neck. An hourglass identical to mine swung from a chain, with the top star-shaped chamber completely empty. Then she narrowed her eyes toward something near the door. *"Tea out to sea, mug back to me."* A warm gold light flashed from the tip of her wand, and dregs of tea gathered off the tiles in round droplets and flew out the door as the mug zipped back into her hand. She set it on a low table next to my cot, not seeming to notice Davy gaping in awe. "I'm sorry. I can't leave a mess in your town, Eva."

"Wow," Davy breathed out. His eyes were wide as saucers as he glanced furtively at my mother. "I still can't believe I've met *the* Nelalithimus Evergreen."

Even Charlotte seemed a little shy around my mother. The tips of her ears burned slightly pink against her crown of braids, and she stuck close to the door.

"Where's everyone?" I asked, swinging my legs over the edge of the cot and stretching.

"They've gone home," Rin said.

"Where do you think *you're* going?" Charlotte said, finally finding her voice. She gasped with alarm as I tottered onto my feet, blood draining from my head. I faintly remembered I hadn't stood in days. But before I knew it, Charlotte and Davy were at my sides, making sure I wouldn't fall.

"I need to go to my cottage to pick up my application. I've got to get it signed by Mayor Taira." I gulped at the thought of approaching her again. Once a lifetime was more than enough, really.

"I'll pick it up," Charlotte said. "I'm running errands anyway."

"And first, eat some pastries." Mother picked up a lacquered box from the low table next to my bed and nudged me and my friends to take pastries. "Your father was terribly worried about you, and you know how he bakes when he's anxious."

I bit into a yuzu cookie, the delicate powdered-sugar topping soothingly sweet, as if Father had wrapped me in one of his warm, steady hugs. Davy gobbled down two in a flash and declared, "These are awesome!"

Ember pranced out from under the cot with my boot in his mouth, eyeing my cookie hungrily. I narrowed my eyes at him, and he opened his mouth in a foxlike grin as he dropped the boot in front of me, as if saying, *What? I waited and waited for you to wake up!* Only one of the laces looked slightly chewed.

The noontime bell rang, resonating across Auteri. To my surprise, it didn't sound from inside the hall.

"Mayor Taira has the bell with her," Rin explained, nodding out toward the docks.

Davy grinned. "And the reason you shouldn't go back to the cottage...is because the festival's today!"

"Today?" I echoed.

"Mayor Taira promised to hold the festival as soon as you woke up," Rin said. "We've been rebuilding the stands and spreading word across the realm that we're ready and open for business."

As I munched on another cookie, the sugar crust crackling in my mouth, Davy explained that the town had minimal damage—all because of the shields, my enchantments on the buildings, and Mother's help as soon as the last drop of sand had fallen out of her hourglass. Ember leaped around, chomping at the air as I tossed him pieces of roasted squab from Rin.

"Rin and your mother woke you up to feed you, but I'm guessing you don't remember that," Charlotte said. Mother placed a hand on Rin's shoulder, mouthing *thank you*, and Rin smiled back. My heart felt as golden warm as the sunlight pouring through the windows.

"Char and I helped, too," Davy said, and Charlotte only blushed more.

"You were drained of magic," Mother said, running her hand across my brow to smooth back my hair. "It was best for you to rest. How are you feeling now?"

I glanced out the door, fighting the urge to race outside. "I want to see how Auteri's doing."

Mother smiled and placed a spare black skirt and gray blouse on top of my blanket. "I prepared another set of that outfit you seem to like."

I wobbled my way to a side room and quickly changed.

Before I returned to the main room, I paused in front of a gold-rimmed wall-length mirror. The fit of the blouse was perfect, and the skirt had two pockets on each side, one the exact length and width of my wand. I looked part-witch, part-girl. Fitting attire for a semi-magical witch.

It was time. Even if my hourglass had drained of its last bits of sand, I had to keep moving. I hurried back into the main room. My legs finally felt like they were working again. "Mother, when's the Novice ceremony?"

"I asked them to wait," she said, and my heart leaped. "It's tomorrow. We can fly out tonight, after the festival, stop a few hours, and then get there early tomorrow morning."

Tomorrow. The thought of being a Novice Witch *tomorrow* made my heartbeat pound in my ears. First, though, I'd have to face Mayor Taira one more time and ask her to sign my application. That *had* to be easier than battling a storm...right?

"But for now," Rin said, as if she could hear my thoughts, "enjoy the festival."

When Mother, Rin, Charlotte, Davy, and I stepped out onto the steps, I basked in the summer sunshine that warmed my skin and blood. The town spread out at my feet, the blue and gold roof tiles gleaming in the sun like jewels clustered in a treasure chest.

Davy nudged me. "Want to go down to Seafoam? Yuri and Edmund are setting up and could use our help."

I frowned, pulling my wand out of my pocket. "I don't have much magic...."

"Only non-magical help. Just setting up a few displays and—my favorite part—tasting their creations for the festival. And they promised you a sugar dusklight flower in return."

"Well, I can't say no to that." I laughed.

Mother nodded encouragingly. "Go on, Eva. This is your town, and they need your help. Just don't tire yourself out. I'm going to drop by that fun-looking shop I saw earlier and pick up a souvenir for your father. I think it's called Corn and Cloudberries?"

"I'll take you there," Rin said, offering an arm, and Mother took it gladly.

Davy beamed at Mother. "Try their Eva Special."

She looked at me quizzically, and I bit down a laugh. "He means the cloudberry popcorn."

"I'm guessing there's a story behind that." Mother smiled. "But tell me later. Go on with your friends now."

Charlotte and Davy tugged me forward, Ember yapping at my feet. My friends led me down the cobblestone street, shiny after the rain, with Ember dancing around us.

ᘒᘖ

When it was almost sunset, Davy and I had finished helping set up the stand for Seafoam Sweets. Charlotte had disappeared earlier to run some errands.

I'd let Edmund, Yuri, and Mister Rydern use my shop space, since I didn't have anything to sell, and my magic wasn't ready to perform any fixes. We were close to the stage that had been built on one of the docks, but I couldn't figure out what it was going to be used for. That hadn't been on my festival scroll. All sorts of stands were setting up, preparing everything from roasted squab to town-hall-shaped contomelon rolls, and the rich smells floated on the gentle winds.

"There you are! Want some glazed almonds?" Charlotte stepped in front of us, waving the paper cone of spicy-sweet cinnamon almonds under our noses.

My stomach growled, even though I'd just demolished a bag of ginger chews.

"Just roasted. The glaze is still soft."

I chewed on an almond, the spices tingling on my tongue. Ember pawed at me to get my attention, his gaze glued on a man surrounded by a few flamefoxes and a bevy of other creatures.

A boy teasing a waterrabbit with a chunk of bread squawked as the creature leaped onto his head, ears twitching and dribbling water onto the boy as it snatched up the whole loaf in its long claws. Vaud calmly plucked the waterrabbit off and put it back in its tank, with a stern warning to both boy and beast.

"Mister Vaud!" I called.

The wild-animal caretaker grinned. "Ah, my favorite

flamefox tamer. And my favorite troublemaking flamefox. So good to see you!"

The pack of flamefoxes gathered around Vaud, stiff and on guard like the last time we'd seen them. They bent down to snuffle at Ember and his flameless tail, their fur prickling. Ember skittered behind me as a few uttered low, suspicious growls.

"Be friendly, now," Vaud told his pack, and they loosened their haunches.

Ember pawed nervously at my ankles, letting out a sharp whimper. His flameless tail sank between his legs.

"You don't need flames all the time to be a flamefox." I smiled and picked him up, holding him close. "I would know. After all, I'm a witch who isn't very magical. But I still can cast some magic. And that magic? It's enough for me."

Ember wiggled his nose, as if testing the air.

"Your witch is a smart one," Vaud said to Ember, reaching out to scratch him behind his pointy ears. The other flamefoxes watched with jealousy.

"Go on," I whispered, as if it was a spell.

Ember wiggled out of my arms, taking one step after another toward the pack of flamefoxes with their burning, fierce tails.

One of the tallest flamefoxes reached out, blinking his dark eyes. He tried to poke Ember's tail with his nose, but Ember batted his paw with a sharp yap, and the larger flamefox jumped back meekly.

Vaud grinned. "Looks like you picked up a trick or two from your witch."

In just a few minutes, I was barely able to tear Ember away from his flamefox friends as they chased one another around the festival, like living, breathing fireworks. Ember teased the other flamefoxes by running underneath them, nipping their ankles, and then sneaking through all the small gaps between people and below stands that the rest of them couldn't fit through. From time to time, Ember's tail spluttered with light, but he was too busy chasing his newfound friends to notice.

As the sun began to set, Davy was trying to get his father to sit by Edmund and Yuri at the stand.

"I don't want that," his father grumbled. "I want... I want..."

"I know," Davy said, and Charlotte's hand curled around mine, tugging me away to give them a moment of peace. "I'll find her for you, Pa. Just come and try some of the new chocolates Edmund has made. It's not safe for you to stand so close to the water in this big crowd."

Davy led his father over to a stool next to the stand, and Edmund offered a plate with thick chunks of fudgy chocolate.

"Have you tried the fudge?" Davy asked, turning to me and Charlotte. "Best in the realm!"

I took a square. The fudge melted smoothly, tasting like sunshine on my tongue. "What's happening on the stage?"

Davy stared resolutely at the ground, scuffling his feet. "Um..."

Charlotte nudged him. "Look, it's almost sunset!"

Davy's mischievous grin lit up his face. "It's about to start!"

"What is?"

Auteri's bell rang, crystal clear, and the crowd hushed. My neck prickled, sensing the weight of a stare.

Davy pointed behind me and I turned around slowly.

Up on the stage, Mayor Taira held my black application tube in her hands. Princess Stella and my mother waited at her sides.

"Please come here, Evalithimus Evergreen, Charlotte of Auteri, and Davy Rydern. And Rin." Mayor Taira's words sounded like a death sentencing. Wide-eyed festivalgoers surrounded us, and I fought the urge to run the opposite way.

Mayor Taira's dry cough echoed over the onlookers, and a path opened. Rin materialized at my side, and Davy and Charlotte pushed me forward, toward the stage. I stopped at the top of the stairs, my heart pounding. Next to the mayor, Mother beamed at me encouragingly.

Mayor Taira dipped into a small, nearly imperceptible curtsy. But it was definitely, absolutely a curtsy. Charlotte leaned over and shoved my dropped jaw back up. The townspeople's eyes nearly popped out in surprise, and I couldn't think of anything to say as I swept into a deep bow. To the delight of the crowd, Ember shifted back on his paws in a bow and sat at the edge of the stage.

Mayor Taira gazed out at the town and then stared me straight in the eyes.

"I believe we owe you our gratitude, Evalithimus. Auteri is in debt to you, and we're lucky to have you as our town witch." She lifted her hand out, and I took it, bobbing my head. I wanted to skip and spin around, but I figured that Mayor Taira would be an unwilling dance partner. And my arms felt more like water than skin and bone.

From over her shoulder, Princess Stella smiled at me.

My eyes burned. "It wasn't only me, it was Charlotte, Davy, and Rin. My mother flew in. It was the whole town, too."

"You did everything you could to help Auteri. You never gave up and fought with all your might until the very end, even through times of doubt." Her mouth curved ruefully, as if Mayor Taira was well aware *she* had been one of the main sources of that doubt. "And for that—I thank you."

I bowed my head, speechless. Even when Mayor Taira

had seemed so proud and haughty, it was because her whole life revolved around one thing: Auteri.

The people of Auteri were everything to her.

My shoulders trembled. I understood, too, finally.

"And," she said, handing over the black tube, "I believe this is yours."

I strained to twist open the top. My hands trembled from weakness, like my arms had become flopping fish. Finally, it came off with a satisfying *pop!*

Pulling out the papers, I smoothed out the wrinkles.

It was odd, though—there were more pages than I remembered.

The application was supposed to be only two pages: one with the rules and the second for the town leader's endorsement.

I turned to the application page, the last piece of parchment. Or, at least, what should've been the last page.

The papers fell from my trembling fingers.

I stared at the pieces of parchment scattered around me. Ember sneezed, and the pages floated up. Charlotte and Davy helped me gather the application, and I gestured with shaking hands. "It's...it's...all filled out."

Next to me, Rin's eyes twinkled. "Charlotte brought it over."

I stared at Charlotte, who shrugged with a sharp, cat-like grin.

Rin continued, "As your guardian, I took it to Mayor Taira for her to complete. And a few of us helped along the way."

Mayor Taira cleared her throat. "Take a look, Evalithimus."

Mother beamed at me, too, her eyes crinkling in the corners. "Go on, Eva. You deserve this."

I gulped, picked up the papers one by one, and started reading.

NAME THE REASON FOR PROMOTION TO NOVICE WITCH

MISS EVALITHIMUS EVERGREEN HAS SAVED OUR TOWN WITH HER MAGIC SKILLS AND HER JUST-AS-MAGICAL CLEVERNESS. AS SUCH, THE PEOPLE OF AUTERI WOULD LIKE TO REQUEST THAT SHE BE LICENSED AS A NOVICE WITCH, IMMEDIATELY.

THIS HAS BEEN PETITIONED BY THE TOWN OF AUTERI, AS SIGNED BELOW.

The page was filled with names: Rin's looping signature, Davy's messy scrawl, and Charlotte's careful cursive. That wasn't the end.

"We had to add a few pages." Charlotte toyed with a new scarlet ribbon in her hair.

Signature after signature was scribbled onto the sheets.

Yuri. Edmund. Trixie. Trina. So many townspeople that I had never met. Some of them had added in their own endorsements, too.

Rin: *Eva's charmed us all and protected our town. What more could we ask for?*

Hikaru: *Eva maykes gud toys.*

Vaud: *Spunky Eva's tamed the wildest flamefox to be her friend,* and *saved the day.*

And others:

Eva saved my house.

Eva Evergreen is the best witch ever.

Eva saved us all.

Mother, too, had signed: *I commend Eva's work for Auteri and fully support her promotion to Novice Witch. As signed by Grand Master Nelalithimus Evergreen, Honorary Auterian.*

Even Princess Stella had added her signature, which was shaped suspiciously like an automobile.

Mayor Taira had signed with a flourish, at the very bottom.

"Look at that," Charlotte said. "Look at that and try to tell me you don't deserve to be a witch." Her eyes sparkled, and in that moment, I felt I'd never seen anyone more beautiful.

"Thank you," I whispered.

I had passed my one-moon requirement to live in

Auteri; I'd gotten my application signed. All I needed to do was fly to the Council Hall to deliver my application, and I'd tick off the last requirement. After that, I would officially become a Novice Witch. I'd finally get my name engraved on a leaf of the Novice tree, even. Mayor Taira clapped her hands. "Guests, dear townspeople of Auteri." She handed me a small bell, holding it tightly so it wouldn't ring.

"Go on," she said.

It was Auteri's charmed bell. The very same bell I'd almost knocked over the first time I'd met Mayor Taira.

"Me?" I squeaked.

"You, Evalithimus Evergreen, soon-to-be Novice Witch of Auteri," Mayor Taira said.

My heart blossomed, feeling bigger than my body, as big as the entire town, as I carefully picked up the bell.

"Ring it three times," Rin said, nudging me.

I flicked my wrist.

The bell rang sweet and clear. Once, twice.

On the third ring, lanterns gleamed bright and a string of lights illuminated the main road, all the way up to the town hall and down to the docks.

Behind us, even the skiffs glowed with lanterns arranged into starbursts, with sailors carefully positioned between the spikes of light. The sailors on the boats tipped pails into the waters, and it looked like they were pouring molten gold into the blue bay.

The crowd alternated between bursting out with delight and hushing one another.

"This is so beautiful."

"There it goes—"

"I hope they'll come. I mean, after the Culling—"

"Look. *Look!*"

The water glowed. Gold and blue lights flickered in the depths of the bay and rose to the surface. I stared closer. The outlines of the fish were almost clear in the waters, but their hearts shone sapphire or gold. It was as if the waters had filled with sparkling jewels.

I was stunned beyond words.

"Lightfish," Charlotte whispered in my ear. "The sapphire fish are looking for their families, and they change colors as soon as they find their fleet."

The crowd oohed as a group of fish shimmered from blue into a deep, rich gold.

Mayor Taira spread her arms out, a proud smile curving across her thin lips. "Welcome to the Festival of Lights!"

With a roar of joy, the crowd began mingling through the stands. Three singers linked arms and broke out into a rollicking melody, with a woman on a huge drum pounding beats that echoed through my bones.

To the Festival of Lights, oh!
To the Festival of Lights we'll go!
To other journeys, o' lands unknown,
But to the Festival of Lights,
We'll always come home!

The ceremony had ended, and Mayor Taira stepped down the stairs, stiff-backed. At the bottom, she paused, briefly, as if she wasn't sure where to go. After a few seconds, she walked over to the nearest counter to check on the workers. Rin watched her with a sad wistfulness in her eyes.

I blinked. The song reminded me of something. I rummaged through my skirt pocket and pulled out the rose-gold compass.

"Rin!" I said, and she spun around, a faintly guilty look on her face. "I repaired your compass."

My guardian took it gently in her hand, opening it up to the glass face. "Thank you, Eva."

"I also tried a special fix. When you're lost, it'll guide you straight toward home."

Rin twisted it from side to side. "A guide? How will it know?"

"Oh!" I smiled. "It's quite simple, really—"

The compass seemed to collect the glow of the light-fish, reflecting off the glass into a brighter ray, and people stepped out of the way, as the ray shone straight at—

"What is this?" Mayor Taira shielded her eyes from the light.

"I'm...I'm home," Rin said quietly. The instant she spoke, the glow faded from the compass.

"Rin?" The mayor frowned, but somehow, the slant of her sagging shoulders made her look old, as if she was tired of fighting.

"Mother, we've lived through the worst storm in the realm." Rin clattered down the steps and hesitantly offered an arm out to the mayor. "I don't want to wait until it's too late to reconcile. Would you like to find something to eat, Mother?"

"Rin..." Mayor Taira breathed out quietly, her lips tilting up into a delicate smile. "Yes, I'd love to."

Charlotte and Davy tugged me by the hand. Mother waved me on. "Go, Eva. I'm going to rest with Mister Rydern and try some sugar dusklight flowers."

"Come on!" Davy said. "Let's go find Trixie and Trina. They promised to save a bag of cloudberry popcorn for me."

"I think they're over by the end of the dock," I said. "They swapped with some shopkeepers to be by the water."

Charlotte laughed. "You know Auteri better than we do!"

Charlotte, Davy, Ember, and I raced around the whole night, feasting on festival snacks and playing games at the stands. Every once in a while, I stopped back at Seafoam's booth for Mother to press a kiss to the top of my head and send me back into the festival with my friends. Occasionally, one of the townspeople would suddenly envelop the three of us in a big hug, shoving a sweet treat in our arms before rushing away, with a choked *thank you*.

I'd never seen a city shine as beautiful as Auteri that night.

CHAPTER 33
The Only Novice

As the last lights of the festival flickered out, Mother and Rin found me, Charlotte, and Davy sitting at the edge of the docks, our feet dangling over the cool water. The three of us wolfed down a box of fried potatoes, thin and crisp with sea salt. Gold lightfish swirled below, mouths gaping for a bite.

Rin leaned over and stole a greasy potato with a grin. "Mm, my favorite!"

Mother rested a hand on my shoulder. "We'll have to head out soon, Eva. I don't want to chance missing the ceremony tomorrow."

Charlotte and Davy stared at Mother with slight horror, until Davy remembered exactly who he was looking at and turned cloudberry-red again.

My stomach churned, and I slowly placed my golden,

crisp potato back onto the pile. "Before we leave, there's something I need to do."

Despite the late hour, Davy's eyes widened, suddenly alert, as if he'd stolen a sailor's mug of tea and downed it all. "Are you saying what I think you're saying?"

I scrambled to my feet, turning to Mother. "I was hoping you might know of a good locator spell...for Davy and Charlotte to find their parents."

Charlotte gasped, a sudden flash of wild, bounding hope gleaming in her eyes, and my heart lurched. What if I couldn't find answers?

But Mother nodded solemnly. "Only if you help me, Eva."

I caught my breath, glancing at Davy and then Charlotte, standing at my sides. Their shoulders straightened, like every bone in them believed in me. Then at Rin, who steadily met my gaze.

Slowly, I flexed my fingers. A sluggish tickle of magic responded, barely there. But it would have to do. "Of course, I'll do anything I can."

"Gather around Eva's counter." Mother pointed her wand toward her knapsack leaning against the wall of Seafoam Sweets, next to her broomstick. *"Map in need, come hastily."*

A sheaf of parchment zipped into the air, unfurling its worn, wrinkled corners, and floated down on my counter. Her map of the realm had been made by a powerful witch, so the enchantment continued even after its maker was long gone.

Rivelle Realm shimmered in all its glory: The snow-capped Sakuya Mountains split the vast land in the middle, and deep riverways curved between the regions. To the west, the Walking Cliffs constantly shifted under the cover of clouds. A few cities were noted, like Okayama City, with a small sketch of the queen's castle, Miyada, and even Auteri. Even parts of Lunea and Constancia were drawn in, north and south of Rivelle.

"Now, this isn't going to be exact," Mother said. "I've tried this only once before."

"Just somewhat exact is better than not knowing anything at all," Charlotte said, and Davy nodded.

"Eva, can you get clippings of their hair?" Mother asked. Charlotte untied her ribbon. Davy procured a pair of scissors from Seafoam Sweets, and then he shook his hair out like Ember, waiting for me.

"Charlotte, Davy, are you sure?" I asked, the shears poised over the tip of Charlotte's hair, glinting gold under the festival lights. "If—if nothing shows up, it means . . . they're gone forever."

"Positive," Davy said. "I promised Pa that I'd bring my mother back. We need to know."

Charlotte nodded firmly. "I've been waiting all my life to find my family."

After a few snips, I carefully laid their locks onto the center of the map.

"Charlotte," Mother said. "Your marks will be scarlet like your hair ribbon. Davy, yours will be gold, like your shirt."

Davy pressed his hands to his flushed face, seeming utterly bewildered with joy that Mother had noticed his outfit.

"Will it be in one spot?" Rin asked.

"If they've moved around in the past week or so, it'll show the different places they've been. And since this spell is for both of your parents, Davy, your father will likely show up in Auteri. Eva, I'll need your help for the spell." Mother whispered her idea into my ear. I nodded, and she straightened. "Ready?"

I poised my wand expectantly, but my throat felt stuck. This was my first time casting a spell alongside Mother—shared spells were so tricky that dual-casters were rare.

She began waving her wand in a circle around the map, like the way I stirred my wand when making potions. *"Birds of a feather, hair of a child."*

I continued the spell, summoning up all my magic. Casting with my mother felt like getting swept into a vast sea, with the power of her hungry, searching spell pulling at my meager, already-drained stores of magic, expecting more and more. My vision spun slightly, but I kept firm. This was for Charlotte and Davy. *"Show their parents, out in the wild."*

The locks of hair gleamed with scarlet and gold light, glowing brighter and brighter, until it was too painful to look.

"W-what's happening?" Davy cried.

A bright gold splotch, like a dab of wet ink, appeared in Auteri.

"Pa!" Davy smiled.

But then lights flickered all over the parchment, covering the entire realm and even the bits of Lunea and Constancia that were visible to the north and south of Rivelle. It speckled Havensea, the landlocked sea in the center of the seven realms, like clusters of rubies woven into gold.

Wherever Charlotte's and Davy's parents could be, it was definitely *not* all over the realm.

They kept their shoulders straight as I bit my lip. "I'm so sorry. I... I don't think it worked."

And when I looked at Mother, worry etched lines in her forehead. "It... it may be too tough right now to track, after the Culling."

"Could we test it to track Rin, or someone we know?" Davy asked, and Rin nodded encouragingly. "We could see if maybe a different spell works?"

"The map was charmed based on your locks of hair,

so it won't be able to track anyone else now," Mother said, and I felt even worse—I'd ruined her precious map, and my spell had completely failed. It couldn't have been Mother's part of the enchantment. I was the weaker witch; it could only be my magic.

"You'll find a way to make it happen," Charlotte said, as if she knew exactly what I was thinking.

I turned to Davy. "I made a promise to you before, and I'll make good on that as soon as I turn in my application."

Davy met my eyes, his gaze steady. He wasn't sad like I'd expected him to be. "Eva, you've given me hope. I know that you'll find answers for me and Charlotte, no matter how long it takes."

I swallowed, turning away to stare out into the rippling, dark waters. I'd thought it was a poor twist of fate when I'd woken up in Auteri, but the people of this town were better than any spell.

"Besides," Davy said, "we've got something else to talk with you about."

He and Charlotte pulled me toward them with serious, expectant looks on their faces, and my heart dropped. I couldn't cast a proper spell to find their parents. Surely they didn't want more of my help?

"What is it?" I asked.

"So." Charlotte crossed her arms. "You've got something really important you need to promise."

"Is there something else that needs a fix?" I scowled down at the map crumpled in my hands, but before I could cram it into my pocket, Charlotte snatched it from my fingers and smoothed it out, folding it into some sort of shape.

Rin tipped the corner of her lips in a smile. "In a way, yes."

Wordlessly, Mother squeezed my shoulder, as if reminding me, *No matter what, I know you'll do good.*

Charlotte clenched the paper in her hands and raised her chin. Her braids glinted like a crown under the flickering lantern light. "We don't want you to leave."

"W-what?" I had to be mishearing things. Was Charlotte actually—

"We want you to stay in Auteri." Charlotte looked down, stubbing her toe on the side of the crate.

"As *our* town witch," Rin said.

"But I'm... You just saw my spell on the map—it didn't work because of me. I know the problem wasn't my mother's magic—"

"There's only one answer to our question, Eva," Charlotte said. "Yes—"

"Or yes," Davy said with an impish grin.

"I..." I searched for what to say, but to my surprise, I already knew. "I want to be Auteri's town witch, too."

Davy wrinkled his nose, turning his head to the side

as if he could sniff out something. "I feel like there's something you're not saying."

"I have to go to the Council Hall to turn in my application," I said. "There's a ceremony, and I'll get my name on the Novice tree, to show the entire realm that I'm a witch."

Charlotte looked down at the ground. A hint of sharp hurt wove through her voice. "And after?"

Rin brushed her fingers against Charlotte's arm, and Charlotte bit her lip, turning to stare south, away from all of us.

I swallowed, glancing northeast to where Okayama and the Council Hall lay beyond the cliffs and expanse of land. "It's not just becoming a Novice Witch, though. I've got other ranks to conquer. Over these next few years, I'll be traveling the realm to earn my place in the Council."

"Come back," Charlotte blurted.

I blinked. "Back?"

She took a slow breath, as if gathering words from somewhere deep in her. Slowly, Charlotte said, "Wherever you go, we want you to come back." Her eyelashes brushed against her cheeks shyly, like she was a frightened cat that had finally begun retracting her claws. "After whatever you need to do, whatever nightdragons you need to battle...come back."

Her eyes pleaded with me to understand. *You matter*

to me. Even if I act prickly, it's because I'm scared, Eva. I'm scared I'm going to be left behind again.

"And if you ever need someone to fight nightdragons at your side," Davy said, raising his arms out, "you have us. You have a whole town at your back."

"The cottage will be waiting for you," Rin said with a wink.

Charlotte's cheeks burned red. "*We* will be waiting for you."

I swallowed. There weren't words to express the strange, beautiful leaping feeling in my heart. But with one look at Charlotte, her gray eyes meeting mine and the tiny smiles on both of our faces, I knew she'd understood enough. She threw her arms around me. "I...I'm glad you're my friend. I'm going to miss you."

I pulled her close. "I promise to visit as much as possible. If you fall in the water, I'll fly back from wherever I am to fish you out, too."

A smile danced across her lips, illuminating her face. She slipped the map into my pocket, before I could see its shape.

"Fly safe," she whispered. "Fly safe, and come back soon."

And Davy put his hands on his hips. "And if you wait too long between visits, we'll just have to adventure out and find *you*."

At that, we all laughed, our grins shining as bright as the lantern light.

Within an hour that went all too fast, I'd packed up my knapsack—Ember immediately jumped inside the moment I brought it out—leaving my cottage empty but clean, and Mother, Ember, and I jetted out on our broomsticks. Charlotte, Davy, Rin, and a group of townspeople who were still awake waved at us as we flew above the docks.

"Don't you dare forget to come back!" Davy hollered so loud that his sailor friends nearly fell off the docks in surprise. Even Charlotte laughed, but her eyes stayed glued to me.

"I'll return." I whispered this promise to the now-calm night sky, the endless ripples of dark water, the beautiful dark blue and gold tiled buildings glowing like a beacon in the night, and most of all, to my friends. "I'll find answers for you, Charlotte and Davy."

I raised my hand to wave and then frowned. I flexed my fingers and magic flowed through my blood, so strong that my vision spun.

"My powers are truly coming back." I breathed out with relief. "I'm not magicless after all!" I looked over my shoulder as long as I could, waving and waving until Auteri disappeared behind the cliffs.

After a quick rest in a small roadside inn, Mother,

Ember, and I woke as buttery-gold sunlight poured over the horizon, coating Rivelle Realm in its warmth. Just a few hours later, we swooped down on our broomsticks, tunneling through the biting-cold wind and low clouds, and dipped toward the Council Hall. Just within sight, through the fog and clouds, faint rays of sunlight sparkled on the twin rivers splashing along opposite sides of the glass building. The sparse leaves still shimmered as clouds shifted and the five trees caught the sun. Somehow, despite the slightly overcast sky, the courtyard seemed to shine brighter than ever.

It was time to show Grand Master Grottel and Conroy my complete, *signed* application.

It was time to become a Novice Witch.

Back in Auteri, Charlotte and Davy were waiting. Waiting for me and Mother to help them. And most of all, waiting for answers. I couldn't let them down.

"Did you—" Mother pulled up suddenly, and I braked, diving to the side to narrowly avoid her.

I wiped the mist off my forehead, my dark hair damp, as I floated up until I was next to her, above the thick clouds and the yellow-orange leaf forests at the edge of Okayama City. Descending to the Council Hall would still take a few minutes, so it was strange of Mother to stop—we didn't have time for a break.

"I thought I heard something." Mother peered down through the clouds moving fast through the sky and covering the lands below us. I shot a glance at her. Was that a tinge of worry in my mother's voice?

From my knapsack, Ember let out a yelp. I twisted over my shoulder to glance at my red-gold furred companion, but his dark eyes were glued to something down below. His pointed ears perked up, listening to something.

I didn't see anything unusual—just the Council Hall and Okayama City, glittering below us. "Ember, what are you—"

Then a cloud moved out of the way, and I gaped. Down below, like little dots frolicking below the clouds, hordes of people were crammed into the courtyard, cheering for something. They held lanterns in their hands—it hadn't been sunlight. It had been something fake, artificial, and fully orchestrated by Grottel. Even from above, the tinny sounds of their yells reached us.

"Three cheers for Novice Nytta!"

"Conroy! Conroy! Conroy!"

My stomach twisted. "They're celebrating Conroy's advancement. *Just* Conroy's."

Mother's face went bone-white. My face already felt frozen.

"*Hayato*," Mother hissed. "I can't believe he *dared* to start without you."

"Well, I guess we're late," I said. "But this is a party I'd love to crash."

Mother shot me a grin. "And crash, we *will*."

We shot down, tunneling through the clouds. My heartbeat pounded in my ears.

Grottel. Grottel. He'd have to give answers. He'd have to grant me my rank, too. Neither Mother nor I would let him get away with this.

⟡

We landed in the courtyard, in between the trees. The fifty or so silver leaves on the Adept tree chimed in the breeze, startling a vendor doling out tin mugs of steaming roasted tea.

I slipped off my broom, water dripping from my damp clothes and soggy boots, and looked around. Everyone around us was celebrating Conroy's upcoming promotion to Novice Wizard, munching on fluffy cinnamon crescents formed in the quarter-moon shape of the Council's emblem, or sipping at mugs, steam swirling above their faces and mingling with the light fog. Across the courtyard, another vendor was offering free mugs of amazake, a hot rice drink currently booming in popularity around the realm. Everyone chattered with excitement, and I heard Conroy's name thrown around in thanks. If my blood wasn't nearly frozen, it'd be bubbling with the urge to charm myself so I couldn't hear his name.

Mother stepped off her broom, not a hair out of place, her charmed clothes warm and dry. "We'll get this sorted out."

I had to hastily smooth out my hair, stiff and tangled after our long flight. Ember hopped out of my knapsack and shook his fur out, tiny sparks of light flying from his tail. He turned to look. Still, unlike other flamefoxes, his fur stayed unlit.

"Someday," I whispered to him, and he padded to my side, leaning into me slightly. His warmth felt like the sun had split through the clouds.

Mother tucked a stray hair behind my ear, and her hand shot back immediately. "Eva, you're shivering."

"I'm fine," I said. Just the thought of becoming a Novice had made me forget the cold.

"May I?" Mother asked, and I nodded. "*Stay high and dry*," Mother said quickly, and tapped my blouse. Water streamed away, wringing out immediately from the threads, even from my socks, and I finally started to feel warm again under the sun.

"Thank you, Mother," I said, smiling.

Turning toward the Council Hall, my smile slid off my face as I saw the obstruction blocking the door. It felt like thick, ink-black clouds had rolled over us. I had a chance at becoming as powerful as my mother someday....

If only Conroy, the peskiest wizard in all of Rivelle Realm, would stop getting in my way.

Conroy's eyebrows furrowed, like angry ink slashes. "Why are *you* here?"

At my side, Ember growled. I curled my fingers

around my Novice Witch application, the paper crackling in my hand. "Let me in."

We stared each other down, the otherwise oblivious crowd milling around us in front of the Council Hall. I squared my shoulders. There was no way I'd let Conroy try to push me around. Not today.

"I heard your mother helped you pass. You don't belong here, Eva." His dark eyes flashed, his eyebrows curving haughtily. He moved in front of the doorknob, crossing the arms of his perfectly tailored black long-sleeve shirt. My black witch's skirt and gray blouse felt sloppy and unofficial in comparison.

I summoned up my words, even if it somehow felt tougher than any spell. "I earned my right to stay, all on my own. Whether you want me here or not. I'm a witch in my own right."

He sighed, shaking his head. "You need your—"

"Signed application?" I raised an eyebrow, waving my papers in front of his face so he absolutely couldn't miss them.

Conroy's jaw dropped.

My eyes narrowed. "Plus, if anyone's had more help, I'd say it was you with your multiple apprenticeships."

Conroy gurgled speechlessly.

"Don't worry, Conroy," Mother cut in. She placed one hand on my shoulder and the other on Conroy's. "Eva's got this handled."

Even Conroy, who seemed as if he'd never accept that I had a pinch of magic, couldn't say no to her. After all, my mother was Conroy's idol just as much as she was mine.

He scrambled into a deep bow. "Grand Master Evergreen. I hope you had a wonderful flight here. I—I've—"

The bell rang, drowning out his words, and he flushed all the way to the tips of his ears.

Mother nudged him toward the door gently. "Come on, Conroy. If you don't watch out, you'll miss the ceremony. The ceremony is for the *two* of you."

There was a sharpness to her voice, and Conroy drew back, as if stung.

I searched his proud face, wondering if he had known I'd passed on my own but had tried to intimidate me all the same. Not that it mattered. He was Grottel's nephew through and through.

Conroy's dark eyes flickered between me and Mother and then lowered. "I...I guess we should go in."

He turned slightly to press against the heavy oak door.

I swallowed, taking a deep breath. Behind the door, my future awaited. If Conroy's cold welcome was anything to judge from, I'd have to battle in a duel of wits to convince Grottel that I deserved to earn my Novice Witch license.

The door screeched loudly as it opened. Throughout the courtyard, the onlookers cheered.

"Hooray!" they shouted. "Cheers to the new Novice!"

I couldn't let the realm forget about me. I wouldn't let them forget about my magic. I brushed past Conroy and muttered, "Cheers to the new *Novices*."

Mother and I strode side by side down the long hallway to the Council's meeting room. We would demand answers.

CHAPTER 34

ᴇVALITHIMUS ᴇVERGREEN

H ello, Hayato."

My hands were like ice, but Mother's voice was even colder.

Grand Master Grottel spun around from where he stood at the front of the Council Hall. Just beyond, past the glass walls, water crashed down the twin rivers, splitting into two separate paths. For an instant, it felt like Mother and Grottel were the two rivers, stemming from the same pool of magic, but using their powers for drastically different futures. Maybe even two drastically different realms.

Then Grottel growled, "*What?*" and all thoughts of the rivers vanished from my mind.

Mother raised an eyebrow, and around us, the other

witches and wizards shifted uneasily, all attention focusing on the two of them—and me.

"I'm about to start Conroy's ceremony," he snarled. His narrow hooded eyes flashed at me. "What are *you* doing here? Didn't your *mother* step in to save your town?"

If he'd asked this just one moon ago, I probably would've tried to cast a spell to melt into Mother's shadow or jumped into the Torido Rivers. But fighting the Culling—and doing everything I could to save Auteri—had nearly washed me out to sea, had nearly taken all the magic from me.

And made me stronger.

Slowly, refusing to let my hands tremble, I unfurled the paper in my hand. "I'm here for the same reason as Conroy."

Like ripples in the Constancia Sea, the room hushed, everyone staring up at us.

"I've completed my Novice Witch quest."

Grottel stiffened. "But—"

"I shielded Auteri, home of the Festival of Lights, from the Culling," I said.

Grottel looked at my mother accusingly. "I'd assumed it was Nela—"

"I was here in Okayama, guarding the capital while you were too busy up north to help." The faintest of smiles danced on Mother's lips. "I did not step foot into Auteri until Eva's quest window was up."

"*I* saved Auteri. Because of *my* magic, Mayor Taira recommends that I receive my Novice rank." I revealed the five pages full of signatures, one at a time, watching the anger on Grottel's face melt into something strange, something I'd never seen before—disbelief. The ink felt enchanted, like I was being filled with the steadfast faith that the townspeople of Auteri had felt when they'd signed my application. "You asked for the town leader to sign. I got a signature from her *and* the rest of the town."

Grottel spluttered. "With just one apprenticeship—I got reports that Nela swooped in to save you, girl—"

A tinkle of crystal chimes sounded through the air, and I frowned in confusion.

I gaped as a familiar-looking woman in a clean-cut uniform, as pale as the crystal walls of the queen's castle, stepped through the side door. Princess Stella had a thin silver circlet resting on her hair. She winked at me, but I couldn't summon up a response. The magicless were not allowed into the Council Hall unless—

"Announcing Her Royal Highness, Queen Alliana, our chosen ruler of Rivelle Realm," Princess Stella declared, pounding a long wood staff on the tiles.

She stepped aside and Queen Alliana swept into the room, her head held high, scanning the hall.

"Queen Alliana," I whispered breathlessly, sinking into a deep bow. All around us, even Grottel, bowed.

The queen took long, proud steps to the front of the

room, her bright robes of the central farmlands, vibrant red-orange and patterned with intricate yellow flowers, floating around her like she was a fireblossom dancing on the sea's waves. It was my first time seeing the queen up close. She had a strong jaw and fierce eyes, and she was strikingly beautiful, almost ethereal. Queen Alliana was only a few years older than my mother, but there were wrinkles at the corner of her eyes and threads of silver in her dark hair, like she'd aged forty years' time, instead of the twenty years that had passed since ascending to the crown. Still, something in the way Queen Alliana carried herself made it seem like she was born to the throne.

The queen met Mother's eyes, and in the flash of a second, I swore there was a sense of sadness radiating from the queen. But I shook my head. *I'm just too nervous about my Novice ceremony. I'm overthinking everything.*

"It seems that Eva deserves her license." Queen Alliana settled into a crystal throne that a few of her attendants had carried out. Her lips, painted a beautiful dark crimson, turned up as she smiled at Grottel. "Thank you for including me in these celebrations."

Grottel looked as if he severely regretted inviting her.

She turned to the hushed crowd and waved her hand, as if casting a spell of her own. Princess Stella announced, "You may now be seated."

We filed to the seats, our clothes whispering like ghosts brushing against the oak chairs as we sat.

At the dais in the center, Grottel was quiet, as if he was still waiting for permission to speak. But he scratched at his wrists as though he could barely wait. Yet the queen held the attention of all in the room, even my mother, who sat with her hands clasped in her lap, and Ember, who peeked out from behind my legs to quietly peer up at her.

She breathed in deep and said, "It is my first time meeting a few of you"—her gaze drifted over to Conroy, sitting across the room, and then met mine. I nearly melted under the strength of her dark brown eyes—"and I am glad to see you all for such auspicious reasons. I thank you all for serving the realm by blood and soul."

We all nodded eagerly. Even Grottel's gaunt cheeks seemed a bit pink, effusive from the queen's praise, as he began reading through the Council's commandments, talking about the quest Conroy and I had undergone over the past moon to earn our new rank.

The ceremony was like a dream.

But it was real, which meant it was better than any dream.

Norya, Grottel's assistant, scribbled out something on stiff, small rectangular parchment cards. Grottel motioned for everyone to clap for what seemed like days as Conroy sauntered up to the dais and accepted his license. With a flick of Conroy's wand, his shirt took on a bronze hue, and the crowd cheered louder.

I kept clapping, but shifted in my seat. Ember poked his nose against me questioningly, as if he was waiting impatiently, too. Finally, Conroy managed to remember that he wasn't actually supposed to stay preening under the attention in the center of the room forever and found his way back to his seat.

Then Grottel said, "The other recipient."

"Evalithimus Evergreen," the queen offered from her throne.

He waved me up with a stiff hand. "Come here."

Grottel shoved the card into my waiting hand. Then he leaned over, and I could smell his peculiar scent, stinging my nose like the antiseptic that Father used to clean my cuts.

"We'll see if you can *keep* your license."

He spoke so quickly I thought I'd imagined it. With that, he poked me in the shoulder to spin me around and sent me back to my seat.

It was all so fast that there was only a smattering of applause.

But then Mother stood up, shoulders straight and tall, clapping louder and louder, and Princess Stella pounded her staff. Then the rest of the witches and wizards joined in until the noise seemed to shake the roof. Even *Queen*

Alliana clapped. I beamed back at the bright faces of my fellow witches and wizards, feeling like the light trickling in through the glass windows had filled my body, warming my heart.

I—I was one of them now.

A low growl from Grottel cut through the symphony of applause. And when I looked over my shoulder, his eyes were still narrowed, as if studying me for a weakness. As if he was a hawk, about to swoop down on its prey.

But receiving my license made me want to float up to the rooftops, above the thick clouds and into the sky.

And seeing my mother's eyes shine back at me?

That—that meant *everything*.

The moment I got back to my chair, Ember jumped into my lap to examine my license.

"Not edible." I took one long look, memorizing every word, before tucking it into the front pocket of my knapsack, far away from Ember's sharp teeth.

> **EVALITHIMUS EVERGREEN**
> **OFFICIAL MEMBER OF RIVELLE REALM'S**
> **COUNCIL OF WITCHES AND WIZARDS**
> **NOVICE WITCH, REPAIR AFFINITY**
> Good until twelve moons' time, when
> aforementioned witch is required
> to undergo the Adept Quest.

Grottel grumbled his closing statement. "Congratulations to the recipient—ah, *recipients*—of the Novice ceremony." His eyes, glued to Conroy, flickered reluctantly to me as he added, "And remember, the choices of our young Novices can define the future of the realm."

Grottel dismissed the meeting by ringing the bell. "It's time for Novice Nytta and Novice Evergreen to summon their leaves outside."

∽

The mist from the Torido Rivers gathered on the branch in front of me, glistening like a gem. I breathed on both water and wood, urging it to life.

On the other side of the Novice tree, Conroy muttered a spell under his breath and prodded the dewdrop in front of him with his wand. It tinkled like glass. His leaf formed instantly with a sharp bronze point, and he looked up gloatingly, meeting my eyes, as the crowd burst into cheers.

Close to my boots, Ember growled, expressing my thoughts exactly.

Of *course* Conroy would get his leaf first.

I curled my fingers around my wand, wishing I could enchant my leaf to diamond and gold like my mother's, which waved faintly in the wind. At the front of the crowd, Mother smiled encouragingly at me.

I turned to my branch and pressed the tip of my wand

to it. I didn't have a clever enchantment, so I spoke the truth. "I've passed my Novice quest. I need to summon my leaf so I can use my magic to help my friends. Please. I *need* to help them."

Thoughts of Davy carefully placing his folded paper flowers into the sea floated into my memory. And Charlotte, her face fierce and unyielding, refusing to show pity for herself, as she'd told me the story of how she'd gotten to Auteri.

This was for them.

And, truthfully, this was for me, too.

To show that I deserved this. That I'd fought for this with my blood, sweat, and tears, through the most frightening of storms and against even the most skeptical of mayors or meddlers. To show that someone like me *could* make her own dreams come true.

A spell finally came to mind. *"The end of a journey is bittersweet. Yet to start anew, let this be complete."*

The water stretched out, mixing with sap from the tree and shimmering into a bronze leaf. It wavered in the faint breeze, tinkling with the rest of the leaves, as lines formed in the metal like molten bronze, spelling out two words I'd waited to see all my life.

Evalithimus Evergreen.

I, Evalithimus Evergreen, a girl with just a pinch of magic, was now a semi-magical witch.

A Spell to Remember

As I stood in front of the Novice tree, trying to memorize every detail of my very own shimmering bronze leaf, Mother wrapped her arm around my shoulders.

"Shall we go celebrate?" she asked.

The crowd had long since returned to their mugs of hot tea and to demolishing the piles of fluffy cinnamon crescents, as fast as the bakers could drizzle on sticky-sweet icing.

I shook my head. "I want just a moment more. I'll join you soon."

It didn't quite feel like it was time to celebrate just yet. A flickering fire burned within me, unquenched.

In my pocket, something rustled, as if answering my thoughts. My fingers brushed against the folded map and a pointed edge poked at my skin, as if admonishing me for forgetting it for so long. Gently, I slid it out, and my chest clenched.

Charlotte had folded it into a shield, like the ones we'd made to protect Auteri.

I wanted, no, I *needed* to help Charlotte and Davy.

At my feet, Ember whined, pawing at me. His wide eyes stared up at me, full of faith. As if Charlotte and Davy had entrusted him to remind me of what they would say.

You've done good for Auteri, Eva.

You have real magic.

"I can do something, can't I?" I said slowly. "I can try the spell again and again, just like my attempts with the waterproofing potion."

Pulling my wand out of my pocket, I stepped behind the cover of the trees, away from the celebrating crowd. For this, I wanted to be surrounded with just the roar of the rivers in my ears and the gentle mist coating my skin. Somehow, it felt like my skin burned under its touch, like the Torido Rivers were testing me, too.

The spell I'd cast on the map with Mother swirled in my mind. But for a spell I'd cast on my own, I had to use only my words, for my friends that meant the world to me. For Davy, who'd always believed in me. And for Charlotte, who'd taught me to believe in myself.

With my wand pressed to the paper, I slowly chanted,

"*A search for two friends close to my heart, show their parents so they will never be apart.*"

A breeze blew through the Council trees, sending the leaves twinkling like a haunting melody, and my skin prickled.

The map was empty. Just the same sharp ink lines marking cities and mountains, landmarks and rivers. This time, it seemed that even Davy's father wouldn't show.

Then, suddenly, the parchment glimmered with a faint golden sheen, and I nearly dropped the map from surprise. Scarlet and gold swirls gathered over a tall, forbiddingly dark tower in the forests of the north. The glowing ink marks twisted and surged like a rising storm, straight toward Okayama and then down to Auteri, where the ink stayed for a few seconds, growing brighter.

Then the moving lights vanished, leaving only the gold marker for Davy's father, blinking faintly in Auteri.

I spun around. Before I could say a word, Mother's eyes met mine through the trees, instantly widening with concern. With a flick of her wand, her tin mug zipped away to a tea vendor's empty tray and she hurried over. "What is it?"

"It's...it's doing something." I lifted the map in my shaking hands, and she stared down with confusion.

Again, scarlet and gold ink blinked from the forests in the north, swirling over the unnamed tower and lake.

The path continued to Okayama and down to Auteri, and then the glowing ink melted away.

Mother tilted her head to the side and tapped her finger against the parchment. "How can this path go over water? Maybe they're on a ship?"

We stared at the map, lost in thought.

I traced my finger along that strange route: from the forbiddingly dark tower, down the coast, and out toward the open sea. I still didn't understand what it meant, yet it was familiar, somehow. I'd seen it before. Or heard of it.

"It's the path of the Culling," I gasped. "It hit the coast by Okayama first and then went down the coast toward Auteri."

Mother covered her mouth with a pale, shaking hand, silent with shock.

"But...but...how can Charlotte and Davy's parents be *in* the storm?" My hands shook as I brushed my fingertip around the tower and wide lake, surrounded by thick trees. "And what's this place to the north, where it's coming from?"

Mother flicked her wand at the map. *"Show me here and now, show me what's all around."*

Light shot out from the tip of her wand like sunrays streaming through the clouds, and spidery gold lines crept over the parchment, listing city names and rivers. I could almost smell Father's buttery croissants when my parents' house appeared as *The Evergreens' home.* I grimaced as a tiny house that formed in the southern farmlands, west of Auteri's cliffs, was marked as *Conroy Nytta's house.*

Then a name appeared above the tower and wide lake in the north. The gold and scarlet ink gathered around the tower, like a pool of shimmering tears and ruby blood.

Hayato Grottel's tower.

Ice filled my chest. "Grottel—and the Culling?"

"*Hayato,*" Mother croaked. "He just went with the queen to the castle. For a private meeting. He barred anyone other than his closest confidants in the Council. I thought it was unusual, but who was I to say...."

It felt like all the air had been cursed out of the world. I looked toward the crystal castle, its shimmering spires sparkling with light. Somewhere inside, Queen Alliana was face-to-face with the person who might very well be responsible for trying to destroy the realm.

"We need to find her, now. If Grottel started the Culling..." I stared down at the illustration of Grottel's tower, and the fading, dying path of flickering scarlet and gold swirls. "The queen's in danger."

Acknowledgments

Thank you, dear reader, for reading Eva's story—thanks to you, Eva can weather the worst of storms.

Sarah Landis, I think the best way to describe everything you've done for me is...you're secretly my fairy godmother, aren't you?! Thank you, Sarah, for making my wildest dreams come true.

Thank you to Alvina Ling, the most magical editor for *Eva* that I could have ever hoped or dreamed for. As Rin said, "To me, that one chance was the world." And, Alvina, that was you, completely. You and the team at Hachette and Little, Brown Books for Young Readers have changed my life.

Sending endless thanks to Ruqayyah Daud—you deserve all the contomelon rolls in the realm!

Thank you to the Hachette and LBYR teams for wholeheartedly championing Eva, including Megan Tingley, Jackie Engel, Tom Guerin, Janelle DeLuise, Cameron Chase, Hannah Koerner, Karina Granda, Sarah Van Bonn, Nikki Garcia, Jen Graham, Andy Ball, Erika Breglia, Emilie Polster, Stefanie Hoffman, Natali Cavanagh, Savannah Kennelly, Valerie Wong, Christie Michel, Paula Benjamin-Barner, Shawn Foster, Danielle Cantarella, Siena Koncsol, the sales team, the publicity team, and many, many more.

Shan Jiang, I am absolutely in awe of your talent and dedication to making the intricate, beautiful artwork that brings Eva to life. Thank you so much.

Sending the deepest appreciation to the booksellers, teachers, librarians, and bloggers who have supported Eva. And thank you for all that you do for your students and readers.

Thank you to Mom and Dad, and my family all around the world, for their steadfast belief in my dreams, just like Eva's parents. And Momo is the best real-world Ember (who decided she belonged in my life).

Sending virtual bottomless fries and genmaicha to Sarah Suk, unimersharks and more ice cream to Chelsea Ichaso, awesomeness and Honey & Butter macarons to Susan Lee and Tara Tsai, a mountain of chocolate mousse to Sarah Harrington and Carly Whetter, an NZ–US teleporter to Graci Kim, oodles of cake and tea dates to Jessica Kim and Grace Shim, endless treats for Daisy and Alyssa Colman, flamefox hugs to Michelle Fohlin and Bridgette Johnson, more game time to Ron Walters, international coffee dates to Meredith Tate, all the hugs to Team Landis and WFC, oceans of hot chocolate to Natasha Buran, and Taehyung to June Tan.

The Author Mentor Match family deserves cloudberry popcorn, especially Sean Easley for taking a shot on a witchy girl and guiding Eva on her journey, my round three mentee family, and the wonderful moderators—Alexa Donne, Liz Parker, and Kevin van Whye.

Fonda Lee, thank you for your words of infinite wisdom. Thank you to SFWA, Julia Rios, and Jessi Cole Jackson for connecting us.

Thanks for supporting *Eva* from the very beginning: Alice MacLennan, Ellen Stonaker, Jenna Rentzel, Lori Tussey, Reese Eschmann, Amber Logan, Paul Janus, Mare Hagarty, and Cassandra Farrin.

To Cindy, Chris, Claire, and Celina, thanks for always cheering me on.

Special thanks to Kaylie and Jude for your help with the table of contents!

Thank you to Conan, whom I can always count on as a real-life anime database and for our fry day adventures.

Thank you to the kiddos for your friendship, even through all the times I disappeared into my cave instead of having a potato party: Ken, Julie-chan, Leon, Dong-saeng David, Jermsies, Jon the Huton, Johnny and his Dang Knives, and that one mysterious K guy. And Mimi, without whom Rin would never have had a motorcycle or be nearly as cool. Also, thank you to Evelyn for our talks and inspirational dinner dates.

Thank you to Eugene for always supporting me. Because of you, I have been able to write—and believe in—this story about fighting for dreams and hopes and brighter days. You are my light in the storm, every day.